MW01134617

The Broken Clock
Book Three of the Deadlock Trilogy

P.T. Hylton

WHAT WE KNOW

On March 27th, 2014, Rook Mountain, Tennessee, was attacked by bird-like creatures called the Unfeathered. A supposed drifter named **Zed** vowed to protect the town…if the residents would agree to a few regulations. The people of Rook Mountain lived in fear for the next eight years, forced to abide by strict rules as a price for protection from the Unfeathered. What most Rook Mountaineers didn't know was their town was locked outside of time. While they lived their eight-year nightmare, time stood still in the rest of the world.

Jake Hinkle fought against the regulations in secret. He and his friends (who referred to themselves as the Unregulated) were dedicated to finding the Tools, powerful objects disguised as everyday items, identifiable only by the broken clock symbol they bore. When Jake's cover was blown, he used one of the Tools, a mirror, to transport himself to an unknown land. He promised to find help for Rook Mountain. Instead, he was trapped in a place he called Sanctuary. He found a book with a strange symbol on the cover, and he used it to save people from life-or-death situations. He brought them to Sanctuary and tried to give their lives meaning.

When **Frank Hinkle** was released from prison after eight years inside, he reignited the fight against Zed in Rook Mountain. Frank learned he had the ability to make locks that could render objects invisible to unwanted eyes, a skill that allowed his friends to hide a number of Tools from Zed. Frank and his friends destroyed Zed's pocket watch, restarted time, and banished Zed. After the victory, Frank went into the mirror to find his brother, Jake.

Frank soon learned time passed differently in Sanctuary. Many years had passed since Jake came through the mirror. Frank met **Mason Hinkle**, his brother's son, now in his fifties. Mason revealed the news that Jake died many years ago. Frank discovered Sanctuary was once a town called Sugar Plains, Illinois. Zed took it outside of time, much like he'd done to Rook Mountain. Over many, many years, the people of Sugar Plains died off, and the town transformed into a strange forest.

Sophie Porter found her way to Sanctuary in her hunt for her sister's killer. After spending months living with Jake and his people, Sophie inadvertently released **Vee**, a mysterious man hell-bent on causing destruction. Vee succeeded in killing most of the residents of Sanctuary, then revealed his ultimate target: Zed. Sophie and Jake made a final stand and temporarily trapped Vee, but Jake was mortally wounded in the battle and died shortly after.

After finally getting revenge on her sister's killer, Sophie travelled fifty years into the future and joined Frank in a face-off with the suddenly very powerful Zed who was now in possession of Jake's book and one of the remaining Tools, a compass. Zed quickly dispatched Vee, ripping off his arms and banishing him from Sanctuary. Zed stated he might have a use for Frank in the future, and he would allow them to live for the time being. He then used a portal in a tree to escape Sanctuary. Using Jake's book, Mason transported Frank, Sophie, and himself back to Rook Mountain. They learned Zed had gone to King's Crossing, Wisconsin, and they headed off to confront him one final time.

Christine and **Will Osmond** were two of the original Unregulated. After Jake and Frank failed to return from their trips into the mirror, Will and Christine assumed them dead. They possess the other remaining Tool, the knife.

PROLOGUE

Boulder Creek, CO
January, 2022

Christine Osmond eased her truck into the driveway, put it in park, and gripped the wheel. There was a stranger sitting on her porch.

She couldn't make out all the details from here, but she could see enough. Stark white hair. A rumpled jacket that was at least a size too large. It was enough to let her know she didn't recognize the man. Yet there he was, sitting on her porch, looking as comfortable as if he'd been here a thousand times.

She hesitated, then got out of the truck and took a few steps toward the house.

"Help you?" she called. She heard the Tennessee in her voice. She never tried to hide it—she was proud of who she was and where she'd come from—but over the past few years she'd noticed it fading ever-so-slightly. God help her, she was starting to sound like a northerner.

The man gave her a weak smile and she saw the deep lines on his face. The guy had to be sixty years old if he was a day. And a hard sixty. Those eyes of his had seen some things. He

4

was thin and sinewy, but he looked strong. She could tell even through his too-large jacket. The way the cords stood out on his neck.

He rose and nodded to her. "Doctor Osmond, I have something for you."

"That so?" she asked.

He nodded and held out a plain white envelope.

She took another step toward the porch. "You selling something?"

He shook his head. "No, ma'am. I'm just here to give you the letter. And to answer your questions, if you have 'em."

She squinted at him. "I don't foresee myself having any questions a stranger could answer. Maybe if you were a little more forward as to the reason for your call…" She let her voice trail off, hoping he'd take it from there.

He stretched out his arm, offering the envelope. "I'd rather you read the letter. It'll make more sense after."

She set her jaw. "No. Tell me why you're here first." Something about the sight of this man made her very afraid.

He sighed. "Maybe you know why I'm here. I think you knew I was coming. Me or someone like me. You keep looking over your shoulder, peeking out your window to see if an unfamiliar car is pulling into your driveway. You look at the sky in the nighttime half expecting to see streaks of white. Because you know it's not over. And you're right."

She said nothing. Her hands were shaking now. The mountain air suddenly felt chilly against the skin of her bare arms.

"Who are you?" she asked. As soon as the words left her mouth she wished they hadn't. She didn't want to hear the answer to her question. She suddenly realized what it was about this man that made her uneasy. It was there around his

5

eyes and in the curve of his chin. It was there in the peculiar angle of his ears.

This man looked far too much like her son Trevor.

He looked her square in the eye. "My name's Mason Hinkle."

"Bullshit." The word sprang to her lips, unbidden. She suddenly wished she had her knife. She would feel so much better if she were holding it now. She wouldn't feel so defenseless and alone. But the knife was in her bedroom and this man, this man who claimed to be a Hinkle, was standing between her and it.

He was still holding the envelope out to her. She stared him down for another moment, letting him know with her eyes she wasn't up for nonsense. He didn't look away.

She snatched the envelope from him and turned it over in her hand. Both sides were blank.

She slid a finger under the flap and tore it open. The letter inside was written on a single piece of legal paper. She unfolded it and started to read.

Christine,

I hope to God this letter finds you and Will.

I don't have time to write it all down. There's so much you need to know. That's why I'm sending Mason. You can trust him. He's one of us. He's a Hinkle. Listen to what he has to say. I was hoping not to involve you, but it's too late for that now. So, I'm asking for your help.

Leave Trevor out of it, if you can. There's still a chance for him. Maybe one Hinkle can get out of this.

Ask the man who gave you this letter where you kept the Tools all those years. That'll be your sign this letter really is from me. Mason's the only one I told about that.

Christine…I'm sorry.

Love, Frank

Christine crushed the paper in her hand. She looked up at the man.

"The freezer," he said. "You kept the Tools in the freezer. The knife, the lighter, the cane. Am I missing any? Oh, and the head of one of the Unfeathered. That part always made me smile."

"You read the letter."

"I was there when he wrote it." The man grinned sheepishly, and her stomach cramped. God, he looked like Trevor. And Jake. So much like Jake.

Christine shook her head violently. "I don't believe you. That answer, it doesn't prove anything. Zed reads minds."

"Not Frank's."

She thought back to that day in Rook Mountain City Hall, when Frank opened the box and unleashed the Unfeathered on the town. It was true. Zed couldn't read Frank's mind.

"He could have tortured the info out of Frank," she countered. "And how do I even know Frank wrote the letter?"

The man sighed. "I don't know what else to tell you. Frank asked you to trust me if I could answer the question, and I answered it. I guess when it comes down to it, you either believe me or you don't."

Christine glared at him. "I don't."

He looked away. "Ma'am, I've come a long way, and I wish you'd at least—"

"Let me finish. I don't believe you. Not fully. But I'm sure as hell not going to let you walk away if there's any chance you're the real thing. So I'll talk to you. But I have conditions. Two of them."

The older man nodded slowly. "I'd like to hear 'em."

"One, I'm going inside to call my husband. He's a part of

this too, same as me. And I wouldn't mind getting his thoughts on this situation. You wait out here on this porch until he gets home. When he does, we'll all three of us have a nice conversation."

"Fair enough. I'll wait. What's number two?"

"I'll tell you when we all sit down to talk."

With that, she brushed past him and went inside. She locked the door and threw the deadbolt.

She touched her phone and said, "Will, come home."

Barely twenty seconds later, her phone chirped in reply. "On my way."

Will didn't have to ask why. In the last eight years, she'd never asked him to come home without an explanation. He'd been looking over his shoulder and peeking out the window at the nighttime sky the same as her. He too knew they weren't out of it. He knew it wasn't over.

Christine's heart was racing and her palms were damp with sweat as she made her way to the bedroom. But she felt something else, too. A tiny something she'd thought had gone out years ago. It was hope.

And with it, relief. She'd been waiting and worrying for so long that someone would find them. Maybe it would be Zed, or maybe it would be the Unfeathered, or maybe it would be someone else altogether, but she'd known it would happen.

Jake hadn't come home. Frank hadn't come home. They would have if at all possible. That meant either they were dead or someone was keeping them away. Or maybe it meant Zed had won.

And now there was a very good chance the answers to the questions that had been burning a hole in her heart the last eight years were sitting on her porch.

She went to her dresser and pulled open the top drawer.

She picked up the knife and ran her thumb over the broken clock symbol. She was doing that a lot lately. It soothed her.

The last time she'd used the knife had been back in Rook Mountain. Sean Lee had brought her a Tool, a hammer. He'd said he'd found it. She knew from the look in his eyes there was more to the story, but, honestly, she hadn't wanted to know. Not then. Not so soon after things had finally gone back to some semblance of normal. She'd been grateful for Sean's lie. So, she'd destroyed the hammer and asked no further questions..

Christine paused, then grabbed her Glock and loaded it. She pulled out the shoulder holster and put that on, too. Yeah, that guy looked like Jake, and, yeah, he claimed to be a Hinkle. That didn't mean Christine trusted him. Her and trust had a complicated relationship.

She walked out to the living room and brushed aside the curtain over the front window. The man was sitting there, looking as serene as if he was on his own porch. She watched him for a long while until she couldn't look at him anymore. The longer she stared, the more she saw Trevor and Jake in him.

For want of something to do, she poured three tall glasses of tea.

When she saw Will's Chevy pulling into the driveway, she opened the front door and carried out the drinks. He leapt out of the car and ran toward the porch. Christine met him at the bottom of the stairs.

Will's voice was shaking when he spoke. "What's going on? Who's he?"

"He says his name is Mason Hinkle." She handed him the letter.

He read it, beads of sweat forming on his forehead. "Is

this for real?"

"That's what I'm aiming to find out." She turned toward the man on the porch. "You want a glass of sweet tea?" She turned so he could see her shoulder holster.

He shook his head slowly, a smile on his face. "No ma'am. But I do appreciate the offer."

Will's eyes were still scanning the letter. "Drink the tea."

Mason shrugged and took a glass off the tray. "You said there was another condition before you'd talk to me."

Christine nodded. "I want to ask you something."

"I believe I mentioned that's part of why I'm here."

Christine paused a moment. She was afraid to ask the question and more afraid what the answer might be. "Mr… Hinkle, do you know where Jake and Frank are?"

A sadness came into Mason's eyes, and Christine's heart broke. "Ma'am, I'm sorry to tell you this, but Jake's dead. And Frank…well, he needs your help."

After a moment, Will said in a scratchy voice, "Start talking. Tell us what happened."

Mason cleared his throat. "Listen, I want you to know we tried our best. All of us did. Frank. Sophie. Me. Things got so messed up."

"We don't know what you're talking about," Will said.

"I'm sorry. There's so much. I'm trying to figure out where to start. Everything went wrong. And now…" He trailed off, staring toward the distant mountains.

Christine gritted her teeth. She'd known in her heart Jake was dead, but hearing it out loud was something else.

Maybe there was still a chance for his brother. "Where is Frank?" she asked.

"He's in a place called King's Crossing, Wisconsin. And we need to save him."

CHAPTER ONE: SWARM

King's Crossing, Wisconsin
May, 2015
1.

Frank, Sophie, and Mason drove north.

Frank adjusted his legs, trying yet again to find a semi-comfortable position. He'd been crammed into the too-small backseat for the last ten hours. Mason had been assigned sole possession of the front passenger seat since he'd thrown up in Kentucky. The man hadn't been in a car more than ten minutes before today, and the fourteen hour trip from Rook Mountain, Tennessee, to King's Crossing, Wisconsin, wasn't agreeing with his stomach.

Frank had offered multiple times to take a turn at the wheel, but Sophie loved to drive. He'd also let it slip he hadn't exactly been driving around these last eight years, so that may have also had something to do with her reluctance to trade spots.

Mason moaned again and Sophie glanced at him. "Do I need to pull over?"

"No," he croaked at her. "Just get where we're going."

Frank shifted in his seat. "Hang on, man. We're only about

ten minutes out."

They pulled off the interstate and onto a road that ran parallel to the Mississippi River. The sign at the city limits put the population at just over twelve thousand, which was three times the size of Rook Mountain. Was that why Zed hadn't made his move?

Zed had a pattern. Show up in town, take it out of time, become the hero, and let the trees slowly take over the town. According to what Frank had read in the book with the broken world symbol on the cover, that's what he had done in Sugar Plains, Illinois, back in 1985, and according to Zed himself, it was what he'd been intending to do in Rook Mountain. How many other towns had Zed destroyed? How many other places had vanished off the face of the Earth, forgotten by the rest of humanity? And why?

Why. That was the big question, wasn't it? Frank still didn't understand Zed's purpose in pulling these towns out of time. He knew they were special, and that specialness had something to do with the books all those towns had…even Rook Mountain.

Rook Mountain did have a book, Zed had told Frank. *You destroyed it.*

Frank didn't like to think about those things. The holes that seemed to exist in his memory. The destruction of the Rook Mountain book. The quarry. What else had he forgotten?

Still, even though Zed had a pattern, it was clear he was being forced to deviate from it. Zed no longer had the watch, so Frank had to assume he couldn't use his usual technique for sucking the life out of towns. King's Crossing, Wisconsin, hadn't been pulled out of time. So what was his new strategy? What would he do now?

It all came down to the *why*. If Frank knew Zed's purpose,

he might be able to figure out what other methods the man would use. Zed had the compass, and he'd indicated it was powerful, maybe more powerful than his old watch. Zed had proven he could use the Tools in ways the rest of them couldn't, or at least didn't think to try.

Frank squirmed in his seat, his eyes scanning the landscape outside the window. All-in-all, it wasn't *that* different from back home. The drive had been strange, particularly the section through Illinois. He'd never seen land so flat. He could see for miles in all directions, the landscape broken only by farmhouses, cellphone towers that jutted into the sky like long, bony fingers, and an eerie fifty mile stretch of slowly churning wind turbines. That section of the drive had made Frank uncomfortable. He'd felt exposed, like a creature in the sky would reach down with a giant hand and pluck him up into the heavens.

But as they'd entered Wisconsin, the flatlands had gradually given way to gently rolling hills. Now, here in southwestern Wisconsin, the bluffs almost made him feel like he was back at home in the Appalachians. Almost.

As they drove north through town, the comforting bluffs cradled the right side of the road, but the left side was something different. Just beyond the edge of the road, the land fell away, and the Mississippi River rolled past.

Frank felt his hand go to his neck for what felt like the thousandth time in the last hour. A small lock hung from a chain there. Mason and Sophie wore similar chains with similar locks. Frank called that model of lock the Beta, because it was nothing fancy. A simple twist would open it. But that was okay. It wasn't meant to lock anything. Not physically. With the compass, Zed could potentially see them coming. The locks would make them invisible to Zed. It

13

preserved surprise, which was the only weapon they had against him.

"Well," Sophie said, "the town's still here. It looks normal. No crazy trees or anything. Maybe Zed's lying low? Waiting for something?"

Frank grunted noncommittally. "Maybe."

They passed a car going the other direction and something tickled in the back of Frank's mind. Something wasn't right here. He just couldn't place what that something was.

"Let's find a restaurant," he said. "Get something to eat. I could use a burger."

"If we can find something open here in the sticks," Sophie said. "It's almost ten. I could go for some fish." She suddenly sat up straighter. "And cheese curds! You have to try the cheese curds."

Frank caught Sophie's eye in the rearview mirror. She was the only one of the group who'd been to this part of the country before. She also seemed the least fazed by this bizarre road trip. Unlike the rest of them, she didn't have a reason to hunt down Zed.

For Frank, it was about getting answers to the questions that plagued him. It was the weight of knowing he might be the only one who had the power to slow down Zed even a little. And deep in his heart he thought it might give him a chance to turn back the clock and save his brother.

Mason had spent his whole life with Zed, only to be betrayed by him when it mattered most.

But why was Sophie here?

Frank hadn't exactly invited her. He'd called to let her know what they were doing, that they were going after Zed, because he felt she deserved to know. She hadn't even paused. She hadn't asked. She'd simply told him she was going. And, truth be told, Frank was glad. He didn't know her well, but they'd been through some crazy things together. There was something about her. He couldn't deny she was pretty, but there was far more to her than that. She had an aggressive, straight-forward quality that fascinated him. Frank was accustomed to living inside his own head, to thinking things through before he opened his mouth to speak. Sure, he occasionally let his hot-headed tendencies get the better of him, but that was the exception. Sophie seemed to rush full-speed ahead as a way of life.

But it wasn't just that. What they were doing, going after Zed, not defending themselves from him, but actually taking the fight to him, terrified Frank. And, while it was great to have Mason by his side, he still wasn't sure the older man wasn't crazy. A lifetime spent in the forest had planted some funny ideas in his head. Who was to say he wouldn't flip back over to Zed's way of thinking when he saw his father figure again?

Some father figure.

But maybe Sophie did have a reason to go after Zed. He'd said she had the potential for great evil. And, if he'd said that about Frank, Frank sure would want to get to the bottom of what exactly he'd meant by that.

Frank slapped Mason on the shoulder. The carsickness had taken it out of the older man, and he looked unnaturally pale in the flickering glow of the passing streetlights. "How 'bout you? Can you eat?"

Mason shrugged. "Maybe a little soup."

"Beer cheese soup!" Sophie said, and Mason grew a shade paler.

A few minutes later, Sophie pointed to a restaurant on the river side of the road. The sign bore the face of a bear, and

15

read *North Country Cafe*. "How's that look?"

Frank answered in the affirmative, and Mason weakly nodded his assent.

Sophie pulled into the parking lot and found a spot near the door. When she shut off the car, Frank said, "Don't forget about the locks. You have to think about it to make them work. Lock yourself away from Zed in your mind, and the lock will do the rest."

"Locked. Got it." Sophie spoke in a way that made Frank think she might be making fun of him. It was at least the dozenth time in the last hour he'd reminded them to have their locks activated.

They opened the forest green doors with the oversized rough wooden handles, and entered the dim restaurant. The place was nearly empty. A classic rock radio station played softly, and the savory smell of cooking meat filled the air.

A balding man with a neatly trimmed goatee stood behind the welcome station. He wore a long apron that perfectly matched the green door they'd just passed through. His smile was warm and genuine.

"Welcome!" he said. And something about his voice made Frank *feel* welcome, like the man was genuinely glad to see them. "Three today?"

"Yep," Sophie said.

He grabbed three menus from behind the counter and snatched three sets of napkin-wrapped silverware from a basket next to him. Sophie nudged Frank with her elbow and nodded toward the man's wrist. It took Frank a minute, and then he saw it.

A Roman numeral III was tattooed on the inside of his wrist in blue ink.

Frank's eyebrows shot up. He remembered what Sean had

told him about the young Zed Heads in Rook Mountain, the way they tattooed the broken clock symbol on the backs of their hands in support of Zed. This was far subtler, but still it seemed to be too similar to disregard as a coincidence.

"Tonight's the night!" he said as he gathered the menus and silverware.

Sophie shot the man a confused look. "Sorry. Tonight's what night?"

Now the man raised his eyebrows. "You haven't been following the news?"

"Apparently not," Sophie said.

"Tonight's the night the mayflies are expected," he said. "The swarm." Then, without pausing to wait for a response, he turned and began walking. He called over his shoulder, "If you'll follow me."

He led them around a corner, past the bar, and to the back of the restaurant. Frank walked behind Sophie and Mason, and he heard them gasp a moment before he saw it.

The table was already set. It was a four top. There was a bowl of what looked to be chicken-noodle soup at one seat. At another, there was a burger and a tall beer. At the third seat, there was a beautifully cooked salmon fillet and a small plate of cheese curds.

And at the fourth seat, behind a steak and a glass of water, Zed sat smiling at them.

"I hope you don't mind," Zed said. "I took the liberty of ordering for the table."

2.

Alice bit her lip as she listened to her parents argue.

They'd hardly ever fought until recently. For the first seven or eight years of her life, her family had been happy. Her parents often looked at her with delight. Sometimes they almost seemed surprised to see her. A couple of times, she caught her mother just staring at her with tears in her eyes. It had seemed normal at the time, but now, at the age of nine, Alice Campbell was old enough to realize most families weren't like hers.

There was something wrong with her parents.

Sometimes she tried to figure out what it was, but she could never put her finger on it. There were the blue tattoos on the insides of their wrists—a *IV* on dad's and a *III* on mom's—but Alice had seen other people in town with those. Mrs. Brandon, Alice's third-grade teacher, had a *II*, and she seemed normal enough.

Alice's parents acted ashamed of their tattoos. It was almost as if they were afraid of them. They usually covered them up with long sleeves, and they looked upset whenever they caught Alice looking at them.

That stuff had been going on forever, but lately the arguing had started. The fights were always about stupid little things: the dishes, money, tones of voice. Young Alice didn't know the word *subtext*, but she understood the concept. She knew her parents arguments weren't really about chores or finances. There was something they weren't saying. Something they never said.

And that was the worst part of it. If there had been a clear reason for the arguments, Alice could have Pulled Back and stopped whatever had caused the fight. It hurt to Pull Back. It felt like a tiny flame burning in the back of her skull every time she did it, but it would have been worth it if it helped her parents be happy.

Today was different. Today she had caused the argument. They'd been sitting at the dinner table eating meatloaf and green beans. Alice hated the meatloaf at school. It was wet and mushy and tasted like something that had been sitting out too long. But the way her dad made it was different. He used barbecue sauce and it tasted both sweet and tangy in a way that made her mouth happy. She wasn't crazy about green beans, but even those were okay if she smeared them around in the extra barbecue sauce a little.

She and her mom and dad had been happily gobbling up their dinners, pausing between bites for a little conversation, her dad making dumb jokes as usual and her mom pointing out how lame they were and how many times he'd told them.

"Hey, why don't seagulls hang out in bays?" her dad asked.

Alice was already grinning. She'd heard this one before. He'd told it only a few nights ago. He was always telling the same jokes over and over again.

"Why?" Alice asked.

"Because then they'd be bagels," her dad said, and he took another bite of meatloaf.

Alice giggled. Mom swatted at Dad playfully, but she was smiling.

Alice felt her mind drifting to the future. School would be out soon. And then…

"How many weeks 'till June?" she asked.

The table grew quiet, and Alice knew she'd made a mistake, though she didn't understand how.

After a long moment, her mom said, "Two weeks," and then went back to her meatloaf.

Alice should have stopped there; the long silence should have been warning enough, but she couldn't help herself. "That means it's only two weeks until acting class!"

19

This would be Alice's third summer in the youth program put on by the King's Crossing theater. It was the highlight of her year. She was generally a shy girl, but something about being on stage, about pretending to be someone or something else, brought her to life. This year they would be performing *Peter Pan* and she could hardly wait.

Alice was a bit tall for her age, and she had a wild head of blonde hair that never seemed to stay in its ponytail. Her enthusiasm and her stage presence had made her popular with the teachers at the theater and helped her win larger roles than most of the other nine-year olds.

When she mentioned acting class, a tiny noise, almost like a gasp, came from her father. Alice looked up and saw her mother's eyes were squeezed shut.

"Helen," her father said. "We have to decide. Tonight."

"No!" her mother answered in a harsh whisper. "We agreed. We can give it another day. We said we'd keep things normal for her as long as we could."

Her father sighed. "You're scared. I get it. I am too. But this....waiting. It's just stupid."

Mom set her fork down, and Alice's heart leapt into her throat. Her mother was angry. She was trying to hide it, but Alice could see it in her eyes.

"Waiting for what?" Alice asked.

Her mother's eyes shot daggers at her father. "You had to bring it up now? At the table?"

"We can't avoid it anymore."

"Okay, then," mom said. "Tell her. Tell her what we're waiting for."

"Seriously Helen, you're just being spiteful."

Her mom stood up slowly and set her napkin on the table. "I can't listen to this. Excuse me." She walked away, and every footstep sent a jolt of worry through Alice. She knew what would happen next.

A moment later, her father sighed and followed her mother out of the room.

Alice sat alone at the table. Times like these, she wished she had a brother or sister. Someone to talk to so she didn't have to sit in the silence. A couple years ago she would have talked to her stuffed panda bear, but she was a bit old for that now.

She took a small bite of meatloaf, but it suddenly didn't taste so good. The sauce seemed harsh and spicy rather than sweet and tangy.

A moment later, she heard their voices. They weren't whispering now; they weren't holding back at all. As if being in their bedroom with the thin door closed would keep her from hearing. Sure, she couldn't make out the words, most of them anyway, but she heard their voices. The anger and fear in their shouts came through to the dining room loud and clear, even if the words were too muffled to make out.

She took a deep breath. This argument was her fault. If she hadn't brought up acting class, this wouldn't have happened. It made her feel bad to know she'd caused the argument, but in a strange way it also made her feel *good*. Because if she had caused it, she could also prevent it.

She knew what she had to do. She needed to Pull Back.

Alice closed her eyes and pictured the rope. It was a thick, coarse thing, as big around as her dad's arm. The type of rope that might be used to tie a big ship to a dock. She pictured it suspended in a sea of blackness. Nothing existed but the rope.

She reached out, not with her hands, but with something else. Something she didn't have a name for. Something in her mind. She gripped the rope, and she felt its prickly coarseness. The heat in the back of her head began as soon as she touched it. It hurt to Pull Back on the rope, but she knew from experience that if she didn't pull, if she just touched the rope for too long, it would hurt far worse. She would get sick and throw up. She'd be weak and wouldn't be able to get out of bed for days. Then there would be more doctors and more tests. And when the first tests didn't find anything, there would be even more. She couldn't let that happen.

She pulled ever-so-gently on the rope, using just the right amount of pressure. The pain shot through her brain and it was so hot she didn't think she could stand it. But it was over in only a moment.

Alice slowly opened her eyes, and what she saw made her smile.

Her mother and her father happily eating meatloaf.

Dad looked at her. "Hey, why don't seagulls hang out in bays?"

Alice grinned, but this time it wasn't from the joke. It was pride.

She never talked about the rope or the way she could Pull Back on it. Not anymore. When she was very young, she'd thought it was something everyone could do, and she'd discussed it openly. Everyone thought she was playing make believe, but a few times she'd seen a worried look on her parents' faces when she brought it up.

When she was four, her best friend Becky had broken her arm. Alice asked her why she didn't just Pull Back to before it happened so her arm wouldn't be broken. Becky had looked at her blankly, so she'd tried to explain. If she Pulled Back to yesterday, she could be more careful in the tree, or not climb the tree at all. Then her arm wouldn't be broken. When

Becky's blank stare had continued, Alice had come to the startling conclusion that not only could Becky not Pull Back, she didn't even know what it was. And if Becky didn't know, maybe other people didn't either.

So, Alice had stopped talking about it. She didn't even mention it to her parents anymore. She took it as fact that no one else she knew had this particular skill.

Since no one else could do it, no one could appreciate how difficult what she had just done was. When she was younger, a single Pull Back on the rope would send her back days or even weeks. It was impossible to control. She'd sometimes worried what might happen if she were to pull a little too hard and get sent back to before her birth. Would she find herself huddled in her mother's womb, complete with the memories of a nine-year-old?

But slowly, over time, she'd gotten better at it. And now she was very precise.

"Why?" Alice asked her father.

"Because then they'd be bagels," he said, finishing the joke, and he took a bite of meatloaf.

Mom swatted at him playfully, just as she had the first time.

Alice felt the familiar tug, the slight urge to say what she'd said the first time, to ask how many weeks until June. Reality wanted to flow like it had originally, and she had to fight it a little to get it to deviate. But just a little. And Alice was used to it.

Alice didn't ask about June or acting class. She just kept eating her meatloaf.

Her mother cleared her throat suddenly. "Hey, isn't acting class starting soon?"

Alice's heart sank. Sometimes reality was difficult to change. Others might fill in the gaps even if she didn't.

Dad's face went pale. "Helen. Don't you think it's time we talked to her about it?"

Alice saw the flush on her mother's face. She knew how this would play out. She'd already seen the argument that was about to happen. She closed her eyes. She'd have to Pull Back again.

She tried not to do it more often than she needed to. Occasionally she would use it if she'd done badly on a test or if something embarrassing happened. But she didn't do it for anything too trivial. And it wasn't just the hot burst of pain that made her reluctant to Pull Back. Ever since she'd learned not everyone had this skill, she'd felt funny about it.

She'd been able to do it for as long as she could remember. The rope had always been there in some dark corner of her mind waiting to be pulled. But something about it wasn't natural, she knew. Something about it felt *wrong*.

There was no time to think about that now. Not while her parents were arguing. Alice took a deep breath and gave the rope the tiniest of pulls.

She let the pain wash over her for a moment, then opened her eyes. Her father was smirking at her.

"Hey, why don't seagulls hang out in bays?" he asked.

Alice reached out as if she were grabbing a napkin and knocked over her glass of milk.

"Whoa!" Dad said, hopping up to avoid the milk flowing off the edge of the table and onto his lap.

There, she thought. That should be enough to knock reality off its tracks. Things would proceed along a different path now.

Alice helped her parents clean up the milk and they all went back to eating their meatloaf.

3.

Frank stood frozen for a long moment, staring at Zed. How was it possible? How had the man known they would be here at this very moment? Had he been tracking them with the compass?

Frank's hand slipped to the lock hanging from the chain around his neck.

He glanced at Sophie and saw she too was clutching her lock, a perplexed look on her face.

But Mason...

Mason stood statue still, staring at Zed. He had a look of fury and concentration Frank had never before seen on his face. His lip was curled slightly, and Frank could see the gaps where some teeth were missing. His fists were clenched in front of him. Frank prayed he wouldn't attack. Not now. It wouldn't do any good.

After a long moment of silence, Zed said, "This is slightly awkward. I can't actually see you at the moment. I have to trust the look on my friend Brian's face that you are standing here at all. Well, him and the others." Zed nodded toward the wall to his left, and for the first time Frank noticed the eight men and women standing along the wall in the shadows.

They were all casually dressed, and they didn't seem to have much in common other than the grim, determined looks on their faces and the guns they all held.

"What do we do?" Sophie asked. "Should we lock ourselves away from the rest of them?"

"Miss Porter!" Zed said with the hint of a laugh in his voice, and Frank grimaced. They'd had fourteen hours in the car and he hadn't covered more than the bare-bones basics of the locks. He didn't think he'd have to. Not yet. He thought they only needed to hide themselves from Zed's compass, that they'd have time to plan things further. He'd been a fool.

Frank locked his voice away from everyone but Sophie and Mason. "Make it so they can't hear your voice. Think about it and it will happen."

Sophie hesitantly spoke again. "Okay. So what do we do? We can make ourselves invisible from everyone and head for the doors."

Frank glanced back and saw two men with revolvers standing in the doorway to this section of the restaurant. And, sure enough, the emergency exit was behind the people lined against the wall.

"Well," Frank said slowly, "we came to find Zed. So... mission accomplished, I guess."

Sophie was staring at Mason. He was still frozen, his eyes locked on Zed. "You okay, Mason?" Sophie asked.

He didn't answer.

Brian, the man who'd led them to the table, spoke. "Their lips are moving, but I can't hear what they're saying."

Zed sighed. "Well, that's just rude." He gestured toward the table. "Would you all care to take a seat?"

Frank paused for a moment. He noticed Sophie waiting for him, letting him take the lead. That surprised him. She didn't seem like the type of person who waited around for anybody.

"Let's hear what he has to say," Frank said.

Sophie's eyes widened. "Really?"

"We can always make ourselves invisible again and head for the doors. Whatever he's going to say is sure to be a lie, but I'd still like to hear it." Without waiting for a reply, Frank mentally turned off his lock.

Zed met his eyes and visibly relaxed. "Here we are again. I ordered you a burger."

Frank wanted nothing more than to ask *how* Zed had known what he'd been planning to eat. But he wouldn't give Zed the satisfaction. Not now.

He pulled out the chair next to Zed, the one with the burger in front of it, and plopped down into the seat.

A moment later Zed's eyes settled on Sophie as she too turned off her lock and sat down. To her, he said nothing. Frank could see something in Zed's eyes when he looked at Sophie. Something that was a cross between hostile, confused, and maybe a little frightened. Frank couldn't read that look completely—it was a complicated thing and Frank could only skim its surface—but it was clear Zed didn't like her.

Sophie met Zed's gaze, and without breaking it, picked up a fork, stabbed the salmon on the plate in front of her and stuck a big bite in her mouth. She didn't bother closing her mouth as she chewed.

Frank had to stifle a laugh. She could be incredibly juvenile at times, but something about her made him smile.

Zed grunted and looked away. "Just waiting for my protege then. How about it, Mason? Join the adult table?"

Mason was still frozen, nearly shaking with rage.

Zed said, "We can't begin if you don't—"

"No," Frank said. "He doesn't have to join if he doesn't want to. You've done enough to him."

"Hell yes," Sophie said through a mouthful of salmon.

Mason seemed to relax a bit at that. Frank could see by the way Zed's eyes suddenly focused that Mason had turned off his lock.

"No," Mason said. "If you're talking, I'm joining." He sat down across from Zed and brushed the soup bowl aside. He leaned forward on the edge of his seat, looking like he might pounce at any moment.

Zed's face softened. "Mason, I owe you an apology. I shouldn't have left you in the woods. I'm sorry for that."

Mason spoke through clenched teeth. "You promised me. We talked about it for years and you said we'd leave together —"

"I've apologized, and that's that." Zed's voice was sharp, like a parent scolding a child. And, to Frank's surprise, Mason reacted like a scolded child, turning a deep red and dropping his eyes.

Zed looked out the window for a long moment before speaking. "Tonight's a special night in King's Crossing. Special and strange."

"Why's that?" Sophie asked. "Half price fish?"

"No, Ms. Porter. Tonight's the night the mayflies come."

Frank felt the sudden urge to grab Zed and shake him. He wanted to force him to tell them why he was here and what he was doing. But he'd had enough dealings with Zed to know the man loved to hear himself talk, and he wouldn't share any information until he'd worked his way around to it. So he asked, "Mayflies?"

"Yes. See, there are millions of mayfly eggs that hatch in the Mississippi River tonight. It happens once a year. It's usually a bit later, generally June or July despite the name, but this year tonight is the special night."

"Fascinating," Sophie said, and she went back to her salmon.

Zed ignored her. "The result is a swarm that is difficult to imagine if you haven't seen it. It's like a living cloud. The swarm is thick enough and large enough that it shows up on weather radar. Imagine a fog made of insects and you'll start to get the idea." He took a sip of his water. "But you won't have to imagine it for long. I expect they'll be out in full force in an hour or so. Probably by the time you leave this restaurant."

"Not sure we'll be staying that long," Frank said.

"The swarm's harmless really," Zed said. "An interesting, annoying anomaly." Zed squinted at Frank. "I still don't know how you do it. The disappearing thing, I mean. I expect that's how your friends hid the Tools from me all those years in Rook Mountain. They must have had some of your locks. But how did you learn to make them? How do you give them their power?"

Frank said nothing.

Zed drummed his hands on the tabletop. "Alright. Down to business, then. I invited you here tonight because I need your help."

Frank tried to wrap his mind around that last sentence for a moment.

Sophie said, "You invited us?"

Zed nodded. "Make no mistake, you wouldn't be sitting here with me, you wouldn't have found me at all, not after years of looking, if I didn't want it to be so."

"Get to the other part," Frank said. "You want us to help you? Why the hell would we do that?"

"Lots of reasons." He paused for a long moment. "I can see by the look on your face you need me to list some of them for you." He counted off the reasons on his fingers as he spoke. "Because the alternative is worse. Because there are people you love on this planet. Because you're not idiots. Because you don't want to be devoured by vicious beasts."

"There you go being vague again," Frank said.

"I'll explain in a moment," Zed said. "But if I can convince you of all that, that the four of us are the only thing standing between this world and its destruction, you would have to at least consider it, no?"

Sophie said, "You make a compelling argument. It's bullshit, but compelling. As far as I can tell, you don't care about anyone but yourself. Why would you save the world?"

"The oldest reason of all," Zed said. "Revenge."

"Might not want to bring up revenge to us," Sophie said. "It won't help your case."

Zed ignored the comment. "It's taken me a long time to plan this. Longer than you might believe." Zed leaned forward and looked each of them in the eye one by one. It wasn't the mind-reading gaze Frank had felt the time Zed knocked on his door long ago in Rook Mountain. No, there was something else in this gaze. Respect. "I've spent centuries planning for what's going to happen in the next couple of weeks."

"And what's that?" Sophie asked.

"Listen. There are things in this world that don't belong here. Terrible things."

"The Ones Who Sing," Frank muttered. He wasn't even sure he'd said it out loud until he saw Zed's face darken.

"They're merely a side effect. The Ones Who Sing are nasty creatures, but they do what they do because it's their nature, as twisted and tainted as it is. We can't hold that against them. Not really. The things I'm talking about are worse. They too destroy, but they destroy for a purpose. They will destroy us all, and they'll start with me."

Frank leaned forward and looked into the bald man's eyes. "Zed, so help me God, if you keep talking in puzzles I'm going to take your steak knife and put it through your eye."

Zed grunted. "Puzzles? You want me to be more straight forward? Okay, I can do that. You remember that man in the forest, the one with the beard?"

"The one whose arms you tore off?" Sophie asked. "Yeah, I seem to vaguely recall that."

"His name was Vee. He's one of them. There are three others like him. They are not happy with me. Vee least of all."

"You think he survived?" Sophie asked.

"Their kind is very hard to kill."

"Maybe you should try talking to them," Frank said. "I thought you were mister persuasive."

"Don't think I haven't tried," Zed said. "But they're stubborn. They won't even consider my way of thinking. So first, we kill those four...they call themselves Exiles."

"First?" Frank asked. "What's second?"

Zed's smile widened. "We save the world."

4.

Alice heard a knock at the door. She rolled over and pushed the button on the pink alarm clock next to her bed. It lit up with a bright blue glow. *3:23.*

She'd been dreaming she was on her way to the beach with Mom and Dad. She didn't know which beach—hopefully not that stinky one over by the river that smelled like fish—but she'd been excited. She'd had on her swimming suit under her clothes. There was a bag on the seat next to her, and she saw a bottle of sunscreen and a towel sticking out of it.

Mom and Dad had been laughing and playfully arguing about who sang the song playing on the radio. It was some old-fashioned sounding song, something about *Paradise City.* Yuck.

The car pulled to a stop and Alice felt her heart leap. She saw a large blue lake out her window, the surface so still it looked like glass. She waited anxiously, and as soon as Dad opened his door, she opened hers. When she stepped out of the car, she felt something cold on her sandaled feet. She looked down and saw she was standing in six inches of snow.

That was when the pounding on the door woke her.

No one had ever come to the door this late. Not that she could remember, anyhow.

She heard her parents' voices in their room down the hall, talking fast, sounding worried. The pounding on the door came again, louder this time, like the person at the door was growing impatient.

She heard her father's heavy footsteps as he walked across the bedroom, through the hallway, and down the steps to the front door. Alice slipped out of her bed, tip-toeing down the hallway after him. She knew he wouldn't be happy if he caught her—little girls were *not* supposed to be out of bed at three twenty-three in the morning, except to go pee or maybe get a drink of water—but she couldn't help herself. She had to know who was at the door. She crouched in the shadows at the top of the stairs, her favorite hiding spot when she wanted to spy on what was happening below. Looking through the wooden railing, she had a clear view of the front door.

Dad flipped the switch to turn on the porch light and peeked out the window. He paused for a moment and sighed, as if whatever he'd seen out there didn't please him. Then he twisted the deadbolt lock and pulled open the door.

The man on the other side of the door was someone Alice had never seen before. She would have remembered. His hair was bright red and it hung down to his shoulders. It was curly, like the way Mom sometimes wore hers, but only if she got up early and spent forever-and-a-half in the bathroom. The man wore a windbreaker and jeans. He was shorter than Dad, but he was thick, like someone had pressed on the top of a tall man's head and smooshed him.

Her father said, "What is it?"

"Can I come in?" the man asked.

Dad paused, then nodded and stepped aside, letting the man through the door.

Alice huddled close to the floor, her hands clutching the rail and her face scooted forward just far enough to see the men standing almost directly below her. Her heart was still racing from the dream and from being unexpectedly woken at three in the morning. She had the feeling it wouldn't slow until she knew what was going on.

The red-haired man said, "It's started, Matt."

Dad chuckled. "You think I don't know that?"

The man sighed. "Jesus. Why you gotta be such a dick lately?"

"I'm being a dick, Willis? You show up and knock on my door at three in the morning to tell me something I already know, and I'm the dick?"

"Okay, geez, sorry." The red-haired man shuffled his feet. "Tomorrow's clutch. And it starts early."

"So you thought waking me up in the middle of the night was the best way to make sure I'm prepared?"

The red-haired man paused. There was something he wasn't saying. Alice leaned out a bit further.

"No, man. It's just…some of the guys are worried. You haven't seemed yourself. And I thought—we all thought—it might be better if you had someone with you."

There was a long pause before Dad spoke again. "Explain how that works."

"I'll just, you know, crash on your couch. Come with in the morning. Instead of meeting you there."

33

Dad leaned close to Willis and spoke softly. "You think I'm gonna flake?"

"No, man. That's not it."

"Yes. I think that is exactly *it*." Dad was talking louder now. He was getting mad, Alice could tell. "Have I *ever* flaked? In all the times we've done this? Have I ever been the reason it failed?"

"No. I mean, not that I know of. But things are different now. And people are worried. We can't let Zed down."

Dad leaned even closer. The two men's faces were almost touching now, but Dad was still shouting. "Don't you say that name in my house. I don't care what that man thinks."

Alice had never heard of this Zed before, but Dad sure didn't seem to like him.

The red-haired man took a step back. His face was growing red now, not as red as his hair, but enough to let Alice know he wasn't taking Dad's yelling very well. "Even still, he runs the show."

"Yeah, he does. And how far's that gotten us?"

The other man shook his head. "You really gonna ask that question? It's gotten us far enough. It's gotten us here. We ain't dead yet."

"No," Dad said, a wicked grin on his face. "Not yet. Not for a couple weeks."

The skin on Alice's arms broke out in goose bumps. What could Dad mean by that?

"So that's it? You're giving up? The solid and dependable Matt Campbell is giving up?"

"You know I'm not. I'm just starting to question the sanity of this plan."

Willis took a deep breath and put a hand on Dad's shoulder. "Think of your kid, man. Think of your wife."

34

Dad brushed off the hand. "It's time for you to leave."

The red-haired man looked around the room, drawing out the moment as if he didn't want to say what he would have to say next. Finally he said, "I can't do that."

Now Dad took a step back. "That's how it is? And what if I say you aren't allowed here? What if I make you leave?"

Suddenly there was something in Willis' hand. Alice realized what it was, and her mouth went dry. It was a gun. Just like bad guys carried in the movies.

"That's not gonna happen," Willis said. "Zed needs us tomorrow. I've got to—"

Dad moved before the man could finish the sentence, rushing Willis. He tackled the man, and they wrestled on the floor. It was too dark for Alice to make out exactly what was happening. All she saw was a dark mass with a streak of red running through it wiggling around on the floor.

Alice felt an arm around her shoulder and almost screamed. She looked back and saw Mom behind her. Mom pulled her close in a hug, her eyes glued on the scene below them.

The world shook as a gunshot rang out. Mom screamed and Alice thought maybe she did too. A grunt and a moan came from the floor below, and one of the figures rose, the gun in his hand. It was Dad.

Dark blood stained the carpet around the moaning man on the ground. The dark spot was growing at an alarming rate.

"Oh, God, Willis, I'm sorry," Dad said. "So sorry."

He let out a sobbing noise, and Alice realized he was crying. She'd never seen her father cry. He staggered backwards. The gun slipped out of his hand and hit the floor with a thump.

Alice whimpered. She scrunched her eyes shut and thought

of the rope. Dad had shot someone! If she let this stand, he would go to jail!

She grabbed the rope inside her mind, but it was slippery. She couldn't hold onto it. That happened sometimes when she was upset. It wasn't fair. The times she needed to use it most were when something upsetting happened.

With her eyes still closed, she drew a deep breath and let it out slowly. She imagined her emotions as a ball of something wet and slimy in her hand. She imagined putting the ball of messy emotions into her pocket. She could deal with them later. They'd be waiting for her when she was ready.

Her mother's arms were still wrapped tightly around her. That, too, calmed her.

She clutched the rope and tugged.

As the blinding pain rocketed through her brain, she had two terrifying thoughts. First, she knew she'd pulled too hard. She gone back hours instead of the fifteen minutes or so she'd intended. Second, she had the realization that she might just return to her sleeping body. If she was asleep, she might not wake again until three twenty-three when it was too late to stop this from happening. Worse yet, what if she remembered exactly what she needed to do but was trapped in a dream and unable to wake up?

As those thoughts passed through her mind, she felt the familiar wave of vertigo as her body changed positions without her physically moving. She lay in her bed, her eyes open, staring at the ceiling. A wave of relief washed over her. She was awake.

She rolled over and punched the button on her alarm clock, washing the room in soft blue light. *10:09.* Geez, she really had gone back farther than she'd intended.

Still, there was no time to waste.

She hopped out of bed and raced to her parents' room. The door was only open a crack. She could hear them talking softly. And another sound beneath that; she wasn't sure, but it sounded like her mother was crying.

She tapped on the door with her knuckles and went in without waiting for a response. Both her parents' faces swung toward her, and she saw immediately she had been correct. Mom was crying.

Now that they were looking at her, she suddenly had no idea what to say.

"Hey," Dad said. "What's up, honey? Can't sleep?"

Mom quickly wiped at her face with her hand, as if she could hide the tears Alice had already seen.

"I…" Alice started, but then stopped. She never talked about Pulling Back. She hadn't for years now. But she was almost certain they knew. Maybe they didn't know *exactly* what she could do, but they had an idea. They didn't talk about it, either. It was like the family had made a silent pact to never speak of how much of a freak Alice was.

But this was different. This was a matter of life and death.

She started again. "There's a man coming here tonight. Willis. He's got red hair. Long, like a girl or a rock star."

Mom looked at Dad. "Willis Eddy."

Dad nodded.

Both their faces were pale as they waited for her to continue.

"He wants to stay here overnight. So he can make sure Dad does something he's supposed to do tomorrow."

"Jesus," Dad whispered.

"And he has a gun!" Alice said. She could feel the tears welling up in her eyes now, as if they'd been bottled up until now and the words were the cork that let them loose. "Dad fights him and gets the gun and shoots him."

"Honey," Mom says, her voice calmer now, "what time does this happen?"

Alice whispered, "Three twenty-three in the morning."

"Holy hell," Dad said. He looked sick.

Mom turned toward him. "Should we leave?"

Dad shook his head slowly. "That wouldn't help. Where would we go? We can't get out of what I have to do tomorrow." He slammed his hand against the mattress. "What the hell have we become?"

Mom put a hand on his shoulder. "No, this is good. We have…" she glanced at the clock by the bed, "…over five hours to get ready for Willis. We can plan what we're going to say. Hide anything we don't want him to see. He wants to stay the night, let him stay the night. Let him report back to Zed on how we're playing our parts perfectly."

Dad nodded. He leaned forward and gave Alice a tight hug. "You did great, honey. So good." He let go and held her at arm's length, looking at her with a serious face. "You have to go to bed now. Mom and I…we have work to do."

Alice wanted oh-so-badly to ask what the work was, who that red-haired man was, what this all meant, but she knew she couldn't. They wouldn't answer her. At best they'd scold her for asking and at worst they'd make up some lie. So she just nodded, put on a brave smile, and went back to her room.

She lay awake watching the clock until three twenty-three when the red-haired man knocked on the door.

THE BOY WHO FOUND THE WATCH (PART ONE)

Topeka, Kansas
May, 1948

The boy sharpened a pencil with his pocket knife.

The process had been going on for quite some time. First, he'd spent a good five minutes meticulously sharpening the knife. He'd used a whetstone he'd found in the shed, doing it just the way he'd seen his father do it. His father had been gone two years now, since the boy was nine; just up and disappeared in the night. The boy got up one morning, and his dad was gone. His mother hadn't seemed all too interested in finding her husband, either. She got angry when the boy brought it up. It had taken the boy a couple weeks to come to the realization that his father had disappeared *on purpose*. And he wasn't going to find his way back. As soon as the boy had the realization, he'd promised himself he'd put his father out of his mind. If it didn't bother his father to leave, then the old man wasn't worth any thought. The boy had done an admirable job of keeping to his word, too.

After the knife was sharp enough to slice clean through a falling piece of paper, the boy had set to work on the pencil.

39

Truth be told, the pencil wasn't all that dull. But the boy liked to write with a pencil so sharp he was liable to draw blood if he poked himself with it. So, he spent the next ten minutes shaving away tiny bits of wood, watching them curl and fall to the floor as he gently moved the blade back and forth.

The work soothed him. He let his mind go. Part of him was completely engaged in the task, locked in concentration on the pencil and the blade. But another part of him was shut off altogether. It was a pleasant feeling, to be both present and absent at the same moment.

"Zedidiah!"

His mother's voice startled him out of his working daze, and the blade slipped, gouging the wood. Zedidiah let out a quiet curse. Ten minutes' work ruined in a moment by his mother's shrill, demanding voice.

"Zedidiah!"

He threw the pencil on his bed, then folded the knife and slipped it into his pocket. It always made him feel better to know it was there, that the razor sharp weapon was within reach at any moment. He paused, then brushed the wood shavings under the bed. That wouldn't hide them permanently; his mother would find them the next time she cleaned in there. But it would save him from being hollered at if she happened to peek into his room tonight.

He left the room and made his way down the wide stairway.

His family wasn't rich. In fact, if his mother was to be believed it was a miracle they were able to keep food on the table and clothes on his back with her measly teacher's salary. But their house *was* the house of a rich family. Not Rockefeller rich, but rich enough that a maid wouldn't have looked out of place. The house had been in his mother's family for more than a hundred years. It was a lonely place for a family of two, and it always felt drafty and cold, even in the summer.

Zedidiah paused halfway down the stairs. His mother sat in the chair near the door, the one she never used unless there was company. She was on the edge of the chair, leaning forward. Her legs were crossed and her hands rested primly on her knee. Most disturbing of all, she was smiling.

In the other chair, the one directly across from his mother, there sat a tall, impossibly thin man. He wore a brown, rumpled suit that looked both expensive and unkempt at the same time. The man looked too tall for the chair; his sharp knees and elbows stuck out at odd angles.

Zedidiah's mother hadn't seen him. Her gaze was glued to the man in the chair. And the man's gaze was glued to her. "Zedidiah!" she yelled again.

The boy slowed his descent. "I'm here, mom." He said it in a soft voice, meant to contrast with her needlessly loud calls.

His mother and the man both turned toward him, their heads moving in unison. The effect was disturbing. There was something odd about his mother's eyes. They seemed a bit glassy, but there was an energy behind them, too.

"Zedidiah, we have a guest."

The boy could think of no response that wouldn't earn him a wallop, so he stayed quiet, instead focusing his energy on coming down the rest of the steps. He stopped directly between the two chairs.

His mother said, "This is Mister...." She faltered for a moment, her face reddening. "Why, I'm sorry. I just realized I don't know your surname."

The man grinned. "Oh, no need for all that. We're among friends. Call me Charlie." The man spoke in a strange accent. Zedidiah thought maybe it was Australian, though he wasn't sure exactly what had led him to that conclusion as he'd never before heard an Australian accent. The man held out his hand.

The boy looked at it for a long moment, temporarily confused. He couldn't recall ever having shaken hands with a grown man. Most grown-ups ignored him or yelled at him. The man's fingers were strangely long, and the boy decided he didn't want to shake that hand. Not at all.

He risked a glance at his mother. Her smile suddenly looked frozen, like the moment was paused and the only way he could unpause it was by doing the thing he didn't want to do.

He grimly took the man's hand. Charlie's grip was strong, and his hand was uncomfortably hot. He gave the boy's hand three quick pumps and mercifully released it.

"May I call you Zed?" the man asked.

The boy didn't much care what the man called him. He was just glad to have his hand back. Something about Charlie's hand felt wrong. This whole situation felt wrong.

And suddenly he thought he knew why. Zedidiah realized this man was his mother's boyfriend.

It was the only possible explanation. Mom had been acting different lately. Dressing nicely. Staying out late. The signs were there, but the boy hadn't wanted to see them. The sudden realization, and the implications of what it could lead to—meals on Saturday night with this man, a wedding, this oddly tall stranger living in their house—made him feel sick to his stomach.

"He's a serious one, isn't he?" the man asked.

"Oh yes," Zedidiah's mother said. "Always has been. Hardly ever smiles."

Charlie looked at the boy for a long moment, then snapped

his fingers as if an idea had just come to him. "We'll see what we can do about that. Want to see a magic trick, Zed?"

Before the boy had a chance to answer, Charlie pulled something out of his pocket. It was a watch.

"Take a close look at this here," Charlie said.

Zedidiah did. He looked at the pocket watch, and after a moment he found he couldn't look away. There was something about the watch. It was like it was calling to him. Singing to him. He couldn't hear anything, not with his ears, but that was how it *felt*. Like the watch was singing a melody so beautiful it might make his heart break. The boy had never felt anything like it. Not even close. It was intense joy and deep sorrow all wrapped together and swirled up.

The man slowly turned the watch and the boy saw something engraved on the back of it. A broken clock. Odd thing, having a picture of a clock engraved into the surface of an actual clock. But it felt right somehow. Beautiful.

It was all too much for the boy. He felt tears welling up in his eyes as the sensations in his brain hummed louder and louder until it felt like he couldn't take it anymore.

"And, there you are," Charlie said, closing his hand and hiding the watch from the boy's eyes.

Zedidiah let out an involuntary moan. He wanted to see the watch again. He wanted to touch it. What he wouldn't give to hold it in his hand, even for a moment.

His mother suddenly giggled, and the spell was broken. The boy slowly looked up. Something was wrong. Charlie wasn't there. He'd disappeared.

The boy realized Charlie was suddenly standing on the opposite side of the room.

"What happened?" Zedidiah asked in a weak voice.

His mother let out another loud giggle.

Charlie winked at him. "Just a little magic trick. Like I said."

Zedidiah's heart raced. "What did you do?" His voice was louder now and there was anger in it.

"He used the watch," his mother said. "He hypnotized us. Like a magician."

Fury rose within the boy, bubbling up so unexpectedly it sent him reeling. "Why? Why did you do it?"

Charlie looked at him oddly. "It's just a magic trick, Zed. Don't you like magic?"

The boy clenched his fists so hard they hurt. This man had used that watch, that beautiful watch, for a parlor trick? That was not right. Not at all.

"Zedidiah, what's wrong with you?" his mother asked. "Charlie's new in town. Is this any way to act to someone who's new in town?"

Zedidiah thought that completely irrelevant and would have said so if he hadn't been too angry to speak.

"Aw, it's all right," Charlie said. "Guess the boy doesn't like magic. There's stranger things." He opened his hand for just a moment, a brief wonderful moment in which the boy was once again able to gaze upon the watch, and then slipped the timepiece back into his pocket. "Maybe cards are more your thing? Care for a game of hearts?"

The boy wasn't listening. Because in that brief flash, the watch had let him know what needed to happen, and he'd instantly seen his only possible course of action.

Zed needed to steal the watch.

CHAPTER TWO: STRAINED

1.

Sophie popped the last cheese curd into her mouth. She'd been eating slowly, if sloppily. When the curd was gone, she would be forced to listen to Zed's insanity unoccupied.

She glanced back and forth between Zed and Frank. In a lot of ways, this was between the two of them. These men hated each other. Or, maybe each of them represented something the other hated.

"I'm sorry," Frank said. "It almost sounded like you were asking for our help."

Zed chuckled. "Not exactly. More like offering mine."

Frank leaned forward, his elbows on the table. Sophie's mom would have cringed. "That's an interesting way of looking at it."

Zed said, "You came here to find me. Not the other way around."

"And you were lying in wait." Frank was talking louder now. Sophie could see by the way he clenched his fists he was getting heated. "If you think we're going to help you, you're sicker than I thought." Frank looked to Sophie and Mason.

Sophie glanced down at her empty plate and sighed. Her

food had been the only thing keeping her quiet thus far. She sucked at keeping her mouth shut. "Hold on. Let's hear what he's got to say."

Frank's eyes widened. "Sophie, you don't know him like I do. There's no point."

She shrugged. "I'm not saying we do what he says. But we just spent fourteen hours in the car. Maybe I don't want to get back in it quite yet."

Frank sank back in his seat. He turned to Mason. "You got anything to say about this?"

Mason did not. His eyes were still glued to his former friend.

Frank sighed and motioned to Sophie for her to take the lead.

Sophie smiled. "What do you want us to do, and what do we get?"

Zed's smile went a bit colder. "You're direct. Tell me, why'd you come along on this trip?"

"You don't seem to understand I'm the only one helping your case at the moment. You gonna answer my questions or not?"

Zed looked at her hard, and she felt...something. Like tiny tendrils crawling across her mind. It was an unpleasant feeling, like something crawling under her skin.

She tore her gaze away from his with a massive effort, and the tendrils let go of her mind, burning as they left her. "What the hell?" she yelled.

Zed tilted his head, suddenly seeming more interested. "Well now. That's curious. Few are strong enough to do that." He glanced at Frank. "I wonder if it really was happenstance that brought the two of you together."

Sophie shook her head hard to clear it. "Don't do that

again. Answer the questions."

"Fine," Zed said. "I need you to do three things for me."

"We're listening," Frank said.

"Remember when I told you every special town has a book?"

Frank nodded grimly. Sophie watched him. She knew how much that conversation had spooked him.

"This town is no different. Thing is, I've had some difficulties locating the book. In theory, I should be able to find it with the compass, but it's not working. I need you to find the book for me."

Sophie squinted at him. "If you couldn't do it with the compass, what makes you think we can find it?"

Zed gestured toward Frank. "This one here has a knack for doing things that have never before been done." He paused, looking back at Sophie thoughtfully. "Both of you do, actually. I figured it was time I started using that to my advantage rather than my detriment."

"There's no way we're giving you that book," Frank growled.

Zed nodded. "I understand. I didn't ask you to. I only need you to find it."

"What's the second thing?" Sophie asked.

"I need Frank to use that talent of his to hide the book. The four who are coming after me want it. If they get it, their job will be much easier."

"Find the book and hide it," Sophie said. "Got it. What's number three?"

"My third request has to do with the four Exiles themselves. When they come, there will be a battle. Even if we are as prepared as I plan to be, the odds will be stacked against us very highly indeed."

47

"That's not a request," Frank said.

"I have reason to believe they'll be here in two weeks' time," Zed continued. "If by that point I have proven myself trustworthy in all things—if I've stayed true to my word and held to the strength of my convictions—I ask that you stand by my side in that final battle and help me kill them."

There was a long silence. Someone shuffled their feet and Sophie turned. She'd forgotten all the men and women standing along the walls. She turned back to Zed. "That answers my first question. As to my second? What do we get out of all this?"

Zed smiled sadly. "I won't lie. All I have to give you is this: best case scenario, you get to save the world. Worst case, you get a front row seat to the apocalypse. You get to see it coming and fight it while the rest of humanity remains unaware that their extinction is moments away. I can't guarantee we'll win, but I do guarantee we'll try our damndest."

After a moment, Frank chuckled. "That's what you sold them?" He looked at the armed people around the restaurant. "The end of the world? Come on, man. At least in Rook Mountain, you had something real for the people to fear. At least they'd seen the Unfeathered. These Yankees handed over the key to the city on nothing but scary stories?"

Some of the people along the wall began to murmur, but Zed held up a hand to silence them. "Frank, you saw Vee. You heard what he said. Saw what he did. If I'm lying, what's the harm? I'm not asking you to give me the book, just to find it. Hide it away from them and me both. But if I'm telling the truth and you don't help me, the world ends."

Frank shook his head. He looked at Sophie and Mason. "You buying this?"

Sophie's eyes searched the room. She didn't consider herself the most level-headed person, but she was beginning to think Frank was even less reasonable. He wouldn't agree to Zed's offer even if it meant they wouldn't leave this room alive. And, from the looks on the faces around them, that might be the case.

She spoke softly. "What do you say we think it over for the night?"

"Sophie—" Frank started, but she cut him off.

"He's right about one thing. We have to at least consider it. Besides, saving the world…seven billion people getting to stay alive isn't a bad payoff."

"No."

The husky voice to her left surprised her. It was Mason.

"No," the older man repeated. "It's not enough. Not for working with him."

Zed turned to Mason and looked at him—really looked at him—for the first time since he'd walked through the door. "Mason, I know I hurt you."

"It's not that," Mason said. "It's the reward." He looked Frank and Sophie in the eye, each in turn. "He can give us more. Lots more." He took a deep breath, and then smiled in a way that was eerily similar to Zed's own smile. "We bring you the book, and you use it to bring us the people of Sanctuary. My parents. The others, too. Everyone who died that night so long ago."

Zed barked out a surprised laugh. "I taught you better than that. I can't just pull them out of thin air. Even with a book."

"You did teach me better than that. With the book and the compass, you can find a soft place and bring them through. Reach back in time and drag them here."

"Okay…" Zed said. "Save a bunch of dead people from

Sanctuary. Is that all?"

"No," Mason said. He nodded toward Sophie. "Save her sister, too."

Sophie's breath caught in her throat. Was it possible? She tried to catch Frank's eye, but he was staring at Mason in disbelief.

Zed drew in a deep breath, then said, "Fine."

Sophie let out an audible gasp.

But Zed wasn't finished. "You find the book. You hide it away. You help me battle my four pursuers. After the battle, if we're all still alive, I'll do as you ask."

Sophie's heart was racing. This was something to fight for. This was something to keep them going. If there was even a chance this was true—

"No," Mason said again.

Zed's smile wavered.

"Not after the battle," Mason continued. "Before. We'll get you the book, but then you save our friends. You do that, and we'll fight for you."

Zed leaned forward. "Impossible." He almost spat out the word. "Even if I could do it in two weeks' time, and I'm not saying I can, I'd be too weak for the battle."

Mason didn't even hesitate. "That's our price. Pay it or don't."

Sophie couldn't speak. She could barely breathe. Zed was offering to save Heather, and the chance was slipping away. She had to find her voice.

But before she could, Zed said, "I'll give you three. I'll bring your mother, your father, and Ms. Porter's sister. You meet my first two demands, and I'll do it."

Mason gave the slightest of nods.

Sophie felt like the room was spinning. She looked at Frank

and saw the same dazed expression on his face that must be on her own.

Zed's smile was weaker than usual. Sophie could tell he didn't respect Mason. And now he'd lost a battle to the old man.

"That's all for tonight," Zed said. "Meet me at eight o'clock tomorrow morning. Volunteer Park. There's something I need to show you. In the meantime, Claire at the Holiday Inn is expecting you. She's got three rooms ready. No charge, of course."

Mason stood up and Frank and Sophie followed. They moved toward the exit, and the men blocking the door parted and let them pass.

None of them spoke until they reached the parking lot. Then Frank said, "Mason. Jesus, how'd you do that?"

Mason shrugged. "I've been dealing with him a bit longer than you have. He respects a hardline."

Sophie couldn't help it; she grabbed Mason and pulled him in for a tight hug. In the midst of all of that, he'd thought of her sister. She was overwhelmed with gratitude. "Thank you."

He awkwardly returned her hug.

Sophie pulled back and looked at both Hinkle men. "He's lying though, right? It's a trick, or a trap? He's going to use us. It's like you said. Whatever happens, we can't trust him."

The Hinkle boys said nothing. The only sound was the buzzing of the mayflies gathering in the sky.

2.

Matt Campbell pulled the truck out of the garage at seven twenty-five the next morning. Willis Eddy sat in Matt's passenger seat, loudly sipping coffee from one of Matt's thermoses. Matt flashed him a grin.

Matt had been doing his best to be extra friendly to Willis. He'd greeted him like the visit was an unexpected but pleasant surprise when the man had knocked on the door at half-past three in the morning. He'd chatted with Willis for a few minutes and then offered to make up the old pull-out couch for him. In the morning, Matt had gotten up early—truth be told, he hadn't slept at all—and scrambled some eggs and fried some bacon.

It had taken an effort of will to sit at his family's table with Willis and have a casual breakfast. Like Willis wasn't an unwelcome intruder. Like today wasn't one of the most important days of their lives. But Matt had done pretty well, if he did say so himself. His dumb jokes had been even more frequent than usual, a nervous habit, but other than that he had managed to act normal. And Helen had been in top form. If Matt hadn't known, even he wouldn't have been able to guess she'd been up all night worried half-to-death about Zed's armed lackey sleeping on their couch. Even Alice had done great, although her eyes showed the lack of sleep more clearly than her mother's did.

Alice.

They'd known, Matt and Helen. They'd known for a long time. Since the girl was, what, three? Four? At first they thought maybe she was some sort of genius, the way she was so hyper-aware of the world around her. Then they'd thought maybe there was something wrong with her. But eventually they'd had to admit she wasn't just aware of the world, she could see things that hadn't happened yet. Not often, but sometimes.

It wasn't something they talked about often, not even to each other. It made them uncomfortable. It led to all sorts of difficult questions. About *why* Alice had these powers. About *what* Alice was. Matt didn't fully understand what she could do. He'd asked her to explain it once a few years ago. She'd tried, but the effort had clearly frustrated and upset her. For her, it was like trying to describe the color blue to someone who'd never seen it. Matt didn't understand what she'd been trying to explain, and Alice didn't understand why Matt couldn't understand. Maybe when she was older, when her vocabulary had grown a bit. Maybe now was the time. It had been a couple years after all, and, God, how she'd grown up during that time. She wasn't such a little kid anymore. She was starting to form her own opinions and views of the world. She had interests now that didn't stem from her parents. Her world had grown as she had, and maybe now she'd be able to explain her abilities in a way even her dumb father could understand.

"Damn mayflies," Willis said, snapping Matt out of his deep thoughts.

Matt grunted his agreement. The ground was littered with their dead little bodies. He thought he could hear them crackling under the truck's tires, but it was probably his imagination. Last year Matt had gone for a run the morning after they came, and he still remembered the way it had felt as they crunched under his feet with each step. And it would be worse where they were going, down by the river.

"Ask you a question, man?" Willis was apparently over his issues with the mayflies. He was like that. One minute, something was a huge deal; the next, he was on to something else.

Matt nodded, keeping his eyes on the road in front of him. He hadn't ever liked Willis much, even before the man had shown up at his door at three-thirty in the morning packing heat.

"Are you dedicated to this…" he waved his hand vaguely in front of him as if indicating the whole world around them, "….thing? What we're doing?"

Matt grimaced. He couldn't flat out say no. He knew from Alice that Willis was carrying a gun, after all. But he didn't have to pretend he was overjoyed either. "I'm here, aren't I?"

Willis shifted in his seat, leaning forward eagerly like Matt had just stepped into the trap he'd laid for him. "See, that's just what I mean. How long we been waiting for this? And you're just *here*? Would you even be here if I hadn't come over last night and prodded you along?"

Matt glanced at his passenger, meeting his gaze as he spoke. "I'll do what I need to do. You don't need to worry."

Willis shook his head. "Man, you used to be something. Remember the fire you used to have? You'd get up for this kind of thing, and I mean *way* up. What's changed for you?"

Matt said nothing.

"Is it Alice?"

Matt snapped his head toward Willis, ready to say something he might regret, and he would have if the other man hadn't spoken first.

"Alright, sorry. Don't get defensive. I'm just asking. Having kids changes people is all I meant. Nothing against yours in particular."

Matt took a deep breath. They were only a few blocks from Volunteer Park, which meant he only had to be cooped up with this redheaded asshole another minute or so. Then they'd be out of the truck and working. It'd be different. He could deal with Willis in the open space of the park. Being cramped up in this vehicle with him was too much for Matt this morning.

After a moment, Willis said, "I'm not the only one

54

wondering about you. You think it was my idea to come over?"

"Whose was it? Zed's?"

Willis shook his head. "Nah, Zed trusts you. He says you're a man who deserves to be trusted, and trust is super important. Something like that, anyway."

"I take it some of you don't feel that way?"

Willis shrugged and sighed. "I don't know, man. You know how tense things are. Nobody wants this to fail. And the way you've been acting…its got people a little jumpy, I guess. And, yeah, it made them wonder. So, here I am."

Matt pulled the truck into Volunteer Park and started down the winding road toward the river. "You think this is really the best time to bring this up?"

Willis laughed his strangely high-pitched laugh. "Hell, man, this might be the only time we've got, we mess things up."

Matt didn't want to think about that. There was too much at stake. He had to succeed. For Alice. "We won't mess things up."

Willis drummed out a *ratta-tat-tat* beat on the dashboard with his hands. "Now that's the Matty I remember! I like your confidence." His voice lowered a few notches. "Though it's not all up to us. Hinkle's unpredictable."

Matt ignored that comment. He pulled into the grass between the road and the Mississippi River. He shut off the truck and opened the door. "Let's do this."

They worked in silence, two men who knew their jobs and didn't need to talk each other through anything. They worked with an efficiency that spoke of competence. For all his flaws, Willis was a great worker. He did his job without question or complaint. And Matt…Matt knew this routine by heart. He'd helped come up with the plan, after all. Back in the days before he hated Zed. Back in the days when this had seemed so much more important. The days before Alice.

They started with the rope. They hauled the heavy coil out of the truck bed and put it in place. Then there was the light.

Matt's forehead was covered with a sheen of sweat by the time they were through, in spite of the cool morning air. He put his hands on his hips and surveyed their work, running through the mental checklist for the third time. If this thing didn't turn out like it was supposed to, it wouldn't be from an oversight on his part. Finally, he gave a satisfied nod and turned back toward the truck.

Now would be the hard part. The waiting.

They got back in the truck and sat for a long while, the silence hanging over them like a spell. Matt was surprised to find his stomach was in knots. Even though he had no love for Zed, he desperately wanted Zed to win this round. He wanted it like he'd never wanted anything.

Willis finally broke the silence. "You ever wonder," he asked, speaking slowly and thoughtfully, a tone Matt had never before heard him use, "how things are going to be? After we save the world?"

Matt shrugged. "I guess it'll be just like it is now, right? That's the goal. Keep everything from dying."

"Nah, man, I disagree. What we're doing, it's gonna change things. One way or another, it'll change them. People are gonna die."

Matt gritted his teeth. He knew this. They all knew it. But he sure as hell didn't want to talk about it. Not now.

"I had a dream about it once," Willis said. "We won. And it was, like, years later."

More out of politeness than anything else, Matt asked, "What was it like?"

"Trees, man. So many trees."

Then Matt saw them. Zed walking along the riverbank with Sophie and the Hinkle boys. Without a word, Matt and Willis got out of the truck and waited to begin.

3.

Sophie turned off the car and glanced at Frank in the rearview mirror. He had that look on his face. It was like he wasn't there. She noticed it happened a lot. She wondered if maybe it happened to him more during times of stress. Come to think of it, she had never seen him during a non-stressful time.

"Yo," she said, and at the sound of her voice his eyes snapped to life, like someone had turned on a light switch in his head. "You ready for this?"

His gaze bore into her, even reflected in the mirror. He nodded sharply. "Yeah. I was just drifting."

They'd talked late into the night, discussing what had happened. They'd considered how Zed could have possibly known they would be at that restaurant and what they'd order. They'd speculated about what Zed had planned for this morning. The one topic they hadn't discussed was Zed's promise to bring back Jake, Logan, and Heather. Sophie didn't even let herself think about it. It was too big to be hoped for.

They'd considered the possibility that maybe Zed had found a way around Frank's locks. But that didn't feel right. He'd claimed not to be able to see them when they'd arrived at the restaurant, after all. And the locks seemed too interesting and mysterious to Zed. He hadn't figured them out yet.

However Zed had managed to determine where they were

going to be last night, the group agreed it had been a genius move. He'd caught them when they weren't expecting him, when they were tired from a long road trip. He'd skillfully manipulated them into showing up this morning.

But, even though they knew he was using them, they also agreed they had to go. They'd come all this way to find Zed, and Zed was going to be here. They couldn't *not* meet him.

Sophie glanced at Mason who sat in the passenger seat. He looked grim but more focused than Sophie had ever seen him. Being here in King's Crossing with Zed seemed to have sharpened him somehow. He wasn't the rambling, scattered old man she'd driven up here with. He wasn't the boy she'd babysat in Sanctuary either, though she saw that boy somewhere deep behind his eyes. This guy was something new. Something almost scary.

Frank cleared his throat. He was back, and now he'd try to take charge again. That was fine with Sophie. She'd invited herself along on this excursion; it was his show. Until she disagreed with one of his decisions, anyway.

"Remember what we talked about," Frank said. "Whatever he shows us, whatever he has planned, we hear him out, and that's it. We don't commit to anything this morning."

Mason chuckled. It was a low, throaty sound. Sophie found it disconcerting. She exchanged a worried glance with Frank in the rearview mirror.

"Something funny?" Sophie asked.

Mason shook his head. "This is what he does. He works people."

"We know," Frank said. "The difference is, we're expecting it. Whatever he's got planned, we're ready to deal with it."

Mason shook his head. "No. You don't know him like I do. This is his *thing*. Whatever he's got planned, it's going to go beyond anything we're expecting. Trust me on that."

Frank just grunted. "Way I see it, as long as we don't agree to anything, we'll be okay. We've got our locks." They'd agreed that at the first sign of trouble, the first act of aggression from Zed or any of the townspeople, they'd disappear and scatter. They had a place picked out on the north side of town to meet if that happened.

"Hey," Sophie said. She nodded toward the riverbank where a tall figure stood, hands in his pockets. He was facing the water, but even from behind, she knew it couldn't be anyone other than Zed. They hadn't seen him arrive. He must have been here longer than they had. "Should we do this?"

Frank grinned. "I've never been partial to asking myself that question." He opened the door and got out.

Sophie turned to Mason. "Guess that's a yes."

The three walked across the pavement toward the riverbank, dead mayflies crunching under their feet with each step. When they reached Zed, he spoke without turning to face them.

"Frank, your brother shot me in the face on a riverbank not dis-similar to this one. Twice actually."

Frank waited a moment before speaking. "Well, good for him. Glad he made the effort."

"It was right after I shot his friend Todd and threatened his family, so I guess I did provoke him a bit."

Frank shifted his weight. Sophie could see he was irritated.

Zed continued. "Your brother disappeared later that night. When I think of all the time we spent looking for him...and he'd escaped through the mirror. I'm honestly ashamed I didn't figure it out."

"Zed," Frank said. "What are we doing here?"

Zed turned toward them, and his smile was alarmingly

large. Sophie wondered how wide that mouth could open, whether it could swallow them whole. "We're talking. Reminiscing. Exchanging pleasantries."

"Your definition of pleasant must differ from mine," Frank said.

Zed chuckled. "This story does have a purpose. See, Jake and I both made the same mistake. We underestimated each other. He thought I could be stopped with a bullet. I thought he wouldn't be able to use the mirror in the unlikely event that he somehow found it. My error cost me years of futile searching and his, in a roundabout way, cost him his life."

Zed gestured toward Frank. "But I didn't learn my lesson. I thought you could never escape the Away, and you did." He turned to Sophie. "And I thought you a pointless troublemaker. But you hid the Rook Mountain tree away from me in Sanctuary." He looked at Mason. "And I thought you had nothing special to offer me. But you figured out how to use the book."

"Damn right, I did," Mason muttered.

Zed's smile flickered. "If I'd realized sooner what you're capable of, I could have made great use of you."

Sophie felt a bit of anger flare up in her. Maybe it was because he was the one and only person she'd ever babysat, but she felt protective of the old guy. "That's the problem, Zed. You're always using people. You see them as currency you can spend or trade. You make me sick."

Frank gave her a worried look, then turned back to Zed. "Get to the point."

Zed nodded curtly. "Point is, I won't underestimate you again. Any of you. And I expect you won't underestimate me, either." He looked out at the river for a moment. The water was calm. "Hard to believe all those millions of mayflies were waiting in this peaceful water, waiting for their chance to hatch, to fill our skies and die on our streets." He gestured toward a gardening shed hidden among a stand of trees fifty yards away. "Come on. What I want to show you is in that shed."

He turned without waiting for a response and started walking. Sophie, Frank, and Mason followed.

When they were about halfway to the shed, they passed a stand of trees, and Sophie saw a pickup truck with two men standing next to it. Zed waved, and they walked over.

Sophie could feel Frank tense next to her.

Apparently Zed could too, because he said, "Don't worry. These are two of my friends. Matt and Willis."

"That's supposed to make me less worried?" Frank asked.

Zed glanced back at him. "You remember the old saying as well as I do. *Trust is a must.* For this to work, I'm going to require just a bit of your trust this morning."

Frank let out a strained laugh. "That's a lot to ask."

"I know," Zed said. "But I promise you any trust you give me will be repaid in full very shortly."

Frank said nothing, but he kept following Zed. Sophie gave Frank a little nod to show her support.

The two men met them at the door to the shed. Their only greeting was a business-like nod at each of the three strangers. One of the men had a bright red shock of hair that fell to his shoulders. The other was a bit taller and wore his dark hair trimmed high and tight. High and Tight opened the door to the shed, reached in and flipped the light switch, illuminating the interior in harsh fluorescent yellows.

Zed waved toward the entrance. "Step inside, please."

Frank paused. Sophie knew what he was thinking. If Zed got them in that shed and locked the door, turning invisible wouldn't do them much good. They'd still be trapped.

Zed smiled at Frank. "Remember. Trust."

An old proverb Sophie had heard somewhere popped into her head, and she said it aloud. "Trust God, but tie your camel."

Zed nodded his assent. "Understood. What I need to show you is in that shed, however."

Frank said, "You and your people first. We stand by the door."

Matt and Willis looked at Zed. He motioned for them to proceed. Sophie followed Frank and Mason into the shed. What she saw gave her pause.

"Kinda makes you wonder where they keep the actual gardening supplies," she said. No one laughed.

The shed was empty but for three items. In the nearest corner, there was a large coil of thick rope. In the far corner stood a spotlight, the kind that was used in theaters. The spotlight was turned off, but pointed toward the last object.

In the center of the room, there was a large hole cut in the floor of the shed. And growing through that hole was a small, twisty tree.

Sophie drew a breath. This was smaller and much, much younger than any she'd seen, but still she recognized the tree.

"Is that what I think it is?" Mason asked.

"Assuming you're referring to the special breed of tree that grew in your home," Zed said, "then yes it is."

"Wait," Frank said. "I thought they only grew outside of time. That's why you took Sugar Plains out of time, right? And what you were trying to do with Rook Mountain. You wanted to grow these trees."

Zed bowed his head a bit like a teacher disappointed in his students. "Not exactly. The ingredients required to grow one of these trees are a great deal of power and a great deal of time. I took Sugar Plains outside of time to provide the second element. It seems good old King's Crossing has had a great deal of power for a long time already. It's a wonder the Exiles haven't found it by now." He lovingly patted the tree trunk. "With this tree, we can access the things that live outside of time. Even without my old pocket watch."

Frank said, "Why would you want to do that?"

Zed ran a gentle hand along the twisted trunk. "You've met some of the creatures that live outside time. The Unfeathered, dangerous in their own way, but ultimately mindless enough to be manipulated. The Ones Who Sing and their young offspring the Larvae are much more dangerous. But they aren't the most dangerous thing that calls the timeless lands home."

Zed stood up straight and pulled the compass out of his pocket. "Now stand back. I'm going to bring one through."

"Why the hell would you do that?" Frank asked.

"I want you to see what we're up against. I don't want you to underestimate them."

Sophie could tell he had something else to say, so she waited.

"And," Zed said, "I need a hostage."

4.

Frank couldn't stop looking at the tree growing through the floor of the shed. Whatever Zed was about to do, it was likely going to come through there. The shed suddenly seemed much smaller than it had a few moments ago. After everything he'd seen, from the Unfeathered in Rook Mountain to the Ones Who Sing in the Away to the Larvae in Sanctuary, he thought he could handle anything. But the idea that there might be something else, maybe something related to those things, something worse, made his skin crawl.

"If this thing is as dangerous as you say, is it a great idea to be trapped in a shed with it?" Sophie asked.

"Probably not," Zed said. "But we've taken great measures to minimize the risk." He nodded toward the spotlight.

"Is it a gremlin?" Sophie asked.

Zed screwed up his face in confusion. "Sorry, I'm a few decades behind in my pop culture references."

"More than a few, apparently. See a movie every once in a while."

Frank reached back and put his hand on the handle of the closed door. If this went south, he wanted to be ready to run. They could use the locks to turn invisible if need be. But who was to say if that would be enough. He remembered feeling safe from the Larvae too because of his lock, until one of them buried itself in his arm.

"Okay," he said. "What happens next?"

"I test a theory," Zed said.

Zed crouched down next to the tree and held his compass near the bark. He tilted his head and moved his eyes around the trunk. Finally he stopped and pointed at one spot. "There! You see it?"

Frank squinted at the place Zed was pointing, but he didn't notice anything different about it.

Zed looked up at Willis and Matt. "Ready, gentlemen?"

Willis said, "You know it."

"I'm ready," Matt said. To Frank's ears, Matt didn't sound nearly as enthusiastic about this endeavor as his red-haired friend.

"Good." Zed turned to Frank, Sophie, and Mason. "Watch close. It'll happen very quickly now. Don't do anything unless

I tell you to, understand?"

None of them answered.

There was still time, Frank knew. He could disappear right now and probably be out of this shed and back in Sophie's car before the mysterious creature appeared. The fact that he was still here at all spoke to his level of insanity.

Zed drew his forefinger across the bark in a complicated pattern. It reminded Frank of the way he'd moved his finger across the pages of the book back in Sanctuary.

"What's happening, Zed?" Mason asked, and for the first time in a while Frank heard that childlike quality in his voice, the one he'd used when talking to Zed in Sanctuary, before he'd been betrayed and abandoned there.

"Trust, Mason," Zed said. "You have to trust me."

Frank opened his mouth to say that was a tall order indeed, but something happened before he could get the words out. A tiny pinprick of light appeared in the tree trunk just where Zed had touched it. It was small but brilliant. The white light cut through the air and shone in a bright circle on the ground not two inches away from Frank's shoe.

Matt reached up and put a hand on the spotlight. Willis crouched down next to the rope.

Zed hopped to his feet and leapt back two steps. "This is the fun part."

Frank glanced at Sophie, then at Mason, checking to make sure they were doing okay and that neither of them were frantically signaling him to use the locks and make a run for it. They both had their gazes fixed on the tree trunk.

The trunk of the young tree couldn't have been more than a foot and a half in diameter. At least whatever was coming through that hole couldn't be too big.

The pin prick of light was growing now. Frank watched the

circle of light grow from the size of a dime to the size of a quarter to the size of a baseball.

"Frank," Zed said, "I need to ask you something."

The light was getting larger at a faster rate. It was as big as a basketball now and Frank could swear he felt waves of heat coming off it. The temperature in the shed must have gone up twenty degrees since they stepped inside.

"What I'm bringing through that tree is going to be very unhappy when it gets here," Zed continued. "It's being ripped from its home, so it'll be startled. We're pulling it through a hole too small for its body, so it'll be in pain. The good news is it will be disoriented enough for us to subdue it. But...if it sees me, it could be a different story."

Frank tore his eyes away from the light streaming through the tree and looked at Zed. "Why?"

Zed grinned at him. "Oh, it really doesn't like me."

Frank thought Sophie would make some joke about how they all had something in common with the creature in that case, but she didn't.

"So I'm going to ask you a favor." Zed moved closer to Frank and looked him in the eye. "Remember when I said I'd pay you back for the trust you gave me in stepping into this shed? This is the moment. I'm trusting you to save my life."

Frank's eyes flicked between Zed and the tree. "What are you talking about?"

"If that thing sees me, it will kill me. And I'm not sure we have a way to stop it. If it doesn't see me, if it only sees a room full of strangers, that'll add to its disorientation."

"I still haven't heard the favor."

"I need to be invisible to the creature. I'd like to borrow one of your locks."

Sophie's voice was cold as ice when she spoke. "You've got

to be kidding."

Zed didn't take his eyes off Frank. "I'm not asking her; I'm asking you. That thing will be here in a moment. You have to decide. I'm asking you to save my life."

Frank paused. His instinct, his gut reaction was to flip Zed the bird, wait for the creature to come through, and watch the old bald bastard die. Isn't that what he'd been dreaming of since the day Zed met with him in the jail in Rook Mountain? The day he told Frank he was sending him to the Away? If he'd had a tree and a crazy, Zed-hating creature coming through it then, things might have turned out much differently.

But he'd survived, hadn't he? As horrible as it had been, he'd made it through. And he'd ended up defeating Zed, after a fashion. He'd stopped the man's plan, anyway.

And now Zed was asking for Frank's help. That didn't much matter to Frank. But the reward Zed was offering did matter.

Frank flashed back to that moment in Sanctuary when he'd stepped through the tree, expecting to hug his brother for the first time in years, and instead found him dead on the ground. If there was a chance he could stop that from happening, he had to take it.

Zed had revealed something in his plea. If the locks could protect him from the creatures, it could protect Frank, Mason, and Sophie too.

Frank held up a finger, the pre-arranged signal to turn on their locks. Mason gritted his teeth, nodded, and quickly disappeared. He'd apparently forgotten to remain visible to Frank and Sophie. That was fine. Sophie squeezed her eyes shut for a brief moment like she always did when activating the lock. It was a bit of a tell, but Frank would never let on he knew. If he were being honest, he had to admit he found it pretty cute. But he wouldn't go there. Not now. Not with the way the world was spinning out of control.

"It's coming." The voice was almost too soft to hear. Zed muttered, as if to himself, "Any moment. It's coming."

Zed had turned away while Frank was looking at Sophie. The man's eyes were fixed on the tree now. The look on his face was more transparent than any Frank had ever seen him display. Zed was afraid.

And that was what sealed it for Frank. As much as he was sure Zed was at least partially playing them, as much as he knew Zed would betray them at the first opportunity if it bought him the tiniest advantage, that look was real. Whatever else he'd lied about, he wasn't lying about the danger that creature coming through the tree posed him.

Then the light in the tree darkened. Something was blocking the hole.

"My God," Zed said. "It's here."

Frank thought of Jake lying on that cold, mossy ground in Sanctuary, his eyes empty.

He reached out and put his hand on Zed's shoulder, mentally pulling him into the protection of the lock.

The tension in Zed's face eased a bit, but he didn't turn away from the tree.

"Come on," he muttered. "Come on."

And then something was pressing through. A face. A human face.

It was misshapen, like a bit of putty squeezed through a hole too small for it. The head popped out and the creature began to howl as it wormed its way through: first its shoulders, then its arms. When its hands had passed through the barrier, it clawed at the floor, looking for leverage to pull itself through. It was hard to make out any distinct features with its body blocking the light through the hole and the thing moving in a panicked blur of blacks and grays.

With one final Herculean pull, it popped through the basketball-sized hole in the tree. It let out one more indignant roar and collapsed onto the floor.

Not it. Him. The creature was a human. A man. Or at least it looked like a man. After everything Frank had seen, he wasn't about to take anything for granted.

The newcomer raised himself up on his hands and knees, and Frank saw his thin face, his jet black hair, and carefully manicured beard. His dark eyes shot up and his gaze darted around the room.

"Who dares?" he asked, his voice a low, quivering rumble.

With that, the spotlight came on. It was aimed directly at his face, and he howled again in pain and surprise.

Zed stood leaning forward on the balls of his feet, looking positively giddy. "Do it, Willis!" he cried.

Willis had the rope in his hand and he quickly threw it over the man. Matt leapt into action, helping Willis wrap the rope around the tree, and then around the man again, circling again and again until the man was secured with his back against the tree. Willis tied the rope off and nodded at Zed.

Zed turned to Frank. "Thank you. Thanks for being worthy of my trust." He stepped forward, pulling away from Frank's hand.

Zed inspected the knots, giving them an exploratory tug before nodding in satisfaction.

Matt turned off the spotlight.

Zed looked at Frank, a wild look in his eyes. "Turn it off."

"What?" Frank asked. He was still struggling to catch up with what just happened.

69

"The lock," Zed said. "It's still hiding me from him. Turn it off."

Frank mentally shut off the lock that hid both him and Zed.

The man tied to the tree drew in a sharp breath as Zed suddenly appeared in front of his face.

"You," the man said.

Zed got within an inch of the man's nose. "Rayd. Thanks for joining us."

The man scoffed. "You've moved beyond insanity, Zedidiah. When Wilm comes—"

"Yes," Zed said. "When Wilm comes. How long will that be? How long until she breaks free of her prison and starts looking for you? How long until she actually finds you?"

"As if you could hold me that long."

Zed helpfully brushed a piece of dust off Rayd's shoulder. "You are secured to a tree. One of the timeless. You know the rules."

There was a long silence, which Sophie broke. "I don't know the rules."

Zed tilted his head at Rayd. "You want to tell her?"

"Go to hell."

Zed nodded politely. "While he's tied to the tree, Rayd is unable to escape his bonds himself. Someone else will have to untie him. And the only people likely to do that are his three friends. Once they find him."

"Yeah?" Frank said. "What happens then?"

Zed turned away from Rayd for the first time since the man had passed through the tree. "They kill us and destroy the world. Of course, if they don't find the King's Crossing book we might stand a chance of defending ourselves a bit longer."

"Why?" Mason asked. His voice was low and scratchy.

"Why are you doing this? If they're going to destroy us, why did you bring him here?"

"It was going to happen eventually," Zed said. "I just sped it along a bit. I told you I'd save your loved ones. That was the carrot. Consider this the stick. Find that book. And find it fast."

THE BOY WHO FOUND THE WATCH (PART TWO)

Topeka, Kansas
June, 1948

Zed waited almost a month.

Charlie often came and sat in their little visiting room. At first, it was all polite smiles and tips of the hat. But as the weeks passed, Charlie became more relaxed around Zed and his mother. A loosened tie. Then no tie at all. Before long it was sleeveless tee-shirts. For her part, Zed's mother always seemed to be racing around. Waiting on him hand and foot when he was there and preparing the house for his arrival when he was away. She talked to Zed less and less. Which, in all honesty, was perfectly fine with Zed. It gave him more time to think. To plan.

And always, there was the watch. Zed could tell Charlie was proud of it, but he rarely took it out. And he never did another magic trick. But how Zed savored those precious brief glances at the watch. He longed for them like a junkie longs for a fix. And, just like a junkie, he had to be careful. At first he hadn't been. On Charlie's second visit Zed had walked right up to him and asked him for the time, as clear as he might ask someone on the street. Charlie hadn't bought it. Not for a moment. He smiled his thin smile and pointed toward the grandfather clock on the other side of the room.

"You're a big boy, Zed," Charlie had said. "Why don't you tell me?"

He'd known. Zed was sure of it. He'd have to work to become more subtle.

So began Zed's quest to befriend his mother's boyfriend. Charlie was odd for an adult. So casual and friendly. Having Charlie there was a bit like having a dad and a bit like having a big brother. The campaign wasn't easy for Zed. He was withdrawn by nature, but he knew in this situation knowledge would be power. His only way to obtain knowledge was to convince Charlie to give it to him. So he asked questions. Lots and lots of questions. Never about the watch, of course, but often *around* the watch. And he learned so much useless information.

Charlie had been born in Florida. He'd given up on school at age ten and gone to work in the groves, climbing rickety ladders and picking oranges for a penny a bushel. He'd learned to work fast and to keep his mouth shut. That was the only way to make a living out in the groves. Somewhere along the way—the when and the how of it weren't entirely clear to Zed—Charlie had fallen off a ladder and injured his leg. Unable to work on his feet, he'd gone to work at a hotel, checking in guests, holding doors, doing whatever needed to be done. And there at the hotel was where he'd met the Boss.

It was always the Boss. No first name, no last name. But boy, how Charlie admired the Boss. It was as if he'd hung the moon, as Zed's father might have said, had he been there instead of wherever men who run out on their families go. The Boss became friendly with Charlie through the course of his regular visits to the hotel. He grew to admire Charlie's work ethic, and Charlie wasn't too humble to say so. One day the Boss approached Charlie with an offer. The Boss was required to travel a great deal. He was sometimes needed in two places at once. Seeing as he hadn't quite figured out the logistics of splitting himself in two, he was in need of a good man. A man who could go to those places he couldn't and carry out the work in his name. The pay, while not extravagant, was enough to keep Charlie afloat. Besides, he'd always wanted to travel.

And that was how he'd spent the last nine years. Traveling for the Boss.

That vague and slightly unbelievable story raised a thousand questions in young Zed's mind. What was this Boss's business? Was it legal? When did Charlie do it? He seemed to hang around Zed's mother's house at all hours leaving little time for any mysterious business dealings. But Zed couldn't ask bluntly like he would have in normal circumstances. Because he wasn't playing the role of *Zed*; he was playing the role of *friend*. Zed had a tendency to come off as aggressive and confrontational when he spoke. *Friend* wasn't like that at all. *Friend* would pry the information out gently and carefully, like a piece of corn stuck in a tooth.

Charlie's story had one implication that made Zed nervous, one that neither Charlie or Zed's mother seemed willing to acknowledge: if Charlie's job was to travel, he would be traveling on from Topeka as soon as his business was concluded. That meant Zed would have to work not only gently, but also quickly.

One afternoon, Zed walked into the formal dining room and saw Charlie sitting at the long table eating a sandwich. Zed hadn't heard him come in that day. For all Zed knew, the man hadn't left the night before. Zed didn't think Charlie and his mother were sleeping together, but one couldn't be too sure.

Charlie and Zed acknowledged each other with a friendly nod, and Zed moved to his seat where his mother had set out a sandwich for him. As he was sitting down, light glinting off something hit his eye. He saw what it was, and his heart caught in his throat. It was the watch. Sitting right there on the table in front of Charlie.

Zed wanted to look away, but he couldn't. It was as if everything beautiful, everything missing from his life, everything he was supposed to be, was caught up in that gold watch with the strange symbol.

"I've seen the way you look at it," Charlie said, talking through the food in his mouth. "I don't blame you. It's a hell of a thing. You'd like to hold it, I bet."

Zed pried his eyes away from the watch. It was like moving a heavy object, but he did it. He knew anything he said would sound desperate. He just nodded.

Charlie reached out his hand, and for one glorious moment Zed thought he was going to push the watch forward. Instead, he wrapped his fingers over the watch and pulled it back away from Zed.

"I can't do that, Zed." There was something wild in the man's eyes. Something terrible lived in there. Either Charlie was very good at hiding it, or Zed had been too consumed by his quest for the watch to notice it. Charlie pulled the watch off the table and gripped it in his fist.

Zed tried very hard to keep the despair off his face. If Charlie knew how badly Zed wanted the watch, he'd keep an even closer eye on it and the boy would never get his shot.

"See, my Boss asked me to hang on to this watch," Charlie

continued. "Just for a little while. I have to give it back soon. And if the Boss asks for it and I don't have it…" His voice drifted off and his face went pale, as if just thinking about it was too much for him. "You ever read *Inferno* by Dante? The stuff they do to those people in the different circles of hell?"

Zed could only shake his head.

"Well, that shit would be downright pleasant compared to what'll happen to me if I lose this thing. So when it comes to the watch," he held it up, and Zed's heart ached anew at the sight of it, "it's look but don't touch. Understand?"

Zed couldn't move. His eyes were drawn to the watch like iron files to a magnet.

"Come to think of it, it's better if you don't look, either." Charlie snapped is hand shut and stuffed the watch into his pocket.

Zed ate the rest of his lunch in silence. He knew he should be making friendly conversation with Charlie. He should try to undo some of the damage he'd done by openly gawking at the watch. But he couldn't bring himself to do it. It was all he could do to keep his jaw working around his sandwich.

He'd learned two important pieces of information. First, Charlie wouldn't allow the watch to be stolen. All Zed's fantasies of pickpocketing it or tricking Charlie into thinking he'd lost it were never going to happen. Charlie would protect that watch with everything he had. All the buddying up to Charlie wouldn't change that. Second, Zed had learned how far he was willing to go to get the watch.

As he choked down his sandwich, he considered how he'd do it. He had to be careful, but he also had to be quick. Charlie's job could take him to another city at any point. Or he and Zed's mom could stop seeing each other. He resolved to act at the first opportunity.

Zed suspected Charlie might be visiting his mother in the night. The idea didn't bother him really; he was too focused on the watch to be distracted by something like his mother giving it up to this traveling salesman or whatever he was. In fact, the idea excited him. Because it gave him a great opportunity. If Charlie *was* visiting in the night, he was always gone by the time Zed woke up. Which meant sometime during the night he would have to descend the stairs.

Zed prepared. Zed waited. And the next night he set his alarm to wake him every hour. And each time it did, he would creep to his mother's bedroom and listen at the door until he heard the quiet snore that convinced him she was asleep. Then he'd carefully inch the door open to confirm she was alone.

The first night was a bust. But the second night, when his alarm woke him at one a.m. and he listened at his mother's door, he heard a combination of giggles, moans, and squeals that confirmed Charlie had indeed come calling.

It might disturb most eleven-year-old boys to hear such noises coming from their mother's bedroom, but Zed just smiled and went to work.

He tied the fishing line across the top of the staircase, securing the ends to the banister on each side with a tight double-hitch knot. He placed the line six inches off the ground which he figured was low enough that it would still trip Charlie but high enough he wasn't likely to accidentally step over it. With that job done, he went to the bottom of the staircase, sat just around the corner, and waited.

It couldn't have been more than an hour, but Zed drifted off into a dream of flying. He suddenly jerked awake at the sound of a floorboard creaking. He was instantly alert. He had to be. The floorboard squeak came again, and he knew it was Charlie creeping through the hall.

Just as Zed hoped, Charlie didn't turn on the light in the hallway. He was probably afraid it would wake Zed. That mistake would cost him.

Zed took a deep breath and let it out slowly, silently counting as he did so, mentally guessing where Charlie was in the hallway, how close he was to the staircase.

Before the breath was gone, a surprised grunt came from the top of the stairs, followed by a series of thumps that shook the house. Then Charlie was lying at the foot of the stairs.

Zed stood, clutching a heavy fire poker in his hands. It was dark, but Zed's eyes had adjusted. He stepped around the corner and saw Charlie lying on the ground. The man let out a moan.

His leg was twisted beneath him at an odd angle, but other than that he didn't appear to be hurt. Zed had hoped Charlie would break his neck. No matter. He had the fire poker.

Charlie squinted up at him. "Zed? Help me—"

He'd barely gotten the word out before Zed brought the poker down on Charlie's head, slamming it into his skull three times, driving the point of it into his face.

Charlie screamed and thrashed, so Zed kept striking until the man stopped moving.

When he was sure it was safe, Zed crouched down and reached for Charlie's right pocket, the one he'd seen him put the watch in a few times. He paused, suddenly sure the watch wouldn't be there, that Charlie had left it at home, that he'd killed this man for nothing. He took a deep breath.

He thrust his hand into the pocket. Relief flooded through him as he touched the watch. He pulled it out and held it to his chest.

Finally. He had it.

He may have stood like that for hours, frozen in rapture, but then Charlie let out a weak, wheezing breath. Zed was suddenly unsure what to do. Rather, he knew what he needed to do but was afraid to do it. He couldn't have Charlie coming after him for the watch. The police, sure. But not Charlie. Worse, if Charlie lived he could tell his Boss about Zed. And Zed didn't want that.

He pulled out his pocket knife, the same one he'd been sharpening on the morning he'd met Charlie, and cut the man's throat. He had never done anything like that before, and the work was far more physically taxing than he would have imagined. Sawing into a person's throat, even with a knife as sharp as Zed's, was no easy task. And the blood! There was so much of it. Zed's hands, shirt and the floor around him where all slick with it by the time he was finished. He surveyed the body with it's gaping neck wound and felt confident he'd done a thorough job. There was no doubt in his mind that Charlie was dead.

Zed washed up quickly in the kitchen, and changed into the clothes he'd left hidden there. He left his bloody pajamas on the kitchen floor, making no effort to hide them. Maybe the police would think he'd been kidnapped by the killer, or maybe they'd realized right away that he'd committed the crime. Zed didn't care either way. Soon he'd be just another nameless runaway.

He grabbed the bag he'd hidden under the sink. It contained a few changes of clothes and the three hundred dollars his mother hid in the basement, all her savings.

Zed paused at the doorway, and he felt an unexpected moment of fear. He was alone now. The police would be looking for him. His mother would be looking for him. Then he felt the cold weight of the watch in his pocket, and he felt at peace.

He walked out the door, boarded the first train east, and never returned to Topeka.

CHAPTER THREE: THE ROUGH-SHOD READERS

1.

Frank looked up at the building in front of them.

"So this is where we start?" Sophie asked.

Frank nodded, but—if he was being honest—he had no idea what he was doing. This was all new to him. Except, that wasn't exactly true, was it? Zed had asked for his help finding something before: Frank's brother Jake. He'd asked through his lackey Becky Raymond, but he'd asked. And look how well that had turned out.

Frank tried to insert some confidence into his voice. "Well, we *are* looking for a book."

The King's Crossing Public Library was a large, modern-looking structure made of glass and steel. It positively gleamed in the morning light. The building looked out of place in downtown King's Crossing, an area that trended toward traditional architecture with a smattering of falling apart thrown in for good measure. The library was unique among its peers.

"So, what, we just check the card catalogue?" Sophie asked. "Or computer catalogue? Whatever they call them now."

"I don't know." Frank sighed. "We have to start somewhere. I'm going with my gut, okay? My gut tells me, you want a book, try the library."

Sophie turned to Mason. "What do you think? You had some sort of mystical connection to the book in Sanctuary. Are you going to be able to work your voodoo on this book, too?"

Frank was curious whether Mason would answer. The older man had been quiet ever since they'd left the shed an hour ago.

"I don't know," Mason said. "I've never been inside a library. I barely even know how to read."

"Seriously?" Sophie asked. "You did okay with that other book."

"That was different. It spoke to me."

Something at the edge of the parking lot caught Frank's eye.

"You two go on ahead and get started," he said. "I need to check something."

Sophie arched her eyebrows. "What are we supposed to get started doing?"

"I don't know. Look around. See if anything seems out of place. Haven't you ever investigated a small town with a secret before?"

With that, he walked toward the man leaning against a tree at the edge of the lot. The man was just standing there glowering like some sort of teenaged rebel who thought he was tough. He wasn't looking at Frank, but he wasn't *not* looking at him either.

It was Matt, the guy with the high and tight haircut.

Frank strode toward him with purpose. "Kinda strange running into you again so soon."

"Not really," Matt said, his face expressionless. "Small town."

Frank stopped a few feet away from the man. A bit of stubble had sprung onto Frank's face over the past couple days of travel, and it itched something fierce. He scratched at his cheek. "You wouldn't happen to be following us, would you?"

Matt coolly met his gaze. "I was here before you."

"That's been happening a lot lately."

"Maybe you're predictable."

This was getting Frank nowhere. This game of *who's cooler* was infuriating. "Okay. If I'm predictable, that means you came here because you knew I'd be here. So, I ask again, are you following me?"

Matt's eyes flickered and a slight smile cracked his face. He was trying to hide something and it seemed to be something funny, maybe even something happy.

"The truth?" Matt said. "Zed sent me. Not to spy on you, exactly. More like to be available if you needed anything. You have any questions, need any local insight, I'm your man."

Frank's gaze caught on the Roman numeral tattooed on the man's wrist. "You know, Zed came to my town a long time ago. Well, maybe not a long time ago, but it sure feels that way. He had a plan, but it didn't work out. He said he was there to help us. Turned out that wasn't the case. Still, some people in my town wear a tattoo to show they're loyal to him."

Matt followed Frank's eyes to his own tattoo. "That's not what ours are about."

"Then what are they about?"

Matt shook his head. There was something in his eye. Vulnerability, maybe. "Not yet. Not here."

"You said you were here to help me if I had any questions."

"I am," Matt said. "Believe me when I tell you I want, no, *need* you to succeed. I have a family."

"And you believe that stuff about the world ending if I don't find the book?"

No hesitation. "Yes." He gritted his teeth for a moment. "And it's not just the book. There's more to it than that." He looked past Frank into the blue sky. "I have a wife. And a daughter. I would take them and leave town if I thought it would help. But in a week I'll be just as dead on the coast as I would be here. At least here I can try to do something about it."

"Seems like you've got a lot of trust in Zed."

"No," Matt said. "I've got a lot of trust in you."

The words shocked Frank. He opened his mouth to reply but realized he had no idea what to say.

"Look," Matt continued, "the book's not in the library. You're wasting your time."

Frank scratched at his neck. Damn whiskers. "Okay. You got a better suggestion where to start?"

"I do." The man glanced at Frank in a conspiratorial manner that would not have been out of place in Regulation-era Rook Mountain. "Thing is, I know some stuff I haven't exactly shared with Zed."

"And you're willing to share it with a guy you just met?"

Again, no hesitation. "Yes. We can go now. We'll take my car."

"I need to get my friends first," Frank said.

"Don't worry about them. They'll be busy for a while."

Frank shook his head. "You might trust me, but the feeling isn't mutual. Not yet. No way I'm leaving without them."

Matt paused for a moment, as if considering it. "Fine. Go get them. I'll be waiting here when you come out."

Frank nodded. There was something strange about the way the man spoke to him. Too familiar.

Just another crazy Zed Head. Even though he claimed he didn't trust Zed, he'd been there at the shed that morning. He'd helped Zed put his plan into action.

But Frank couldn't completely dismiss the look in the man's eye. Frank considered himself a pretty good judge of character. He had needed to be in prison, where looking at the wrong person at the wrong moment could start a beef that would lead to someone ending up in the infirmary, the SHU, or worse.

Matt might be crazy, but he believed what he was saying. Of that, Frank was certain.

Frank turned and walked toward the library.

2.

The best part about being able to Pull Back time was that there were no consequences. It was also the worst part.

Alice had recently read the first couple of Harry Potter books. She'd loved them, but the one thing she'd thought about the most was the Invisibility Cloak. It had felt so familiar, but also so sad. To have to wear that cloak in order to find out secrets...

Whenever Alice wanted to find a secret, she just nosed around until she found it. If someone saw her, well, she'd just Pull Back time a little and she'd still have the information. She'd like to see Professor Snape try to bust *her*. Not likely.

She knew in her heart consequences were, deep down, a good thing. They existed to keep people safe. You didn't jump off a building because, while the falling part might be kinda fun, the landing definitely wasn't.

Alice's problem was she could experience the fall and not have to deal with the landing. She was often tempted to try things, things she definitely shouldn't, things that were dangerous, even to her. Like, when she'd been swimming last week. Something inside her had wanted very badly to sit at the bottom of the pool until she couldn't take it anymore, until she just had to breathe in water. And as the darkness closed in on her, she would Pull Back. Then she would know what it felt like to drown without the messy dying part. Or even the having to get mouth-to-mouth from that pimply-faced teenaged lifeguard part.

Dangerous things like that attracted her and frightened her at the same time. What if the day came when she couldn't fight them? What if she'd given in and accidentally drowned herself? Or what if she jumped off a bridge, miscalculated, and hit the water before she thought she would? Then she would be dead, just like so many other dumb daredevil kids. And she couldn't Pull Back from death.

At least she didn't think so.

Alice woke up at ten-thirty that morning. It was, as far as she could remember, the latest she'd ever slept. She woke up just as tired as she'd been when she'd gone to sleep four hours earlier, when her dad and Mr. Willis had left. She'd listened at the top of the stairs as they went out the door, just as she had earlier that night when her dad had killed Willis.

She guessed she was skipping school today. That didn't bum her out too badly. It was like a surprise snow day.

She tried not to think too much about the times with double memories. At three thirty that morning, she'd technically been both sitting at the top of the stairs watching her father kill a man *and* lying in bed thinking about that killing. It made her dizzy, but she found if she picked one memory and pushed the other one away, she was usually fine.

When Dad and Willis left that morning, Alice had heard the words *Volunteer Park* and *shed*, so it didn't take a third-grade science fair winner like Alice to figure out where they were going. The question was *why*. And she didn't like unanswered questions.

After she got out of bed, she headed down to the kitchen. Mom tended to cook when she was nervous; most other times she let Alice's dad do it. This morning she must have been leaning over the edge of insanity, because she'd made waffles, fruit salad, sausage, *and* bacon.

Alice stopped at the door to the kitchen, plotting her next move. That food smelled *really* good. She wanted nothing more than to sit down and eat until she couldn't eat anymore. But…wouldn't that food taste even better when she got back?

Her mind made up, she turned and walked out of the kitchen.

"Honey?" Mom asked. "Where you going? Breakfast is ready."

"I'm going to the bathroom, Mom."

Alice headed toward the nearest bathroom, the one off the living room, went inside, and turned on the light and the fan. As a final measure, she pressed the button lock on the doorknob. Then she left the bathroom and pulled the locked door shut behind her. That would buy her some time.

She walked to the front door, eased it open, took a final look back to make sure Mom wasn't watching, and slipped out, closing the door as gently as possible.

A clean escape. Ha. Who needed an Invisibility Cloak?

It was a six block walk to Volunteer Park. She moved quickly and with purpose. If she dawdled, some well-meaning stranger might think she was lost and offer her help. What a pain *that* would be. So she moved as if her destination was right around the next corner.

As she walked, she couldn't help but feel just a little bit guilty. Mom hadn't had an easy night, and now Alice was kind of piling it on her. She might have realized Alice wasn't in the bathroom by now. She wasn't above popping the lock to the bathroom door and coming in if Alice didn't answer her calls. She was probably searching the house, starting to get a little frantic. Yelling things like, "Come out! This isn't funny!" and "Okay, you win. Hide and seek champion of the family." Soon she'd be calling Dad. Then maybe the police.

It wasn't like Alice felt great about it. But once she saw what she needed to see, she'd Pull Back and sit down for breakfast with Mom, being sure to act extra friendly and cheerful. From Mom's perspective, it would have never happened. So there was nothing wrong with that, right?

She made it to Volunteer Park and spotted the gardening shed near some bushes. She wasn't one hundred percent positive that was the place, but she couldn't think of any other shed in the park. Her suspicions were confirmed when she saw Willis leaning against the shed, smoking.

Wouldn't you know it? After acting so superior, she could have used an Invisibility Cloak after all.

Still, there was a good chance she could remain unseen if she slipped around the back of the shed and was extra careful not to make noise.

She circled around the back of the shed, creeping slowly and softly. As she turned the corner and spotted the door, she saw it was shut, but not latched. Maybe Willis was supposed to be doing something in there and was out on a smoke break?

She reached for the door and gently pulled it open. What she saw inside was so unexpected it made her gasp.

A tree was growing right in the middle of the shed. And a thin man with black hair and a neatly trimmed beard was tied to that tree. His eyes were on the ground.

She stood frozen, just staring at him for a long time.

Finally, he looked up and saw her.

Surprise flashed across his face, but it was quickly replaced with a smile.

"Hello," he said.

"Hello," she answered, her voice barely above a whisper.

"What's your name?"

"Alice," she said, and instantly wished she hadn't. It was automatic, though, giving your name when someone asked for it.

"Alice," the man said, "I have a bit of a problem. As you can see, I'm tied to this tree. Some very bad men put me here. I need your help to get out."

She stood frozen, unsure of what to do.

"You know about bad guys right?" he asked. "Like Snidely Whiplash?"

She had no idea who Snidely Whiplash was.

"I just need you to come over here and untie the rope."

Suddenly, Willis' voice was coming from behind her. "Alice? What the hell are you doing here?"

She panicked and Pulled Back on the rope in her mind, just a little.

Then she was standing on the other side of the shed again, peeking around at the door.

She should leave now. She should Pull Back to when she was standing in her kitchen. She should enjoy the breakfast Mom had made and forget all about this man tied to the tree.

But she couldn't. She had to see one more time. Because that man had said bad guys tied him up. Her dad had been here this morning. Was her dad one of the bad guys? Was that why he hadn't wanted to go?

She had to take one more look.

She crept around the corner and pulled the door open again.

And, again, she gasped. Because, for the first time in her long and storied history of Pulling Back on the rope in her mind, things were different this time. Not everything. Only one small detail. The man wasn't looking at the ground. He was looking at her. And smiling.

"Clever girl," the man said.

She froze. He couldn't know. He couldn't.

"That was a neat trick," the man said. "A very neat trick. Surely someone as clever as you can untie a simple rope."

She shook her head slowly and took a step back.

"If you like tricks, I have some I could show you. Lots and lots. I could teach you things that would make your little time refold look like kid's stuff."

Her heart was racing now. She wanted to run away, to Pull Back, but the man's gaze seemed to be holding her somehow, making the rope in her mind too slippery to grasp.

"I'm a very good friend to have," the man said. "But a very bad enemy." His voice dropped to a lower register. "If you don't help me, I'll pop your eyeballs out of your head, and no simple time fold will save you. I was born in a place where time was no more than a color. You can't fool me, and you can't make me forget."

She turned and ran out of the shed. She brushed past a shocked Willis, who yelled after her, "Alice? What the hell are you doing here?"

90

When she was fifty yards from the shed, she stopped and tried again. She was relieved, oh-so-relieved, to find she could grip the rope again. She Pulled Back.

A moment later she walked into her kitchen and sat down at the table.

Mom smiled at her. "Just in time." She handed Alice a glass of orange juice.

Alice hoped her mother couldn't see her hand shaking when she took it.

3.

Sophie was not a fan of libraries. All these books, wrapped in weird shiny plastic coating. And there was the musty smell. The decay of old paper. Even in a modern library like this one, with bright lights and dozens of computer screens lining the walls, they couldn't hide that old-as-sin book smell.

Or maybe it was just the memories of Mrs. Wexel, her high school librarian who'd run detention. Mrs. Wexel had possessed impressively pungent body odor and a stare that could shame even the most shameless of note-passers and spitball shooters.

Mason didn't seem to carry Sophie's baggage when it came to libraries. He turned in slow circles as they made their way through the stacks. "My God," he kept repeating. "So many books."

Sophie was thinking much the same thing. How were they ever supposed to find the right one? What if it was hidden on a shelf? Were they supposed to look at every spine? Worse yet, what if it was wrapped in the dust jacket from some other book? What if the book that held the power to save the world looked like something by Danielle Steel? Would they have to pull every book off the shelf and look inside each one? How many days would *that* take?

Mostly, she was frustrated with Frank for ditching them. He'd been out there five minutes already. But when he came back in, she didn't want him to find them standing around waiting for him to save the day. They had to take a proactive approach.

"Okay," she said, "let's assume for now it isn't on one of the shelves. I mean, they wouldn't want just anybody walking up and checking it out, right?" For the moment, she put aside the question of who *they* were.

Mason was still doing his slow spin, taking in the new sights and smells. It had to be an assault on his senses. Sophie felt a bit sorry for the guy. His voice was distant when he spoke. "Then we check the perimeter?"

"Good a plan as any. Come on."

She led him away from the east side of the library, where the fiction section and the banks of computers with free Internet access drew the majority of the weekday morning patrons. They walked west, past the graphic novel section and the travel books, until they reached the far wall. Small meeting rooms lined this side of the building. Each had a table and a couple chairs that looked entirely uncomfortable. All the rooms were empty and their doors were wide open as if waiting for someone to come into the municipally-provided comfort of their open arms.

Sophie tried to think who would use such rooms, and why, but she came up empty.

At the end of the room was a staircase leading to the second floor. Sophie paused, unsure if patrons were allowed up there, but Mason, who didn't have her years of institutional brainwashing on following rules, didn't pause and nearly ran into her back. She reminded herself the book was just as likely to be in an employees only section as anywhere else, and headed up the stairs.

In the end, she needn't have worried. The upstairs was open to the public. The walls of the long hallway at the top of the stairs were lined with paintings which Sophie assumed were probably by local artists. Some of them were pretty good, but some were clearly hanging there because a library employee didn't have the stones to say no to a desperate local artist.

They passed a pair of restrooms and a drinking fountain before reaching a set of glass doors. She glanced at the sign next to the door. *The Rough-Shod Readers Book Club. Tuesdays 10am. All welcome. Doughnuts provided.*

Sophie felt Mason move next to her.

"What's going on in there?" he asked.

"Book club. They read a book and then all try to sound smart while talking about it." She glanced at her watch. Ten-oh-three. She looked through the glass doors. There were maybe a half dozen people inside, and they appeared to be settling in. A number of distinct conversations were happening. One man was carrying two precariously balanced doughnuts back to the table. Everyone in the room appeared to be in their sixties, if not older.

She was about to turn away when something caught her eye. A familiar green paperback book sat in front of almost every seat. Sophie recognized it.

She'd never been much of a reader, but the weeks she'd spent in Sanctuary had included a lot of downtime. In her bored desperation, she'd dug into Jake Hinkle's small collection of science fiction and fantasy books, and she'd been surprised to find how much she liked them. She'd even read a few more since she'd been back from Sanctuary. She had a harder time concentrating now, though. Every time she started to get lost in a story, some memory popped into her head, pulling her back to the real world. Mostly they were memories of her final fight with Taylor, her sister's killer. But there were other things, too. Vee's arms being pulled from his body. The Larvae burying itself in her friend's arm. A man being turned into a tree. They came to her as still images, frozen pictures of the worst, most gruesome moments of her life. She had to close her eyes and put the book aside until it passed. It took her a long time to get through a book now.

Of all the novels she'd read in Sanctuary, her favorite was *Old Man's War* by John Scalzi. It was the story of a future where the Earth was at war with aliens. For reasons unknown to most of the people on Earth, you weren't allowed to join the fight against the enemy until your seventy-fifth birthday. If you decided to do so, you would be taken away to fight and never see Earth, your family, or your friends again.

Old Man's War was the green paperback on the table.

Sophie looked at Mason. "Let's go in."

He raised his eyebrows. "Really?"

She nodded to the sign. "All welcome."

"I mentioned I can barely read, right?" He looked toward the people inside. "How about I wait out here?"

"You fit the demographic better. Don't worry, I'll do the talking." Without waiting for a response, she pulled the door open and walked inside.

She found two empty seats near the end of the table and sat down, motioning for Mason to join her.

She suddenly realized the conversations had stopped, and everyone was looking at her. After a moment, a man with a wide smile and thinning but neatly combed hair walked over, his hand out.

"I'm Joe Cantor. I'm the director of the library. Welcome."

She shook his hand and introduced herself. After an awkward pause, Mason did the same.

"If you don't mind me asking, what, er, brought you to our little group?" Joe asked.

Sophie tilted her head. "Book talk. Can't get enough of it."

"What he means to say," an older woman on the far side of the table said, "is how'd you hear about our group?"

"Ah," Sophie said, doing her best to turn on the charm. "Oddest thing. Mason and I were just hanging out, taking in the library, and we stumbled across your room here. I saw you were reading *Old Man's War* and thought I'd join in."

After a long moment, Joe said, "So, you've read the book, then?"

"One of my favorites."

Though she wouldn't have thought it possible, the tension in the air grew thicker.

Joe moved to his seat. "Okay, well, let's...get started, I suppose."

More silence.

Sophie glanced over at Mason and was surprised to see he looked like the most comfortable person in the room. He'd snagged a jelly-filled doughnut—probably while she was awkwardly engaging with Joe and his bookish oldsters—and was happily munching away.

After another long, heavy silence, Sophie said, "How's this work? Do we just give our thoughts on the book?"

Joe's smile widened a bit. "Yes! Excellent. Since you're our guest, feel free to go first."

She wasn't expecting that. She was hoping to listen in a bit, maybe get a feel for the flow of conversation. And maybe pick up a few juicy bits about King's Crossing. But she went for it. "Yeah, okay. I liked it a lot. It was funny, and sad, and exciting. My favorite part was when they first get into space. When there's all the mystery about what's actually going on."

She looked around the table as she spoke, and she noticed something odd. The copy of the book she'd read at Sanctuary had been beaten up, the spine lined with dozens of creases and the cover starting to tear. She could see three spines from where she sat. Not one of them had a single crease. The others looked to be in perfect condition, too. Their covers held the sharp edges of a book never once banged against anything. Either every person here was a super careful reader, or these books had never been read. One way to find out.

"I'm a little conflicted on the shark monster scene, though," she said. "I guess I can see how it fit into the plot, but it was a bit graphic for me. Shark sex is not something I was really expecting."

A murmur of agreement went around the table.

"That was very odd indeed," an old woman said.

"And can we talk about the twist?" Sophie asked. "How it was all a dream? I was *not* expecting that! So original."

The smile fell from Joe's face. Clearly, he'd figured out she was messing with them.

Sophie had her hands folded on the table in front of her, and she noticed they were all looking at them. No, she realized, remembering the Roman numeral tattoos. Not her hands. Her wrists.

She unclasped her hands and laid them palms up on the table, exposing the untattooed skin of her inner wrists. "Show them your wrists, Mason."

Mason grudgingly put down the doughnut, brushed the powdered sugar from his hands and followed her lead.

She looked at Joe. "Guys mind if I see yours?"

Joe slowly unbuttoned his cuffs, rolled up his sleeves, then showed his wrists. The others did the same. None of them had a tattoo.

Okay, so this wasn't really a book club. What was it?

Joe buttoned his cuffs. "Why are you really here?"

The truth was she was here to talk about the book, but it might sound more impressive if she let them assume for the moment she'd uncovered their covert little group on purpose.

She took a deep breath before speaking. "I'm looking for a book. An old book. It might have a broken world on the cover. Like a sketch of the earth with a crack through it. Or it might have a cracked clock."

"Like the compass Zed carries," another man said. Joe shot him a look.

Sophie nodded. "I'm not sure exactly what it looks like. But most of the pages would be blank." She decided to take a shot. They'd wanted to make sure she didn't have the tattoo Zed's followers had, so they weren't likely to be Zed Heads, right? "Zed wants the book. We want to find it and keep it from him."

The people around the table looked at each other. The mood in the room changed from suspicion to...maybe hope?

"I'm sorry," Joe said. "I know every book in this library. There's nothing like that here."

Sophie found herself believing him. That wasn't something that happened frequently with her.

"Who are you?" Joe asked.

"My name's Sophie Porter. Me and my friends are here to stop Zed."

"And how are you planning to do that?"

She shrugged. "We've had dealings with him in the past. You know Rook Mountain?"

"We do get CNN up here," Joe said.

"Okay, well, Zed did that. He's done it to other places, too. He's got similar plans for King's Crossing."

They were still all looking at her, not saying anything.

Mason finished his jelly doughnut and wiped the excess powdered sugar on his shirt. "Okay, our turn. What's this group really all about?"

Joe rubbed his chin for a moment. "Strange things have been happening in King's Crossing for a while now. Zed's part of it, but not the only part. People here seem to know things—"

"Joe!" the old woman next to him barked. "You gonna reveal our secrets, we gotta vote them into the group." Her voice was a strange combination of raspy and high pitched.

"Is that really necessary? They have information—"

"It is," a man to Sophie's left said. He'd been silent until now.

"Okay…" Sophie said. "Do we need to step out or something?"

"That won't be necessary," the woman croaked. "Hands of those who oppose allowing these two strangers into our group?"

Every hand but Joe's went up.

The woman flashed her dentures at Sophie. "Sorry, dear. That means you'll have to be going."

Sophie put her hands on the table and pushed herself to her feet with agonizing slowness. "Fine." She looked Joe in the eye. "If any of you change your mind and want to talk, we're at the Holiday Inn. Sophie Porter and Mason Hinkle."

"I highly doubt—" the woman began, but Sophie turned on her heels and marched out of the room, missing the rest of whatever snide sentiment the woman hurled at her.

When they reached the hall, Sophie turned to Mason. "Dude, I kinda miss the Larvae. I wasn't cut out for this reconnaissance stuff. This is Frank's thing."

Mason nodded. "Good doughnut, though."

They found Frank wandering the stacks. He hurried over when he saw them.

"Come on," he said. "I've got a lead."

Sophie nudged Mason with her elbow. "What'd I tell you?"

As they were about to exit the library, someone called Sophie's name. She turned and saw Joe trotting toward them in a most un-librarian-like fashion.

When he reached them, he said, "Can we talk? It's about what you said up there. About Zed."

THE BOY WHO FOUND THE WATCH (PART THREE)

Charlotte, North Carolina
September, 1948

A bright light shone into Zed's eyes, and he woke with a start, blinking furiously against the powerful beam. His mind spun with disorientation.

"That's the last show, kid. Go home. Your mom's probably worried sick."

The light moved away from his eyes and Zed got his first look at the speaker. It was a pimply faced teenager dressed in a red uniform. An usher.

Zed blinked hard as he remembered where he was. A movie theater. In, what, Atlanta? Nashville? He couldn't remember.

It had been three months since he'd taken the watch from Charlie. Three months of trains and buses. Three months of looking over his shoulder for the police or Charlie's mysterious boss or whoever else might be after him. He'd found he liked traveling. He liked the solitude. And he still had over half his money, so he could keep traveling for at least a few more months.

The thing he hadn't counted on before leaving home was how difficult it was for an eleven-year-old to travel on his own. People asked so many questions. What was he doing? Where was his mother? Why was he riding the train alone? He had a slew of stories he used, never too elaborate. He kept his answers to a sentence or two when he could help it.

One other difficulty Zed hadn't anticipated was the constant struggle to find a place to sleep. He could buy his own food without anyone raising an eyebrow, but sleeping... motels didn't rent rooms to eleven-year-old boys. The few times he'd tried had led to questions that were difficult to answer.

He'd found a few solutions. Trains and buses made for excellent places to sleep. He'd spent much of his time traveling from city to city just for a semi-quiet place to rest his head without anyone bothering him. The downside was that the constant travel was a major drain on his money roll. A cheaper alternative was movie theaters. He could buy a ticket to the first show and happily sleep his way through the last. It was loud—he often had ringing in his ears after a day like that and he always seemed to smell of stale popcorn—but when he got tired enough, it was worth it.

The usher's flashlight beam was still pointing at him, though mercifully not in his eyes. Zed stretched and slowly got to his feet, dreading another cold night of walking the city streets.

As he stood, his hand slipped automatically into his pocket, and a wave of peace passed through him as he touched the watch. His watch. Despite all the hardships of the past three months, he had to admit it had been the happiest time of his life. He had the watch, and he could touch it as much as he wanted. He could look at it anytime he wanted. He'd killed to get the watch, and he'd happily do it again. It was his.

If there was one thing about the watch that bothered him, one annoying little thing that grated him like a pebble stuck in his shoe, it was that he hadn't been able to get the watch to do anything out of the ordinary. He wasn't sure what he was expecting of it exactly, but he remembered back to Charlie and the way he had made himself go from one part of the room to another in an instant. Zed hadn't been able to get the watch to perform any of those feats of magic.

Maybe his mother had been right. Maybe Charlie had just hypnotized Zed. Maybe it didn't have anything to do with the watch itself. But Zed didn't believe that. He could feel the power in the watch when he held it. It was like a pulse. Or maybe a building pressure. Zed sensed it had an energy different from anything he'd ever experienced, and something told him it wanted to get out.

Zed left the theater, and stepped out on to the dark city street. He remembered where he was. Charlotte, North Carolina. It was a nice town. Small enough that it wasn't overrun with crime, and large enough that he was able to wander the streets at night without attracting too much attention. Still, he thought he'd probably move on soon. He wanted to see the ocean. He thought of the map that had hung in his classroom and wished he'd paid more attention to it. What was the closest coast town of any size? Savannah, maybe? That was on the ocean, right?

The smell of cooking meat suddenly hit him like a bag of bricks, and his stomach cramped in painful hunger. He looked up and saw a diner on the corner. It had the beautiful words *Open Late* painted on the window. He stopped under a street light and considered. Did he dare? Would the waitress insist on calling his mother? Or, worse yet, would she call the police to report this boy out after curfew? What time was it, anyway?

He pulled out the pocket watch and flicked it open. *11:04.* Late for a boy his age.

He ran his finger over the broken clock symbol on the back of the watch. The diner and his hunger were momentarily forgotten. He felt suddenly strong. Powerful. He squeezed the watch.

There was a click.

For a terrible moment, he was certain he'd broken it. If that had happened, he didn't know what he'd do. He imagined it would involve stepping in front of a train. But, no, he hadn't broken the watch. He'd simply pressed the broken clock symbol and it had depressed.

It was a button, he realized.

Three months, and he hadn't realized the symbol was a button that could be pressed. The watch held too much import for him. He'd always handled it gently, reverently.

Something felt different. There was a strange hum in the air, a feeling he'd never felt before. The watch buzzed with energy, but it felt different somehow. He'd always assumed the energy was imaginary, his way of externalizing the specialness he saw in the watch. But maybe it wasn't. Maybe the energy was real and he had just used some of it.

A shiver passed through him. And with it, his stomach resumed its angry complaint. He shook his head to clear it and walked toward the diner.

The quiet hit him first. He walked in the door and heard nothing. It was still. As quiet as his old childhood home when his mom had been at work. Quieter even. At home there'd been the sounds of the radiator and the occasional car horn out the window. This was different. There was nothing.

For a terrible moment, he thought he'd gone deaf. He made a pathetic wordless vocalization, and was relieved to hear the sound of his voice.

Then he noticed the people.

The diner wasn't full, not by a long shot. But six of the tables were occupied. Two waitresses stood behind the counter. None of them, patrons or workers, were moving. They were still as statues.

Zed wandered through the diner for five minutes, observing the strange frozen figures. A man in the booth in the back corner held a fork with a bit of pumpkin pie on it, headed toward his gaping mouth. Zed plucked the pie off the fork and stuck it in his own mouth. He didn't normally like pumpkin pie, but this bite tasted especially sweet.

It was the stillness of the clock on the wall that finally made him realize the truth. He stared at its motionless second hand and realized he had stopped time.

Or, the pocket watch had.

No, he decided after a moment's thought. The pocket watch was just a tool. A beautiful and life-changing tool, but a tool nonetheless. It was Zed who'd stopped time.

He realized he could very likely counter the effect and restart time by pushing the button again, but he wasn't ready to do that yet. There was something peaceful about all this. Something soothing.

He left the restaurant and walked around the block checking to see how far the effect went. Everything outside was just as frozen as the diner. Which meant, what, the whole world was frozen? Everything but him?

If so…it was wonderful. There would be a million uses for this power, a million ways he could use it to his advantage, but the first that came to mind was sleep. If he stopped time, he could walk right through any person's front door, lie in their bed and sleep until he woke up naturally. How long had it been since he'd slept in a bed? The mere thought of it made his knees weak.

But first he had to take care of a more pressing issue: his stomach. He went back in the diner and walked through the door to the kitchen. Next to the motionless cook, there was a large cheeseburger sitting on a plain white plate. He picked up the plate, walked to the nearest booth and sat down to eat.

He picked off the tomato and took his first bite. The meat was cooked perfectly, and Zed sighed in pleasure as a bit of juice dribbled down his chin. He quickly swallowed and took another too-large bite of the greasy, delicious burger.

"You're a very stupid boy."

Zed froze at the sound of the unexpected voice. A woman sat across from him. He hadn't seen her arrive. One moment, he was alone in the booth, and the next she was there.

He started to speak, but the woman held up a hand to stop him.

"Please, finish chewing your food before you speak."

He dutifully chewed his food, and as he did, he inspected the woman more closely. She had a face of sharp angles, and her most distinctive characteristic was her head of long, curly blonde hair. If asked, he wouldn't have been able to even guess at her age. She looked both older and younger than his mother. There was an ageless quality about her. Her eyes were a blue so deep they were almost purple.

The woman stared at him, not moving, not speaking, just waiting for him to swallow his food. As soon as he thought he could do so without choking, he gulped it down.

He started to speak, but the woman stopped him with a hand once again.

"Do you know who I am?" she asked.

He was surprised to realize he did. He nodded.

"Who am I?" she asked.

His voice sounded weak and childish in his own ears. "Charlie's boss." He had assumed Charlie's boss was a man, but looking at her…he somehow just knew.

She nodded grimly. "Good. So you probably realize how unhappy I am with you right now."

That wasn't exactly a question, so he elected not to answer it. Instead, he said, "How'd you find me?"

She raised an eyebrow. "We are sitting here with time paused around us, and that's your first question? Truth is, we've been on your trail for a month now. We would have had you within a week. There are those in our…organization who can track the Tools. But you used the watch, which made things quite a lot easier."

He asked the only question that mattered, the one that had been burning a hole in his heart since she appeared. "Are you gonna take it away from me?"

Her mouth was a thin grim line. "That watch is only to be used by people in the employ of my organization. Are you in the employ of my organization?"

Zed slowly shook his head.

"Then there's your answer."

Zed considered bolting for the door, but something about the woman made him think that would be a very bad idea. She had an air about her, a feeling of power. The same feeling, come to think of it, he felt when he held the watch.

She tilted her head and regarded him for a moment before continuing. "As much as I disapprove of your actions against our man Charlie, it did show a certain initiative. And it did create an opening in the organization. The very fact that you were drawn to the watch shows a lot about your aptitude." The hint of a smile played on her lips now. "Tell me, young man, how would you feel about coming to work for me and my friends? If are able to dedicate yourself fully to the tasks we set before you, and if you demonstrate absolute loyalty, you could find yourself with a *very* profitable and *very* lengthy career. I'm even prepared to let you hold on to the watch. On a trial basis, of course. How does that sound?"

Zed thought that sounded very fine indeed.

CHAPTER FOUR: THE KEY WITHOUT A LOCK

1.

After Frank and Mason left the library, Joe led Sophie through the stacks. Her friends had gone to follow up on whatever Frank had found, but Sophie had insisted on staying behind to talk to Joe. She had to admit, she was suddenly feeling very good about this whole thing. She'd uncovered a lead! Frank could take his smug, *Haven't you ever investigated a small town with a secret before*, and shove it.

As they were walking, Sophie felt a hand on her arm. She turned and saw a little old woman holding a thick historical novel. The woman looked at Sophie with wide eyes.

"Where are the others?" the old woman asked.

Sophie paused, confused. "I'm sorry, I don't—"

"The others!" the old woman barked at her. "Mason and Frank! They're supposed to be with you."

Sophie felt her mouth fall open. It took her a moment before she could respond. "They...they had to leave."

The woman grew a shade paler. "Oh, this isn't good. This isn't good at all. They're supposed to be here."

Joe turned toward the woman. "Mrs. Gilbert, are you alright?"

Mrs. Gilbert shook her head. "They're supposed to be here and they're not. I have to tell someone. But who? Who should I tell? What if they make me do it again?"

Joe motioned for Sophie to follow him. "She'll be okay."

As she turned to go, Sophie noticed a tattoo on the veiny flesh of the woman's wrist. The Roman numeral *VII*.

Joe led Sophie behind the circulation desk and into a small office. He pointed her to a chair in front of the desk that dominated the room.

"I'm sorry about before," Joe said. "Some of the Rough-Shod Readers are a little...paranoid. And not without reason. No doubt they're less than happy with me for slipping out in the middle of the meeting."

Sophie nodded. "No worries. I gotta ask, though, if the club's a big secret, why the '*All welcome*' sign?"

Joe thought for a moment before answering. "There's something to be said for hiding in plain sight. And a book club on Tuesday morning at ten a.m. doesn't bring in a lot of random stragglers, believe it or not."

"Maybe try bringing a book at least one of you has read, though," Sophie said with a smile.

Joe nodded. "Yes, that was a bit embarrassing. Actually, I've been meaning to read *Old Man's War*. It's just...difficult to concentrate lately."

Sophie could relate. "You wanted to talk about Zed?"

"Yes. Well, him and some other things. The others might not agree, but I think your outside perspective might be able to shine some light on what's happening in King's Crossing."

Sophie leaned forward. She was suddenly feeling every inch the detective. "And what is happening here?"

Joe shook his head slowly. "Strange things. Very strange things."

"That tends to be the case when Zed's around."

"Actually, Zed's only been here a few months. This started well before that."

Sophie bit her tongue. She'd seen enough movies to know she'd broken the cardinal rule of sleuthing: if your source is talking, shut up and let them talk.

"It started a couple years ago," Joe continued, "with a tree. This weird little tree started growing down by the river at Volunteer Park. It's hard to describe if you haven't seen it. It's small, but it's—I don't know—twisty. Something about it isn't right."

Sophie reminded herself of the cardinal rule and didn't respond. Man, it wasn't easy.

"Then the weirdness started. All of the sudden, a bunch of people in town had those Roman numeral tattoos on their wrists. And people started knowing things they shouldn't. I don't know how else to say it. It was like the people with those tattoos suddenly knew the future."

Sophie couldn't help herself. "Give me an example."

Joe grinned like he'd been waiting his whole life to be asked that question. "I can give you hundreds. That's what the Rough-Shod Readers do. We collect examples of the weirdness. We're trying to piece together what's going on."

For the next half hour, Joe told her about some of the things the Rough-Shod Readers had uncovered.

There was the story of Nate Sanders, the part-time movie reviewer for the *King's Crossing Tribune*. One day about a year-and-a-half ago, he had emailed a movie review to his boss Cheryl, who happened to be a member of the Rough-Shod Readers. Thing was, Nate had accidentally attached his master file which contained reviews of over fifty movies, twenty of which hadn't yet been released. As the movies came out, the

Rough-Shod Readers carefully checked the reviews and found them to be amazingly accurate, including many details about character moments and special effects that would have been impossible to know from just reading a leaked script. It was clear Nate Sanders had somehow seen these movies months —and in some cases over a year—before they were released.

Six months ago, someone had made an anonymous call to city hall, demanding someone inspect the bridge at Fourth Street within thirty days. The inspector had gone out and discovered structural damage that would have caused the bridge to collapse in the very near future. It was certainly possible the call had been placed by some concerned citizen with structural engineering knowledge. But was it likely?

And then there was the sports gambling. A strange number of King's Crossing residents had suddenly become eerily accurate at predicting Super Bowl winners and filling out March Madness tournament brackets.

On and on it went. Mostly it was little things, a comment here, a strangely worded email there, and the Rough-Shod Readers collected them all. Most of these things could have been coincidences if taken alone, but when considered as a whole they made a difficult-to-refute case that some sort of psychic ability had taken hold of some of the residents of King's Crossing.

The ability seemed to be tied to those with tattoos. The Rough-Shod Readers had spent a lot of time trying to understand the connection. What did the tattoos mean? Did those with higher numbers have greater psychic ability? Were the numbers some sort of leveling system? The Rough-Shod Readers believed less than two-hundred people had the tattoos, but two-hundred people with psychic ability could make a pretty noticeable impact.

And then, a few months ago, Zed had arrived, and the tattooed people of King's Crossing had welcomed him like a conquering hero. Like he was the savior they'd been waiting for. They'd built a shed around the tree in the park as if they were trying to hide it away, to keep it for their own.

Joe was still discussing Zed's welcome in King's Crossing when Sophie's phone rang. It was Frank.

After she hung up, she looked at Joe. "I'm sorry, but I have to go. My friends will be here to pick me up in just a minute. Can we finish this later? I know my friends are going to want to hear what you have to say."

Joe nodded. "Indeed. And I want to hear what you have to say, too. I just realized I've done all the talking."

Sophie couldn't help but smile. Maybe she wasn't such a bad sleuth after all.

2.

They followed Matt through town—he in his truck and Mason and Frank in Sophie's car—past schools, churches, and houses, large and small. Now that they were away from the river and getting their first real look at the heart of town, Frank thought this place wasn't all that different than Rook Mountain.

For the first time in years, Frank was behind the wheel. He suddenly realized he'd missed driving.

He looked at Mason. "How am I doing?"

Mason raised an eyebrow. "You're asking me?"

Matt turned onto a small road that twisted up a bluff.

Mason asked, "Can we trust this guy?"

"I have no idea," Frank said.

Mason's gaze was fixed to the window. As they moved away from town and deeper into the forested heights of the bluff, he seemed to relax by degrees. They were going into his element.

Finally, they passed a sign that read, *Castle Bluff Park*. A few moments later, the road ended in a parking lot. Matt parked his truck, and Frank pulled into the spot next to him.

"Same signal as before if we need to run?" Mason asked before getting out.

"Same signal as before," Frank answered.

When they got out, Frank turned to Matt. "Okay, why'd you bring us here?"

Matt smiled weakly. "We're not quite there yet. Follow me."

He led them on foot through the parking lot and up a well-trod, paved path up to the top of the bluff. It was a short walk, clearly designed to allow people of all abilities to make it to the summit.

They rounded a final bend and came out onto a vista. A flag pole stood in the middle of the clearing, the American flag at the top whipping in the wind.

Matt moved to the wooded fence at the edge of the vista. "Take a look."

They were looking out over King's Crossing. Every house, every church, every road was laid out below them like some sort of miniature town.

"It's beautiful," Frank said.

"That's why I brought you here," Matt said.

They stood in silence for a few moments, looking out over the town.

"I've lived here my whole life," Matt said finally. "It can be a strange place. Sometimes a petty place. A dangerous place, too. But mostly it's a good place. The people here can surprise you in a million wonderful ways."

Frank let that hang in the air for a few moments before he

---

said, "What did you want to talk to us about?"

Matt looked at them both in turn, and there was something like fondness in his eyes. "This is going to sound strange."

"We saw a grown man get pulled through a hole in a tree two hours ago," Frank said. "I think we can handle it."

Matt smiled. "Yeah. I guess you're right. Okay, here goes." He put his hand on the wood fence. "I'm pretty good friends with both of you."

"Okay…" Mason said.

"I'm friends with Sophie, too," he continued. "She and my wife are practically inseparable."

Frank suddenly realized he'd never introduced Mason. Matt had acted so familiar with him right off the bat that Frank hadn't felt the need.

Matt pointed down toward the town. "A pretty big fight happens down there in the very near future, and we're in it. We watch each other's backs and make a pretty good showing of things."

"Can you explain this a little more clearly?" Mason asked. "I grew up in the woods, so I don't always catch on to things as fast as some."

"Yeah, explain it for Mason's sake," Frank said.

Matt grinned at that. "Okay, sorry. Let me try to do this another way. I can explain how Zed knew you'd show up at that restaurant last night. How he even knew what you'd order. It's the same way I knew you'd go to the library this morning after you left the shed." He looked Frank in the eye. "It's because we've done this all before. Lots of times, actually."

"Still not following," Mason said.

"Okay, look, it's like this," Matt said. "Zed's figured out a way to send someone back in time. Not anywhere in time,

The Broken Clock

mind you, but back along their own timeline. So, he could do his thing and send me back, say, two years. It would be 2013, and I'd still be me, just as I was in 2013, but with all the knowledge I have now."

He let that take hold for a moment.

"So let me see if I understand," Frank said. "If you went back to 2013, there wouldn't be two of you, right? Just the one guy with this future set of memories?"

"You got it."

"So you're *Quantum Leap*ing into your past self?" Frank asked.

"Err, yeah, I guess," Matt said with a grin.

Mason leaned against the fence. "How's Zed do it?"

"It's that compass of his," Matt said. "That's part of it, anyway. And you've seen how he can teleport?"

"I've seen it," Frank said. "Some of his cronies in Rook Mountain had the power too. It was pretty gross."

"Well, he says it's like that. But he's moving people through time rather than through space. The compass tells him who to send and when to send them. And then he touches them and they go back."

"Okay, then *why's* he doing it?" Mason's voice was as confident as Frank had ever heard it. Now that they were away from the unfamiliar ground of modern society and talking about a topic he knew something about, Mason was like a whole different person.

"Now that," Matt said, "is an excellent question. Here's the thing. All that stuff he said at the restaurant last night and in the park this morning? He was telling the truth. Mostly. A version of the truth anyway. He does have powerful enemies, and they are coming in two weeks' time. And we will have the fight of a lifetime on our hands. Zed has a plan to defeat them, but for it to work, everything has to go exactly as planned. So far, it hasn't."

Frank was starting to get the picture. "Sending people back in time gives him unlimited do-overs."

Matt nodded. "Exactly. A couple problems, though. From what he says, Zed can't go back in time himself. He has to send somebody else. And when that person goes back, only that person retains their memories of the most recent try. Everyone else loses them. That person explains to Zed what happened. He always sends back someone who was actually there when it went wrong, but still…it's all subject to the interpretation of the person telling the story. It's a bit like shooting darts in the dark for Zed."

Frank shook his head. This was crazy, but it was also pure Zed. He couldn't help but believe what Matt was telling them. "How many times has this happened? How many times have we tried and failed?"

"I'm not sure of the exact number. I don't even know if Zed knows. Maybe a hundred? More? I don't know. Because the only person who knows is the person who's sent back. But we've come up with a little way of keeping track."

A light went on in Mason's eyes. "The tattoos!"

Matt nodded enthusiastically. "Exactly." He rolled up his right sleeve and showed them the Roman numeral *IV*. "This means I've been sent back four times."

"Jesus," Frank said. "You've experienced this conversation four times?"

Matt rolled his sleeve back down and shook his head. "I told you we were friends before. And we were. I mean, as close as people can become in a couple weeks, anyway. But we've never had this talk. I'm changing things up this time."

"Why?" Frank asked. "Did Zed—"

Matt cut him off. "Zed doesn't know I'm doing this. I'm going behind his back. First time ever."

Mason echoed Frank's last question. "Why?"

"Let me give you a little background. I was a dyed-in-the-wool Zed supporter from the start. He showed us what he could do with that compass and I believed him. Then I met you three. You started telling me what I now believe is the truth about Zed. By the third time I was sent back, I was sure you were the good guys. The fourth time I went back everything changed."

"How so?" Frank asked.

Matt scratched his chin. "Normally, Zed only sends people back as far as he needs too. A few weeks. Maybe a month or two. However far back he wants to send them to adjust whatever it is that needs adjusting. But the last time…he sent me back ten years."

"Why so far?" Mason asked.

Matt shook his head. "I don't know." He turned and looked out over the vista. "The town looks so small. Like a set of toys or something. That's the way they see it, Zed and the Exiled. King's Crossing is just another battleground. But it's more than that to me."

"Tell us what changed your mind about Zed," Frank said.

Matt took a deep breath before continuing. "My wife and I never had kids. Doctors told us we couldn't. We thought about adopting, but we decided we liked the freedom. We liked the ability to do anything and go anywhere without being tied down. But when I went back this time…I got my wife pregnant." His eyes lit up as he talked. "Her name's Alice. She the sharpest kid you'll ever meet. She's changed my world. Our world. She's the best thing in our lives." He reached out and grabbed Frank's arm, gripping the sleeve.

"So you see my problem? What if Zed sends me back ten years again? Or sends my wife back? Or, hell, sends someone else back and it sets off a chain reaction that changes things. Alice might never be born. Or maybe a different sperm will fertilize a different egg, and we'll have a kid, but it won't be her."

Matt looked back and forth, meeting their eyes. "There can't be any more do-overs. We have to get it right this time."

Frank put a hand on the man's shoulder. "We'll do what we can to help. Tell us what went wrong the other times."

Matt nodded. "Yeah, that's a good place to start. I don't really know how to say this, but every time I've lived this... you three have been the reason we couldn't beat the Exiles."

"Wait, what?" Mason asked.

Frank drew in a deep breath. "What do you mean? Was it because we couldn't find the book?"

Matt shook his head. "You had the book. All four times. The first time, you tried to destroy it. You said something about a quarry and burning the book. I don't know, I didn't trust you back then, so I didn't really try to understand. The second and third times, you hid the book far away from the fight with one of your locks. You tried to help us kill the Exiles, but the outcome was never good. The last time, Mason tried to use the book. They killed us before he could make it do anything. Every time the Exiles ended up getting the book. Zed says we've also tried *not* asking you to find the book, but the Exiles find it even more quickly in those cases."

"Wait," Frank said. "If you know we found the book those other times, why bring us into it at all? Why doesn't Zed just get the book? It's in the same place we found it those other times, right?"

"That's a complicated question," Matt said. "To answer the

first part, you never told him where you found it. You were never honest with him and you never handed over the book to him. As far as I can see it, that's the *only* thing you haven't tried."

The air suddenly felt a few degrees cooler to Frank. "So that's your angle. You're telling us all this so we hand the book over to Zed."

Matt slapped the wooden fence. "No! That's not it at all. I'm just giving you the history. Future history. Whatever. After I give you the book, you can do whatever you want with it. I still believe in you three. I think we can find a way. Whatever that way is, it's not Zed's. Because even if we win that fight, what then? What's the world like after Zed wins?"

Frank squinted at him. "You said *after I give you the book*. You have it?"

Matt nodded slowly.

Frank frowned. "I thought you said we never told you where the book was."

"That's true," Matt said. "But I also told you things are different this time. My daughter is a special girl. She found the book. We've been hiding it for three years."

3.

Alice was drawing when they arrived. She wasn't the best artist in town, or even in her class, but she enjoyed it. Drawing released a certain kind of energy that always seemed to be trapped inside her. Taking it out and putting it on the page was a relief, kind of like sneezing. It had to be done, even if the results weren't always pretty.

Today she was watching *Adventure Time* on the iPad while she drew, so she wasn't paying much attention to what she was drawing. She was just letting it flow through her. She didn't like the results, though. First she'd drawn a dog, a cute little one, maybe a beagle. But after she'd finished she'd noticed his teeth were a bit too sharp, and the sparkle in his eye was a bit too lively. He looked like he was hungry and maybe he didn't mind so much if the meat he got happened to be human. Then she drew trees, but the wrinkles in the bark looked like screaming faces. Then it was bunnies, and landscapes, and people, all with the same odd, slightly frightening result.

It seemed everything she drew today turned out twisted. Maybe that wasn't surprising. Maybe that was because *twisted* was exactly how she felt. She'd felt that way for the past two hours. Ever since meeting the man in the shed.

He'd seen her. Really seen her in a way she couldn't erase. She'd Pulled Back, and it was as if he'd Pulled Back with her. That knowledge, the knowledge that there was someone out there that could do what she did, or at least could see through what she did, was like a lead ball in her stomach.

She might feel better if she could talk to someone about it, but who? Her parents got uncomfortable and acted weird any time she even hinted around the topic of her special abilities. Who else was there? Marcy? Yeah, right. All she ever wanted to talk about was soccer.

There was something else that was bothering Alice about the man in the shed. He'd been scary, yes. Terrifying, actually. She'd be surprised if she could sleep any night for the next week. But he also understood what she could do. He'd understood it better in five seconds than her parents had in nine years. What if he could help her understand it? What if he could tell her why she was this way?

These were the thoughts running through her head when the front door opened, bringing her back to the real world.

She set down her pencil, only barely noticing that the flowers she'd drawn had pretty mean thorns sticking out of their stems, and scurried to her usual observation place atop the stairs.

Dad was walking through the door, which was a little surprising considering it was a work day and all. Just as surprising, he was not alone. Three people followed him. The first was a woman in a tee shirt and jeans with an impossibly cool haircut that made it look like she didn't care when clearly she did. The second was a man with black hair streaked with grey. Neither of them looked up and noticed Alice at her perch atop the staircase. No one ever did.

Then the third man, an old guy with leathery-tan skin and wrinkles around his eyes looked right up at her, like he'd known she was there. His eyes lit up when he saw her, and he gave her an enthusiastic wave.

No one else noticed.

"Helen," Dad called. "They're here."

Mom came out of the back room. She ran toward them, then stopped awkwardly. It was like she was meeting strangers and seeing old friends all at the same time. "Hi," she said. "I'm Helen."

"Frank," the younger guy said.

"Mason," muttered the old guy, barely loud enough for Alice to hear.

"Sophie," the woman with the cool hair said.

Helen smiled crookedly at Sophie. "Oh, what the hell," she said, and she pulled Sophie in for a hug. "I know you don't remember, but we've had some fun times, you and I. We got drunk together the night before the Exiles attacked last time."

Sophie held herself awkwardly though the hug as if not sure what to do with her hands. "God, this is weird."

Mason said, "How about this one?" He pointed up at Alice.

The others lifted their gazes and searched for her a moment before settling on her.

Dad did a double take when he saw her. How many times had she hidden and watched from up there? And no one had ever noticed. Until now. "Come on down, honey."

She descended the stairs, suddenly feeling a bit shy. They were all watching her, like she was something special. It felt like they expected her to do a trick or something.

She reached the bottom of the stairs and her parents introduced her all around. As if she hadn't been watching the first time everyone had given their names.

After Mason introduced himself, he said, "Sorry I gave away your hiding spot."

She was none too happy about it, but what was she supposed to say? "It's okay. I don't mind at all."

"Well," Mom said. "This is very…strange."

Sophie smiled. "For all of us."

"It doesn't have to be," Dad said. "Besides we don't have time for strange. There's lots of work to do and not much time to do it."

That was Dad's way, Alice knew. Anytime he was feeling uncomfortable he started working on something. That was probably why he always got so many projects done when Grandma and Grandpa were visiting.

Dad reached down and put a hand on her shoulder. "Alice, I want you to go get the book."

She paused, her hands suddenly ice cold. She wouldn't have been more surprised if he'd said, *Alice, I want you to stab me in the throat.* They never showed the book to anybody. Ever. That was the rule. And if someone saw the book, she was to Pull Back and keep it from happening. Her parents never said that directly, of course, but they'd firmly implied it. It was the closest they'd ever come to openly speaking about her abilities.

She looked back and forth from Dad to Mom, waiting for confirmation that she'd heard correctly.

Mom smiled at her. "It's okay, honey. Get the book."

Alice walked upstairs as if in a dream. She went to her parents' bedroom, opened the closet, and reached into the back corner behind the shoe boxes. It was wedged in there pretty tightly, but she gave it a couple of yanks, and it came free.

And was it ever heavy. It wasn't just the physical weight of the book, though that was part of it. It was tall and wide and as thick as Alice's leg. But there was something *heavy* about the content of the book, too. It made her feel uneasy to touch the book. It made her upset. It made all sorts of strange thoughts come into her mind, thoughts about fires, and destruction, and trees. Now, that she thought about it, the trees she thought of when she held the book were very similar to the one she'd seen in the shed that morning.

When she reached the group waiting silently at the bottom of the stairs, she handed the book to Dad. A wave of relief passed through her as her fingers lost contact with the leather-bound book.

"This is it," Dad said, handing the book to Frank. "The book that saves the world. Or damns it."

Frank took it, and Alice watched as he inspected it. He ran his fingers over the symbol on the cover. It was the rough image of a man with a crack running down the middle of him.

Frank said, "The one we saw had a broken world on the cover."

Alice tilted her head. There was another book? A book like this one?

"I wonder what it means," Sophie, said. "The broken clock on the Tools. The broken world on the book in Sanctuary. And now the broken person on this one. Why are they different?"

"Mind if I..." Frank raised the cover a hair.

"Go ahead," Dad said, "for all the good it will do you."

Frank opened the book and slowly started flipping through the pages. "It's blank."

"Funny thing, isn't it?" Mom asked. "All this fuss about a blank book."

Frank handed the book to Mason. "Take a look."

Mason flipped through it, a look of concentration on his face. "It's not blank, exactly. I can see, I don't know, impressions? Like there used to be words here but they faded away or something."

Now it was Sophie's turn to flip through the book. "Blank for me, too. Maybe that's for the best. I don't have the best record when it comes to using these books."

Mason looked at Dad. "You said that I used the book once?"

"Yes," Dad said. "You holed up with the book for a few days and eventually you were able to see some of the words. That's what you told us, anyway. Then you used the book."

"Where'd you find it?" Frank asked.

"We didn't," Mom said. "Alice did."

"We were out hiking," Dad said. "All of a sudden Alice ran off the trail and into the woods. She'd never done anything like that before. We went after her and by the time we caught up, she was sitting under a tree, holding the book in her hands."

"So what now?" Sophie asked.

Frank looked at Dad and Mom. "Maybe you should start by telling us how this all ends."

Dad nodded. "You're right. It's time for you to hear my story."

4.

It's raining when Matt goes out the door. Normally, he'd wear a hat or grab an umbrella. Today he doesn't care. Because today is the day the world ends.

He opens the back door to Sophie's car and lets Helen get in first. He squeezes in beside her. Mason's already back there, the big leather book, the one with the symbol of the broken man on the cover, clutched to his chest.

The door's barely shut before Sophie squeals out of the driveway.

"It's getting bigger," Frank says, by way of greeting.

No need to say what he's referring to. They all know.

Matt just nods absently. He glances down and sees the Roman numeral III tattooed on his wrist. This isn't his first time. He knows how this will play out.

He turns to his wife and gives her a reassuring smile. He sees steel in those eyes. She's handling all this much better than he is. Maybe she's just a stronger person. Looking at her, he wants to weep. He wishes they had more time. They've had twelve years together, but it doesn't seem like enough. Not nearly. He wishes they'd gone on more dates. He wishes they'd spent more time just talking instead of spending their evenings watching dumb TV shows.

Helen's holding the revolver awkwardly. Matt's doing the same. He wishes they would have bought holsters. On the other hand, he's not even sure why they have guns. They had them last time, and it didn't make any difference. The Exiles are bulletproof.

But it had felt better to go out shooting than to wait like he had the

125

first time, just staring up in the sky until the fire devoured him.

They pull into the lot at Volunteer Park. The lot's full. Matt thinks maybe next time they should set up some kind of carpool situation. The thought almost makes him laugh. Almost.

Sophie parks in the grass. It's not like she's going to get a ticket.

She turns around and looks at each of them. "We all ready?"

Everyone nods. She turns to Frank. "How 'bout you, big guy?"

He nods absently.

Sophie's taking the lead. Usually it's Frank who fills that role. Frank has a distant look in his eye and a nasty cut on his cheek. Matt notices Frank's knuckles are badly bruised.

"What happened to you?" Matt asks. He saw Frank just yesterday, so whatever it was must have happened between then and now.

Frank doesn't answer. Instead he tosses something to Matt; one of his locks. He tosses one each to Mason, Helen, and Sophie, too.

Matt turns the lock over in his hand. It looks like a normal enough padlock, but he knows it's not. Frank showed them yesterday how to use it.

Without a word, Frank steps out of the car.

"Last time he gave an inspiring little speech," Helen says. "I was kinda looking forward to hearing that again."

"I'm sure Zed will do enough speechifying to make up for it," Mason says.

They get out of the car and move toward the riverbank where a crowd is gathered. There must be two hundred people out here. All of the people Zed trusts.

Zed pushes through the crowd toward them. "About time." His signature smile is missing today. Worried lines crease his face. "The crack's getting bigger. They'll be through soon." He grabs Willis Eddy by the shoulder. "You and Matt bring Rayd from the shed."

Matt's heart skips a beat. Willis nods toward Matt, and Matt follows him to the shed.

This thing with Rayd is new since Matt's last time. Bringing one of the Exiles through that tree in the shed. The last time Matt saw Rayd, he'd been floating in the sky with the other three Exiles, raining hot white light down on the town.

Willis throws open the shed door. Rayd is tied to the tree. He's recently taken quite the beating. His eye is black and blood is crusted under his nose.

Matt remembers Frank's bruised knuckles and wonders.

They haul Rayd to his feet and untie him from the tree. They secure his hands behind him with a smaller rope and bring him out of the shed. The strange man can hardly walk. Zed told them he'd be weak from having been tied to the tree for so long.

Matt has to admit, capturing and weakening one of the Exiles was a pretty good idea. Now they'll only be facing down three godlike beings instead of four. Still not the best odds in the world, but...for the first time today, Matt allows himself to hope they might make it.

They bring Rayd before Zed. Rayd chuckles softly.

"You could have lived forever."

Zed's face is stone. "Better to reign in hell." He turns to Frank. "You ready?"

Frank scowls at him. "What about Jake? And Mason's mom? And Sophie's sister?"

"There isn't time," Zed says absently.

"You promised. You said if we found the book—"

"After," Zed says. "We survive, and you'll have your brother back. The rest of them, too."

Rayd looks around, squinting. "I can feel the book. It's somewhere nearby, isn't it?"

Matt looks at Mason who is holding the book not ten feet from Rayd. He must be using his lock to hide himself.

Matt's eyes drift to the spot out over the water. There is a black tear a few feet above the surface of the river, maybe three feet long and a foot wide. It hurts his eyes to look at it. It is a thing that should not be.

"Everybody ready?" Zed asks.

That surprises Matt. No speech from Zed this time, either. Maybe he isn't so confident in their chances of success.

Frank looks at Matt and the others. "Turn on your locks."

The crack over the water begins to shiver.

Mason has the book open now, and his fingers are poised over the page.

Then, with a terrible ripping noise that chills Matt to the bone, the crack widens. Now light is pouring through, and three people step out. Two women first, then a man. The man, Matt can't help but notice, has no arms.

The older of the two women looks down at Rayd for a long moment. "Zed. What have you done?"

"The book's here," Rayd bellows, his voice quivering.

"So it is," the older woman says. "But where?"

Mason's fingers are tracing the page in the book now, his hand moving slowly and carefully.

"Wilm," Zed says. "You and yours have lived long enough."

The older woman looks distracted. "Someone's trying to use the book." She turns to her comrades. "Do you feel the power pulsing out of it?"

Mason's hand is moving faster now. He looks toward Zed. "It's not working like it's supposed to."

"Mason," Zed says, "I'm going to need you to finish now."

Sweat trickles down Mason's face. "I can't...it's not doing what it should."

Wilm shakes her head. "Nice trick. You're hiding things from me. People. The book. I don't know how you're doing it. But your man is concentrating too hard on the book." She squints...directly at Mason.

Matt realizes she can see him. He reaches out and takes Helen's hand.

"We've been patient," Wilm continues. "There's plenty of power in this town. We finally have what we need."

"No," Zed says. "Wait. Listen to me!"

But it's too late.

The three Exiles move toward Mason. He doesn't even have time to look up before they're on him.

Zed is holding the compass now, and Matt knows he's using it, asking it who he needs to send and when he needs to send them to in order to fix whatever went wrong here. Then Matt feels Zed's hand on his shoulder.

The world dissolves into white light.

5.

Dad made Alice wait in her room while he told the story. They were always making her wait in her room. It wasn't fair. She was the one who'd found the book.

And what was up with that guy Mason blowing her secret like that? He'd revealed her hiding place at the top of the stairs. It was like he'd seen straight through her.

She didn't like it. It was too similar to that weird guy in the shed.

Ugh. That guy in the shed. She shuddered just thinking about it.

Whatever they were talking about down there, it had to be juicy. She lay on her bed, clenching her fists and wishing she could hear what they were saying. If only Mason hadn't told about her hiding spot!

After a few minutes, she decided she didn't care. She was going to listen.

She crept out of the room and to the top of the stairs. She crouched in her usual spot, but back a little. That way even if they looked up, if that jerk Mason looked up, they wouldn't be able to see her. She couldn't see them either, but she could hear them.

Dad said, "Then Zed touched me and suddenly I was ten years in the past."

There was silence for a long time after that. It was so quiet, Alice was afraid they'd hear her breathing.

"That was the most recent time?" Frank asked.

"Yeah," Dad said.

"Zed betrayed us," Mason said. "He didn't bring back our families."

The room was silent for a long moment.

"You ask me, only one thing's changed since then," Sophie said. "Alice. Alice is the key to all this. She has to be."

Alice felt her heart beat quicken.

"Now hold up," Mom said.

"No, it's gotta be," Sophie said. "Look, Mason was born outside of time in Sanctuary, right? He could read that book and use it. He had a huge connection to that place. What if Alice's the same way with this place and this book?"

"She wasn't born outside of time," Dad said.

"No," Frank said, "but she was born in a—what did you call it—redo. In a strange way, she never should have been born at all."

Alice felt her face redden. What were they talking about? Of course she should have been born. She waited for one of her parents to defend her.

After a moment, Dad said, "You're right. God, I hate it so much, but you're right."

What did *that* mean? Dad agreed she should have never been born?

She had to find out what they were talking about. She needed to hear the rest of the conversation, the part she'd missed the first time.

She grabbed the rope in her mind and Pulled Back.

For a terrifying moment, it didn't work. It was as if it were stuck on something. Then she pulled a bit harder and felt the rope move, and with it came a burning pain in her mind.

Then…she was somewhere else.

She blinked hard, trying to orient herself to her surroundings. She wasn't in her room. She wasn't in her house. She was standing on a street in a downtown. But it wasn't King's Crossing.

And there was a woman standing in front of her, a woman with curly blonde hair and a wide smile.

"Hello, my dear," the woman said. "My name is Wilm. You and I have quite a lot to discuss."

THE BOY WHO FOUND THE WATCH (PART FOUR)

Santa Cruz, California
December, 1956

Zed stepped off the train and onto the dusty sidewalk. The air smelled like salt and it tasted bitter. Over the past few years he'd come to hate the ocean. He was born and raised on the plains of Kansas, and he felt all land should be like that of his home. Mountains and oceans were just being showy.

Zed had been working for Wilm and her organization for over eight years. He was nineteen, and his years of travel had left him weathered; he looked older than he should have. Though, with the amount he used the pocket watch, he sometimes wondered how old he really was. Had he paused time for a total of a year? Two years? If there was a book he wanted to read, he would pause time, and read the book, stopping to eat and sleep when the mood took him. He did the same for many things. If the swimming pool was crowded and he felt like taking a dip, he'd pause time moments before it closed and swim to his heart's content. If he became ill, he'd pause and wait it out until he was feeling better.

He sometimes felt a little guilty using the awesome power

of the watch for such mundane purposes. But if Wilm disapproved, she never let him know her feelings. Not that he saw her often. In fact, he'd only seen her five times since she'd hired him in the diner that day so long ago.

Most of his work for Wilm had been bizarrely simple and straight forward. He'd get his assignment mailed to him, always in a square white envelop with an ornate letter *W* as the only return address. The letter would succinctly describe his next job. It would always involve traveling to a new city and performing some minor task. It was often passing along a message that—it seemed to Zed—could just as easily have been delivered via post. But occasionally it was something slightly more substantial. Attend a series of public meetings and take detailed notes on the proceedings. Go to a town library and dig through the records in the local paper to research a certain event. The envelopes also contained a bit of cash that was expected to cover his expenses through the end of the assignment.

After the job was done, he was to wait in that city until further notice. He stayed in nice guest houses and hotels. His lodging was always paid for through means that weren't revealed to him. He used his cash to pay for meals, clothing, and any entertainment. It was a bit nerve-wracking at times because he never knew when his next job was coming, so he never knew exactly how long he had to make the money last. But he hadn't run out yet. After a week, or a month, or occasionally a few months, another white envelope would show up and he'd be off to his next assignment. Trust was a must.

It was a strange job in that, technically, he wasn't being paid. His expenses were covered, but he wasn't given any take home salary. Zed didn't think about that much. For one, he'd never had a job before this one, and—while he understood the concept of a paycheck—paying for his keep as he travelled around the country seemed fair enough. But, if pressed as to *why* he thought it was fair, he would have admitted he thought being allowed to keep the pocket watch was more than payment enough.

To Zed's mild surprise, he had yet to be asked to do anything illegal or even anything that required the use of the watch. When he thought about it, he wasn't sure why they allowed him to hang onto it. Either he was being groomed for some greater purpose or they had so many of these watches lying around that they didn't mind giving them out. He doubted it was the latter. He'd been waiting for his opportunity to prove himself on a bigger assignment. And now, finally, it looked like he was getting his chance.

He'd been in some backwater town in New Mexico for two months when he'd gotten his latest envelope. The note inside had read:

There is a man named Henry Rankin in Santa Cruz, California. We need to learn where's he's been the last three years. He will be reluctant to tell you. Use all means at your disposal. - W.

Under the message, as always, there was the address of the boarding house where he was to stay. There was also three hundred dollars. The most he'd ever received in one of these envelopes by half.

Zed wondered at the amount. Three hundred. The same amount he'd taken from his mother when he'd left home that bloody night. Was Wilm trying to send some kind of message? Remind him of his humble beginnings? Inform him she had information about what he'd done that night? Or was it a coincidence?

Enclosed was a picture of a stocky man with a bushy

mustache. The picture was yellowed and frayed along the edges.

Zed looked at the letter for a long time. *Use any means at your disposal*, it said. Well, he had quite a few means at his disposal. He'd been practicing.

He made his way to the boarding house and settled in, allowing himself to relax for the night before starting the job the next day. It only took him three days to find the man, though they were three days of his least favorite type of work: the kind that included human contact. Over the last eight years he'd been able to skate by with only talking to people once or twice a week, not counting the service people he had minor interactions with on a daily basis. And that was the way he preferred it. He liked to be alone with the watch.

Still, he did what the job called for.

So, picture in hand, he canvased the streets of Santa Cruz. He started with the bars. Knowing that some people, likely the type of people who frequented bars, might assume he was a lawman and be reluctant to help him, he concocted a story about having been hired to find Henry Rankin about a confidential matter involving an inheritance. If he saw anything in anyone's eyes that said they might know something about Henry, Zed was quick to slip them a dollar or two. Once, he even passed a five dollar bill to a man who hemmed and hawed just the right amount. But they all turned out to be dead ends. It was happenstance—or was it?—that finally gave him the man's location.

The woman who ran the boarding house saw the picture and asked him if he was a friend of old Hank. A few carefully phrased questions later, he had his quarry's place of employment, which was less than a block from the boarding house. Zed was beginning to realize Wilm wasn't really trying to locate Mr. Rankin. This was a test, and one Zed was determined to pass.

Zed watched Rankin for two days, taking particular note of his route to and from work, which passed right by the boarding house.

On the third day, he stepped in front of Rankin as the man was passing the house. Just before he got to Rankin he noticed Nancy, the woman who ran the boarding house, striding toward him with purpose. No matter. She'd be right there when he was done with Rankin. He pushed the broken clock symbol on the pocket watch and time stopped.

One of the more frustrating aspects of the watch's ability was that it didn't allow you to move people while time was stopped. Objects, yes. Anything not alive. But people and animals became immovable statues.

However, Zed had a theory. One he'd been too afraid to test until now. He believed that the watch released the power to stop time, but that he himself could shape it. Expand it.

He concentrated on expanding the bubble that allowed him to move while everyone else around him was frozen. He pushed the circle until it reached Rankin. In a moment, Rankin was blinking. Zed felt a smile creep across his face.

Rankin continued walking and almost bumped into Zed.

"You mind?" he asked.

Zed's smile widened. He couldn't help it. This was just too much fun.

"I do," he said.

The man looked confused so Zed gestured toward the street, indicating the frozen people around him.

The man's eyes widened. "What the hell?"

"I need to ask you a question, Mr. Rankin. Where have you been the past three years?"

Rankin shook his head, his breath coming in quicker gasps now. He took a step backward. "No. I already told them I'm not going to talk about that."

Zed stepped forward, closing the distance between them once more. "I'd suggest you revise your position."

Now Rankin drew his chest up, like he was making an effort to look tough. "I don't care what you do. You and all your tricks. I won't talk."

"Very well," Zed said. He imagined the bubble in his mind contracting ever so slightly.

Rankin's face grew pale. "Wh-what are you doing? I can't feel my feet."

Zed continued to contract the bubble.

The man looked around in panic. "Help! Someone help me!"

"Believe it or not, Mr. Rankin, you and I are the only living creatures in the world at this moment. There's no one who can help you. By the way, have you tried wiggling your fingers?"

Rankin looked down at his hands and the horrified look on his face answered Zed's question.

"Okay," Rankin said, his voice choked with emotion. "I was in Rook Mountain. Rook Mountain, Tennessee."

Zed couldn't help but be the tiniest bit disappointed the man hadn't held out longer. He would have liked to have frozen all but Rankin's head. He thought for a moment, trying to think of something else to ask, but he came up blank. He had the information he'd been asked to get.

He touched the broken clock symbol on the watch, and time resumed. Rankin gasped and crumpled to the ground in a shivering heap.

"Take a moment to compose yourself," Zed said, "then

go." He was surprised to realize he was still smiling. He rarely smiled, a habit that he'd carried with him since childhood.

Zed felt a tap on his shoulder. He turned to see Nancy standing behind him. He'd forgotten she'd been walking toward him when he stopped time.

She said, "This came for you. Delivery man said it was urgent." She held out a white envelope. She noticed Henry Rankin on the ground. "My Lord, is that Hank? Is he hurt?"

"Just a little excited to see me," Zed said. "It's been a long time."

He could see the elegant *W* in the upper-left corner of the envelope she held. He nodded, took the envelope, and walked away without a word. He tore it open, standing in the middle of the lawn, and was surprised to find there was no money inside. Just a letter. He took out the piece of paper and unfolded it with a shaky hand.

We are pleased with your progress. Our man will pick you up in the morning to bring you to see me. Then your education will be begin.

Regards,

Wilm

It was the first time she'd signed a letter with anything other than her first initial.

He returned to his room and lay awake until morning.

CHAPTER FIVE: FRANK'S DILEMMA

1.

They sat in silence for a long moment after Matt finished telling his story about how the world had ended.

"You ask me, only one thing's changed since that last time," Sophie said. "Alice. Alice is the key to all this. She has to be."

Frank looked at Sophie. It was one of the things he liked best about her, the ability to cut through to the heart of the matter. Frank felt like he always had to think his way around things a dozen different ways before he gained any perspective. Not Sophie. She bulldozed right through any emotional baggage or strange implications. Some of the time, the things she blurted out were wrong. But more often than not, she was right. And Frank had an idea this was the latter.

Alice *was* the key. She had to be. He didn't know how he felt about using a nine-year-old girl in a fight against ancient evils, but he had a feeling she'd be important by the end of this.

No matter what happened, they had to keep Alice safe.

"Now hold up," Helen said.

"No, it's gotta be," Sophie said. "Look, Mason was born outside time in Sanctuary, right? He could read that book and use it. He had a huge connection to that place. What if Alice is the same way with this place and this book?"

"She wasn't born outside time," Matt said.

"No," Frank said, "but she was born in a—what did you call it—redo. In a strange way, she never should have been born at all."

He hoped Matt wouldn't be offended by the way he'd said it, but there was a certain truth to it.

After a moment, Matt said, "You're right. God, I hate it so much, but you're right."

"No," Mason said. "Trust me, I have some experience with this. It's not that she shouldn't have been born, it's that nobody was expecting her to be. It gives us an advantage. The bad guys, Zed and these mysterious Exiles, they'll underestimate her. If they even notice she exists at all."

"You really think so?"

"Look," Mason continued, "I spent upwards of fifty years in Sanctuary with Zed. Never once did he say anything about these great enemies of his. He didn't care enough about me. I was just a tool. No different than that compass he carries."

Anger flared in Matt's eyes. He looked from Mason to Frank to Sophie. "And now you're talking about using Alice in the same way. It's like you think she's some kind of weapon."

Frank didn't deny it. Neither did the others. The fact was, that was exactly how Frank was thinking of her. And the worst part was, that didn't bother him. He'd seen his hometown torn apart by the Unfeathered. It had nearly killed him. He didn't want to imagine what it would be like to watch the whole *world* burn. If turning one little girl into a weapon was the price that had to be paid, then so be it.

Frank wasn't crazy enough to say any of that out loud, even though Matt seemed to think they were best buddies from previous lives. For once, Sophie was smart enough to keep quiet, too.

Matt must have seen something in Frank's eyes though, because he said, "She's a nine-year-old-girl!"

Helen put a calming hand on his knee. "Honey, it's okay. We're just talking is all. If we want to keep Alice safe, we have to understand."

Frank could have kissed her.

Helen continued. "How do we know what she can do? If you're right about her being the key to this thing?"

Matt shot her a look that was half surprised, half hurt, but he didn't interrupt.

"Well," Frank said, "it could be she's using the book already and we don't know it."

"I highly doubt that," Matt said. "She hates the thing. Did you see her face when I asked her to get it? There's no way she's flipping through it without us knowing."

Frank frowned.

"There is one thing," Helen said. "It doesn't have to do with the book, at least I don't think so, but she does have a certain…strange knack."

Matt's face went pale. "Should we really be talking about this? In front of strangers?"

Helen pursed her lips. "These aren't strangers, and you know it. You said yourselves they're our friends. We've died beside them how many times? Besides, I'm sick of not talking about what Alice can do. It's like this dark cloud hanging over our lives and we never acknowledge it."

Matt's eyes narrowed. "You think I don't want to talk about it? Of course I do. But what's there to say? I'm scared, okay? Scared for her. Scared of what will happen to her if we don't find a way to win."

"I am, too," Helen said. "But it's time to talk about it, to figure out a way to handle this thing. But we're a team, so if you don't want me to tell them about it, I won't."

Matt looked at the floor for a moment. "No. You're right. God, I hate it when that happens." A sad smile curled his lips. "Tell them."

Helen nodded, her eyes filled with love for the man. Then she turned to her guests. "Alice has this knack for...knowing what's going to happen before it does."

"Sounds like what Joe at the library said about you guys with the tattoos," Sophie said. "She can tell the future?"

"Not exactly," Matt said. "I mean, yes, but only in specific circumstances. It's like she knows when there's gonna be trouble and manages to avoid it. She's never once scraped her knee or broken anything. And sometimes she warns us before something happens."

"What do you mean?" Frank asked.

"Like last night. She told us Willis was going to knock on the door at three in the morning, and he did."

"She used to talk about it," Helen said. "She called it Pulling Back. I think she meant fixing things that have already happened. Or making it so they never happened. I don't know. But once she realized not everyone could do it, she stopped talking about it. And, cowards that we are, we didn't bring it up again. I think we were *relieved* she stopped mentioning it."

Matt sighed. "It scared us. It's too much like what Zed can do."

Frank ran his hand through his hair. "Could we bring her down here?"

Matt and Helen exchanged a look.

"We won't mention that Pulling Back thing," he continued

before they could voice their objection. "I want to talk to her about the book. I want to know if she can see the words. And, if so, whether she can figure out how to use it."

After a moment, Helen and Matt both nodded.

"I'll go get her," Helen said.

As she headed up the stairs, a cellphone buzzed. Matt pulled it out of his pocket and looked at the screen. "It's Zed."

"I wonder what kind of cellphone Zed rocks," Sophie said. "I'll bet it's a flip phone."

Frank watched Matt's face closely as he spoke with Zed. In the distance, he heard Helen calling for Alice.

Matt said, "Okay. Yeah, I understand." He ended the call.

Helen's voice drifted down to them, more frantic now.

"There's something wrong at the shed," Matt said. "Some kind of problem. Zed said it could ruin everything." His eyes were wide. "I'm scared, guys. Whatever's happening has him spooked. He's on the verge of pulling the plug and starting over. We need to get down there."

Before Frank could answer, Helen stuck her head over the railing, a look of terror on her face.

"Alice," she said, her voice a husky whisper. "Alice is gone."

2.

Alice stared at the woman standing in front of her. The world felt like it was spinning. She had to remind herself to breathe.

She reminded herself to focus on what was real. On the things she could see.

The woman who'd introduced herself as Wilm was tall and thin. She looked strong in a reedy way. And hard.

Not wanting to meet the woman's gaze, Alice looked

around. This was definitely not King's Crossing. The street seemed a bit wider. The shops were different. Even the color of the pavement under her feet seemed off a few shades.

But that wasn't all that was different. There were strange, white, featherless birds walking the streets. And dark, shadowy shapes circling in the sky.

The not knowing got her panicking again. She wanted to get out of here, and she wanted to do it now.

She imagined the rope in her mind and imagined grabbing it. Normally she was careful when she Pulled Back, exerting just the right amount of effort to go back to some exact moment. But not now. She was too scared. She just wanted out of here. If that meant going back a month or two, so be it. She gripped the rope and yanked it hard.

A spike of pain shot through her brain, but the rope didn't move. For the first time in her life, it didn't move.

The woman took a step toward her. "None of that, now."

Alice pulled again. Another spike of pain, sharper than before, but again the rope didn't move.

She pulled a third time, and she cried out as the pain rocked her like it never had before. She fell to her knees.

And then Alice felt true fear. She'd thought she'd been afraid before, but what she felt now was a whole different level. She couldn't leave. She couldn't go home. She couldn't Pull Back.

"Now you're just being silly," Wilm said. She held out a hand, then said in a softer voice, "Come on. I'll explain."

Alice looked at the hand for a long moment. Finally, not knowing what else to do, she took it and let the woman help her to her feet.

"You're trying to pull on time, yes?" Wilm asked.

Alice paused a long moment. She'd never had it put to her

so plainly. She nodded.

Wilm said, "Well, that's your problem, then. Time doesn't exist here."

Alice was starting to feel sick now. She tried unsuccessfully to keep the quiver out of her voice when she spoke. "I don't understand. If time doesn't exist, how am I breathing? How are we talking?"

Wilm waved a dismissive hand at her. "You people. You have it all wrong. You think time is some sort of protector. Or a necessary thing for your survival. Time is the chains you don't even know you're wearing."

Alice tried to understand. She thought maybe this woman was crazy. But this place seemed all too real. Maybe it was Alice who was crazy.

"Where are we?" Alice asked.

Wilm put her hands on her hips and looked around, as if for the first time. "A place called Ferman Creek, Montana. I live in a little cabin outside town."

A tiny part of Alice's mind was thrilled at that. She'd never been out of the Midwest.

"I've been here for what you would consider a long time," Wilm said. "A very long time. Tell me, do you know a man named Zed?"

Alice shook her head. "I've heard of him, but I've never met him."

"Zed trapped me here." She frowned and a shadow fell across her face. "He doesn't even fully understand what this place is, but he still managed to trap me."

After a moment, Alice asked, "How'd I get here?"

"I brought you, of course."

"But how?" Alice asked in a shaking voice. "If you're trapped, how'd you bring me here?"

"Zed has it all wrong. He thinks that by putting me outside time he's cut me off from my power. In fact, he's put me in my natural habitat. I was born outside of time, and here I can see time as if it were a parchment laid out before me. Possible pasts, presents, and futures are all there for me to read. Understand?"

Alice didn't, but she wasn't about to say so.

Wilm continued without waiting for a reply. "But I can't leave. I can't get back into time. And, though I can see time, it's murky. Difficult make anything out. All I can see clearly are the occasional bright spots." She looked at Alice pointedly. "Like you."

Alice knew her hands were shaking, but she was powerless to stop them. Wilm was talking about her power, her ability to Pull Back. Alice had always known deep down that the power would get her into trouble one day. But she'd never imagined it would be something like this.

"I saw your life stretched across time like a beam of light. But I couldn't be sure you were important. Until I noticed something strange. I noticed a friend of mine, a man named Rayd, was in King's Crossing in 2015. I recognized his light immediately. It was strange, because he was supposed to be locked out of time. Like me. And then I saw your light next to his. And that's when I knew you must be important."

Alice thought for a moment. "The man in the shed?"

Wilm smiled thinly and nodded. She reached out and put a hand on Alice's shoulder. Alice had to force herself not to pull away.

"It wasn't easy to suck you out of time," Wilm said. "It took most of the power I had left. But it was worth it. You're a very special girl."

Something about this woman—the air of authority she

146

carried—made Alice flush with pride when she said that. Alice was terrified and angry with Wilm for bringing her here. But, for some reason, winning her approval seemed very important, too.

Alice waited, not sure what to say. As much as the strange conversation upset her, it did keep her mind off those scary, featherless birds.

Wilm followed her eyes to the group of birds standing down the street. "Oh, don't worry about them. They're pretty harmless this far outside of time. It's the other ones you have to worry about." She cocked her thumb up at the shadow creatures over her head.

Somehow, this didn't make Alice feel better.

"No need to worry about them, either, though," Wilm continued. "I can handle those rascals."

"The thing is," Wilm said, "my friends and I keep an eye out for special people. They're surprisingly rare. Every time we think we've found someone, they end up letting us down." She looked at Alice, and Alice felt like the stare was boring into her brain. "You wouldn't let me down, would you, dear?"

"No." The word passed through Alice's lips unbidden. But it was true, she realized. She didn't want to let this woman down.

"Good," Wilm smiled. "Then we'll get along just fine. Come with me." She turned and walked down the street.

Alice hesitated. Now that the woman wasn't looking at her, that strange urge to please her lessened. Alice considered making a run for it. But where would she go? If time didn't exist here like Wilm said, did that mean people didn't exist here, either? There were some cars parked along the road—a few parked right in the *middle* of the road, which was weird— but she didn't see any people.

What she did see were the featherless bird creatures. Wilm had told her not to be afraid of them, but saying it and doing it were two different things. And she saw the swirling shadow creatures in the sky.

As she watched them, she heard a strange, singsongy voice say, "*Alice.*"

It was as if many voices were all singing her name at once.

She took off running toward Wilm.

Wilm didn't look back as Alice followed at her heels. "Don't let them bother you. They know better than to mess with one of mine."

Is that what Alice was? One of this woman's students? Her friends?

As if reading Alice's thoughts, Wilm said, "I have a feeling you and I are going to be great friends. We can help each other."

"Help each other do what?" Alice asked.

"That's what I'm going to show you. It's just a few blocks ahead."

As they walked, Alice saw the swirl of shadows overhead. It was growing.

"*Alice,*" the singsongy voices called, and a chill ran through Alice.

"Oh for the love of Pete," Wilm said. "One new arrival and they lose their manners."

"*Alice. Come to us as a friend, and we will feed you.*"

"Really now." Wilm stopped and thrust her hand into the air. The creatures froze. The mass of shadows stopped swirling. "Enough, all ready! The girl's under my protection."

The voices were whiny when they replied, almost like they were begging. "*She is fresh from the river. We can smell time on her. It's dripping off her. Let us have a taste.*"

"I won't ask again." Her voice was stone. "Behave. Or there will be consequences."

The shadows dispersed into a hundred smaller shadows and scattered in every direction.

Who was this woman that even the stuff of nightmares listened to her?

"I want to go home," Alice said. She knew she sounded like a baby, but she didn't care.

Wilm smiled at her. "Good! That's very good. I was counting on that. Come on, we're almost there."

They rounded a corner, and Wilm stopped. "Do you see it?"

Alice looked around, trying to figure out what the woman was talking about.

Wilm pointed. "Right there."

Alice still didn't see it. Wilm seemed to be pointing at the pawn shop across the street.

"Not over there," Wilm said, following her gaze. "In the air. Right here."

Then Alice saw it. A black dot the size of a dime hanging in the air just past the end of Wilm's finger.

"What is it?" Alice asked.

Wilm smiled. "It's what I've been working on these many years. It's a hole into time. A tiny one, but a hole nonetheless."

Alice looked at it. A hole in time? What did that even mean?

"It was nasty work," Wilm said. "Difficult and monotonous. Most wouldn't have the stomach for it. The good news is there's two of us now. And I'm locked in on where we need to go and when we need to get there. When we're done, it will open on a very specific time and place.

149

King's Crossing, Wisconsin. No matter how long we work on this, we'll arrive only an hour or two after you left."

"You want me to help you make this hole bigger?" Alice asked.

"Exactly," Wilm said. "Adding your power to mine will make the work go faster. And while we work, I can teach you so many things. I'll bet being able to pull on time is just the surface of your abilities."

Alice felt a sob rising in her throat. She couldn't help it. She said it again. "I want to go home."

Wilm patted her on the shoulder. "I know, dear. That's why we have to get to work. See, I brought you on a one way trip. I'm locked out of time, and now so are you. You can't get home unless I come with you."

3.

They drove to the park in silence.

It was just Frank, Sophie, and Mason in the car. Helen and Matt were too busy frantically looking for their daughter. Though, to Frank, it seemed unlikely the two events—Alice disappearing and Zed calling to say there was trouble at the shed—were unrelated.

"Anybody have a plan?" Frank asked.

"I was about to ask the same thing," Sophie said. "Let's play it safe like last time. No big decisions in there. Hell, no small ones either. Don't agree to anything."

Frank nodded. Sophie was right, of course. There was a better than average chance this was all a trick. Some further manipulation by Zed.

"What about the book?" Mason asked.

"Leave it here," Frank said. "Use your lock to hide it. No, actually use your lock to hide the whole car. The last thing we need is somebody stealing the car with the book in it."

"Seems unlikely," Sophie said.

"So does a girl who can tell the future."

She shrugged as she parked the car. "Fair point. Let's go."

The door to the shed was closed, so they knocked when they reached it. The door opened a crack, and they saw Willis staring out at them, his deep red hair giving him away even through the tiny opening. When he saw them, he opened the door a foot or so and motioned them inside.

They squeezed into the shed.

It was much the same as they'd left it except for the smell. A sickly sweet funk hung in the air.

Rayd was still tied to the tree, but his skin was an alarming shade of pale green. A strange wheezing noise came from his chest when he breathed.

Zed was kneeling beside him.

"What happened?" Frank asked.

Zed looked back at him. He was wearing his usual smile, but it looked thin and forced. "I don't know."

Frank raised an eyebrow. "Pretty sure I've never heard you use that phrase before."

"It gives me no pleasure, believe me." Zed grabbed Rayd's chin and lifted it, inspecting the man and his half-closed eyes from a myriad of angles. After a moment, he looked up at Frank. "Matt told you about the time loop? That I've been sending people back in time to get redos?"

"He told us," Sophie said.

Frank knew it drove her crazy how Zed always addressed him and never her or Mason. He didn't blame her.

Zed glanced at her, then back to Frank. "Yes, well, this is the forty-sixth time we've run this iteration where I bring Rayd through the tree. This has never happened before. Him

151

getting like that."

"How do you know?" Sophie asked.

"What do you mean?" Zed asked, a bit of irritation in his voice.

"How do you know it's been forty-six times? Matt said you can't go back yourself. You can only send others."

"The people I send back report back to me." He waved away her question. "I just wish I understood. I wish he'd tell me what's happening to him."

Rayd let out a weak cough. "Waiting...for...you to ask."

Mason chuckled. "You never were the asking type, Zed. More of the telling type."

Zed ignored this. "Rayd. Please tell us what's happening to you."

Rayd chuckled. "Isn't it obvious?" His voice sounded stronger now. "I'm dying."

Frank had never seen Zed look so shocked. Whatever he'd been expecting to hear, it wasn't that. Frank wondered if this man was the same type of creature Zed was. Maybe this man's mortality was making Zed question his own.

"Sorry, I don't believe it," Zed said. "The tree should weaken you, of course. That's the reason I tied you to it. But it won't kill you. I know that."

"Oh, the trees can kill us. If we aren't strong enough to protect ourselves."

Zed rose to his feet and looked down at the man. "But you are! You've survived this."

Rayd chuckled. "Right. Your redos. Interesting idea. Have they gotten you any closer to beating us?" Zed didn't take the bait, so Rayd continued. "I can't speak to those other times. I can't remember them. You must have done a good job covering your tracks. And you're right, maybe I could have survived this, but I had to use some of my power." He smiled up at Zed.

Zed shook his head. "We have to reset. Try again. Willis, come here. I'm sending you back."

"No!" Frank hadn't meant to shout the word. But Alice... if Zed sent Willis back as far as he'd sent Matt last time, there was the chance Alice might not exist. "What good will sending him back do? The same thing will happen next time unless we figure out what changed and how to deal with it."

Zed said nothing. He just glared down at Rayd.

Frank decided to keep things rolling before Zed decided to act on his threat. "What did you use your power to do?" Frank thought he knew the answer, but he asked anyway.

Rayd chuckled. "The girl wasn't like you, Zed," Rayd said. "She was clumsy with her powers. Not her fault. She's young. But I was able to see through her redos. It's rather humorous. All this work you went to, and you didn't know you had a weapon living among you."

Zed looked up as if slapped. Something about those words struck a nerve. "Who? Who is it?"

Rayd fell into a coughing fit before he could answer. The others waited.

Sophie nudged Frank's arm and nodded to the other side of the room. Mason was slowly making his way along the perimeter.

"It was a little girl. Her name was Alice."

Frank's heart sank.

"She came to see me the other day," Rayd said. "I have no idea why. She just came to the shed and showed me what she can do. Funny how life works, isn't it? A little while ago, I felt the girl's power starting to fade, and I knew Wilm was trying to pull her out of time. I used my power to help things along."

"That didn't turn out so great for you," Sophie said, "with the dying and all."

"How do we get her back?" Frank asked.

"Oh, you don't have to worry about that part. She's coming back. Wilm's bringing her. Should be here by the end of the day."

Zed took a step back. "No. That's not possible. She doesn't break through for two more weeks. She escapes her prison and opens a portal over the Mississippi two weeks from now."

Rayd grinned, a smile that revealed his teeth were speckled with blood. "Maybe before. But now Wilm's locked in on me. And she's got the girl to help her break through. Before she didn't know where to go, not precisely. The tree muted my power, but we connected when I helped push Alice through. Wilm's locked in on me now. Alive or dead, she'll be able to find me. She'll want to give you as little time to prepare as possible, so I wouldn't be surprised if she's here in a few minutes."

Zed looked at him for a long moment, and then an expression of calm washed over his face. "So what you're really saying is, if you weren't here, she wouldn't be able to find us as accurately. She'd still arrive two weeks from now."

Rayd barked out a weak laugh. "What are you gonna do? Throw me in the river? It won't matter where in the world you are. It's where in *time* that matters. All she needs to do is track me to a location in time. She can easily find you from there."

Zed's smile widened. "And what if you weren't in a certain location in time? What if you were outside of time? With her?"

Rayd shook his head. "You can't make that happen. You

don't have the book."

Zed smiled. "Maybe you don't know everything. Maybe I've found a way to open the portals without the books."

"Impossible." Rayd practically spat out the word.

"Wait," Sophie said. "What happens to Alice if you do this?"

Zed glanced at her for a moment, then licked his lips. "She'll be trapped with Wilm. Outside of time until they can break through. There are unfortunate casualties in any war."

Frank said, "Mason."

Suddenly, the compass disappeared from Zed's outstretched hand.

Zed's eyes widened, realizing what was happening. He lunged out wildly behind him, but his hands went through empty air. "Where is it?" His voice was crazed. He took a deep breath and spoke again, sounding more like Zed this time. "Mason. Don't do anything rash. After all we've been through, please hear me out."

Mason remained silent.

Zed turned to Frank. "You and your damn locks. So that's it then? You're going to let the world die to save one girl? No, that's not even right, is it? The girl won't survive this, she'll just die with her parents by her side."

"Not necessarily," Rayd said. "I doubt Wilm would let a talent like that die. I expect she'll take Alice to wherever they go next."

"Zed, we just need to think this through," Frank said. "We need to understand the consequences."

"What's there to think through? Rayd dies here, the gates of hell will open. We'll all be killed."

"So why not reset things?" Sophie asked. "Isn't that what you do when things go wrong?"

Zed shook his head slowly. "You all don't understand what's happening here. We might have a chance to beat them! For real! If I send him back through, I might be able to close the hole. If I do that, they'll be trapped outside time."

"Can't they just dig their way out again?" Frank asked. "Isn't that what happened this time? And they're outside time, so they'll still get here at the same moment no matter how long they dig."

"Yes, but they will be much weaker by the time they break through. We may have enough power to defeat them."

"And Alice?" Frank asked.

"Alice stays with them. It's not ideal. But she's not dead. She's just…"

"Away," Frank finished. He remembered his time Away. The untold years he'd spent living off the meat of the Unfeathered, battling daily to survive against the Ones Who Sing, the strange shadow creatures who seemingly wanted nothing more than to strip the flesh from his bones. "There might be worse fates, but I can't think of many."

Zed nodded sadly. "I've been there, too. It isn't pleasant. But it's necessary. Just hand me back my compass and I'll do the rest.

Frank looked at Sophie. "What do you think?"

Sophie's teeth were gritted and her eyes were fixed on Rayd. "It's not my decision." She turned to Frank. "If we do this, Alice will be cut off from time for who knows how long. She'll be trapped with a person who, if we can believe Zed, is evil. The only person qualified to decide is the only person who's experienced that. Mason, what do you say?"

There was a long pause as they all watched and waited. Mason had hid himself from all of them so Frank couldn't see his face, couldn't even read the non-verbal cues as to the emotions he must be going through.

Slowly Zed held out his hand.

After a long moment, the compass dropped into it.

Zed grinned and clutched the compass.

Mason appeared, his face streaked with tears. "I'm sorry, Alice. We have to do this. We have to."

Zed looked at Mason with something like pride. "You made the right decision, son."

Mason turned away. "Don't call me son. Not ever."

If Zed cared about Mason's words, he did an excellent job not showing it. He held the compass up to the tree.

Rayd looked up at him. "You send me through, you kill me. I'm not strong enough to survive."

Zed shrugged. "You said you were dying anyway." He lifted the compass and muttered, "Show me Wilm."

From where Frank was standing, he saw the needle spin wildly for a moment, then come to rest pointing roughly southeast.

"You kill me," Rayd said. "You might regret it."

"I doubt it," Zed said. He touched the tree and drew a pattern with his finger.

A light burst forth from the tree, filling the shed with hot white light. Rayd cried out in pain as he was pulled backwards into the tree. It was the reverse of the process they'd seen this morning. This version seemed even more painful. Rayd's torso folded as he was pulled into the tree. His feet were the last part to go through, and, as they did, the hole closed with an audible snap.

The shed was quiet. It seemed so dark now after the blinding bright light was gone.

"There now," Zed said. "We've done it. We've killed one of them. That is our first step toward victory."

Five minutes later, they learned what a terrible mistake they'd made.

4.

Alice was walking behind Wilm when suddenly a man fell out of the sky and landed in the middle of the road.

For once, Wilm looked as shocked as Alice felt.

Wilm ran to the man and crouched down next to him. His skin was a strange green color, and his limbs were twisted at all sorts of unnatural angles. He had broken bones, a lot of them. Even Alice could tell that much.

Wilm touched his face, brushing his neatly trimmed beard with her fingers. And suddenly Alice recognized the man. It was the man from the shed. The one who'd seen what she could do.

Had he been the cause of all this? Had he somehow sent her here?

"Rayd," Wilm said. Her voice caught with emotion.

Rayd looked up at her. His eyes were large, too large, and there was dreamy, far off look in them.

"I had them send me here," Rayd said. He spoke slowly, as if each word was an effort of concentration. "I thought you could use me. Sorry I didn't do more."

"No," Wilm said. "You did well."

"I just wish it wasn't that boy with the watch who got me. He was always so smug."

Wilm leaned forward and kissed his forehead. "You'll be revenged. He will pay. His whole world will pay."

Rayd nodded contentedly and closed his eyes. He let out a great wheezing breath and breathed no more.

Wilm choked out a sob. "Forgive me," she said to Alice. "It's been a long time since one of my people have died. "

Her gaze was a little too intense. "Now you'll see something," she said. "Something none of your kind has ever seen before."

As Alice watched, Rayd began to melt. It happened quickly and smoothly. One moment, he was a corpse, and the next he was dissolving into a pool of metallic liquid.

Alice drew in a sharp breath. "What's happening to him?"

Wilm watched the pool grow. "Energy can neither be created nor destroyed. Didn't they teach you that in school?"

"I'm in third grade," Alice said.

Wilm grunted. "At any rate, it's a fact of science. And my kind contains a hell of a lot of energy."

A thought occurred to Alice. "You keep saying *our kind* and *your kind*. Aren't you a person?"

Wilm shook her head, her eyes still fixed on the metallic pool. "Not remotely. We're from somewhere very far away."

"Like…aliens?"

Wilm looked at her sharply. "That's a rather geocentric description, don't you think? Come on, I'll show you something cool."

The older woman walked to the pool and knelt down next to it. She put a finger to her lips for a moment, thinking. "We'll need a compass. That much is certain."

She scooped up a handful of the metallic liquid and squeezed.

Alice should have been grossed out—she knew she should have been. But she wasn't. Not in the least. There was something about this liquid that drew her. Something that made her feel happy.

Wilm opened her hand, and in it was a perfectly shaped compass. She turned it over for Alice to see. It had a strange symbol on it: a mountain with a crack running through it.

"Rayd always did want to destroy the Earth," Wilm said, a hint of sadness in her voice. "Now then, I'll make something for you. What would you like?"

Alice thought for a moment. She would like something made of that liquid. She'd like it a lot. But what?

"A sword." The words just popped out. For some reason, a sword felt right.

Wilm smiled, clearly pleased. "Good. Very good."

This time she scooped up two handfuls of the stuff and shaped it. A moment later, she handed Alice a beautifully thin sword. It had the same broken mountain symbol on the hilt.

Alice took it and held it proudly. She didn't think she'd ever held anything half as cool, even her baby cousin Ben.

"Thank you," Alice said, her voice weak with gratitude.

"You're welcome," Wilm said. "I can't wait to see what you can do with it." She suddenly snapped her fingers. "I have an idea." She took another handful and shaped a pair of scissors.

Alice was a bit disappointed, but she didn't let it show. There was nothing very cool about scissors.

"Now follow me," Wilm said.

She led Alice through the streets to the library. As they walked, they passed a few people, but they were all frozen like statues. Alice wanted to ask about it, but this didn't seem like the time.

Inside the library, Wilm pulled a large United States atlas off a shelf and set it on a table. She flipped pages until she found Wisconsin.

"Can you show me where King's Crossing is?" she asked Alice.

The girl looked to the far left side of the page and found her home town.

"Good," Wilm said. "Take these and press the broken

mountain." She handed Alice the scissors.

Alice pressed the broken mountain and felt it click, like a button on her PlayStation 4 controller. Suddenly it was as if the scissors were buzzing in her hand. It was the power Wilm had been talking about, Alice knew. She felt it.

"Now," Wilm said. "Cut out King's Crossing."

Alice raised an eyebrow. "Out of a library book?"

Wilm nodded. "Trust me. It's okay."

It was hard to trust someone she'd just met but...it was as if the scissors wanted to cut. And Alice wanted to use them.

She cut carefully, feeling the power in each clip as she squeezed the scissors closed again and again. In a moment, the piece of the map that represented King's Crossing lay on the table, a sad little scrap.

But it was more than that. Alice could sense something bigger had happened when she'd used the scissors.

"What did I just do?" she asked in a quiet voice.

Wilm smiled, "My dear, you just removed King's Crossing from the Earth. Now what do you say use these scissors to cut our way back into time?"

THE BOY WHO FOUND THE WATCH (PART FIVE)

Santa Cruz, California
December, 1956

The car that came to pick up Zed was a faded yellow Chrysler. It pulled up to the curb, and the driver rolled down his window.

The driver was a square-jawed man with a few days' stubble. He was chomping noisily on some chewing gum. His face was devoid of emotion. He was just a man doing a job.

"You Zed?"

Zed indicated he was, then held his hand out to the man.

The driver glanced down at it, then looked back up at Zed's face. "I've been told not to talk to you, except for this here conversation."

Zed lowered his hand to his side.

"You're to sit in the back. There's a cooler with some beers and sandwiches back there. Water, too. Make it last. We'll be in the car about twenty-four hours."

"Where we going?" Zed asked.

The driver ignored the question. "You have to use the restroom, you knock on the back of my seat. You don't like what I've got playing on the radio, well, tough luck. I'll pull over to catch forty winks in sixteen hours or so. We sleep in the car." With his speech concluded, he rolled up the window.

Over the past eight years, Zed had learned Wilm had a fairly large network of people working for her. He'd come into contact with many of them. He'd passed messages to some of them, and some of them had passed messages to him. But in his experience, none of the workers were keen on sharing any more information than they had to. If Zed had to guess, he'd have said they all knew as little about the organization as he did.

The driver was just another one of Wilm's worker bees. Now that Zed had been invited to visit her, he couldn't help feeling superior to this man. He wondered if this guy had a pocket watch, or something like it. He highly doubted it.

Since the driver hadn't popped the trunk, Zed carried his bag into the backseat with him. The windows were blacked out on the inside, and a divider separated the backseat from the front. The blacked out windows made Zed reconsider how much Wilm trusted him.

Zed felt the car lurch forward as soon as he'd shut the door. Apparently the driver was in a hurry to get Zed to his destination.

For the next twenty-four hours, they drove. Zed sat in the dim backseat, bored out of his mind. Even holding the watch didn't help, and that was something that comforted him in nearly all situations. He wished there was a way to speed time up using the watch, but he hadn't figured out a way. Whenever Zed knocked on the partition, the driver pulled off the road and Zed got out to answer the call of nature. It was always in a field, never in gas station. Though the driver did stop at gas stations, Zed knew instinctively he wasn't allowed to get out at those stops. He didn't know what the punishment would be if he did, but he wasn't eager to find out, not when he had finally won Wilm's favor.

As the time passed, the landscape changed. Near sundown, Zed saw mountains in the distance when he left the car to urinate. They were moving into the Rockies.

Eventually, the driver pulled over and slept for six hours or so. Zed heard his gentle snores through the barrier. When he woke, he started driving again without a word to his passenger.

Zed was sitting in the backseat, having let his mind go blank. He may have been dozing—the difference between awake and asleep was purely academic in that darkened car. He was startled to attention when the door opened and pale sunlight streamed into the darkness. The driver, once again chomping his gum, stood out there holding the door. That same bored, blank look on his face.

This, Zed realized, was it. He had arrived.

He grabbed his bag and stumbled out of the vehicle. His legs felt weak, though whether it was caused by the lengthy car ride or his nerves, he didn't know.

He blinked quickly, his eyes adjusting to the midday sunlight, and looked around. They were high in the mountains. Pine trees dotted the landscape of the peaks. The smell of pine was heavy in the air. The only signs of humanity were the dirt road he stood on and the modest house that stood twenty yards in front of him. The house looked like something you might find in the country in Kansas, the type of home where you'd find Ma and Pa and the three kids gathered around the breakfast table for some freshly scrambled eggs and some newly smoked bacon. The house was well-kept, but there wasn't much more to say about it.

Could this be Wilm's house? He didn't see any other possibility. Disappointment crept up within him; he'd expected something grander.

He turned to thank the driver, but as he did he heard the sound of the door shutting and saw the car rolling down the dirt road. The man's job was done and he was anxious to get on to whatever Wilm had planned for him next, apparently.

Zed sighed and walked across the rocky soil toward the house.

A man sat in a rocking chair on the porch, his right foot perched high on the railing. Zed hadn't noticed him until now, which seemed impossible. The man had jet black hair slicked back and a neatly trimmed goatee.

He didn't move as Zed approached, but he watched him with suspicious eyes.

When Zed reached the porch, the man said, "You're the new boy, then?"

Zed had long ago stopped thinking of himself as a boy, but he nodded. "I'm Zed."

"I know," the man said.

Zed felt his frustration growing. After three days in the car with the silent driver, he'd about had it with people who didn't shake hands or offer their names. These people obviously hadn't been raised in Kansas.

"I hear she gave you the watch," the man said.

Zed knew he should be polite. Whoever this man was, he surely had higher standing in the organization than Zed. But he couldn't help himself. "She didn't give it to me. I took it."

The man took his foot off the railing and leaned forward, a smile playing across his face. "Is that what you think? And you don't think any one of us could take it back at any time?"

Zed realized he'd gone too far. "I didn't say that."

"Go ahead. Stop me." The man stood up and began walking toward Zed.

Zed didn't want to have an altercation with this man, but he certainly wasn't going to let him take the watch. He reached into his pocket and pressed the broken clock symbol, freezing time. And the man kept coming.

"See what I mean?" the man asked.

Zed's hand was shaking, whether from fear or anger he didn't know. But he was not letting this man take the watch. He imagined the bubble that surrounded him, the thing that kept him moving while the rest of the universe was stopped, and he pulled it away from the man.

The man kept coming, but he was moving more slowly now. Zed pulled harder, and it was like the man was moving in slow motion. A look of surprise came across the man's face in comical slow motion.

"Enough!" The voice came from the doorway. Wilm.

Zed clicked the symbol on the watch, restarting time.

She looked at the man. "Rayd, stop harassing the boy."

The man nodded. He glared at Zed.

"And you," Wilm said to Zed, "need to be more careful. You'll get yourself killed before you walk through the door."

She waved him inside, and he carefully stepped around Rayd.

The house looked for all the world like the interior of the dozens of farmhouses he'd seen as a kid. Even the knick-knacks were spot on. He had the strange feeling this was all for his benefit.

Wilm showed him to his bedroom, a modest room with a twin bed, a small dresser, and nothing else. She followed him into the room and sat on the bed.

"Now," she said, "we can talk."

He wasn't sure how to respond, so he just nodded.

"We like your work," she said. "You have initiative, but you can also follow instructions. That's a rare combination. And you're skilled in using the watch. You figured it out on your own. So I've decided it's time to tell you some things. But you have to agree to ask no questions. I'd rather you find the answers yourself than have me give them to you. This is just the baseline of what you need to know right now. Understand?"

He understood well enough to simply nod rather than answering aloud.

Wilm looked pleased. "Good. Would it shock you to learn your world is not what you think it is?"

Zed thought for only a moment before shaking his head.

"Of course it wouldn't. You've been playing at the edge of the truth for eight years now. You've seen how frayed the borders of reality really are." She leaned forward and put her hands on her knees. "You and your kind consider yourself the highest form of intelligence. You pride yourselves on your scientific discoveries the way a baby prides itself on being able to find its own feet. But your kind will never learn the truth of existence. You don't have the tools to prod at reality, and you don't have enough sense to know the right questions to ask.

"But this world *is* a special place. Parts of it are, anyway. Think of the Earth as a mountain. It's mostly rock and dirt, worthless rubble piled on top of more worthless rubble. It exists only to support itself." She smiled now, and there was a glint in her eye. "But within this mountain, there are jewels! Special places. They can't be used by your kind. But for us, these places contain something necessary for our very survival."

Zed desperately wanted to ask what she meant by *us*. If she and her people weren't human, what were they? Who had he been working for the past eight years? But he couldn't ask those questions. Not now. She wanted his silence.

"These special places can, for lack of a better word, *feed* me and mine. But we have to wait until they're ready. Perhaps a better analogy is that of a fruit rather than a jewel. We have to wait for it to ripen."

Wilm paused a long moment before continuing. "But there's a problem. The power we need is hidden away from us. It's locked in books, and that makes these special places very difficult to find. That's why we created the Tools. Your pocket watch is one of them, but there are others. We put a bit of our kind's power into them so that very special people sympathetic to our cause could use them to help us. Sadly, most of those people haven't worked out. You humans are not built to handle that kind of power, not for long. But we sense that you might be different.

"You are a special young man. We had to find all the others. Not you. You found us when you stole the pocket watch. Charlie was our best prospect in a long time, but at age eleven you showed us what a real prospect looks like." She reached out and took Zed's hand in her own. "We can offer you so many things, Zed. All we ask in return is that you help us find these towns and prepare them for their destruction."

CHAPTER SIX: SEVEN YEARS IN KING'S CROSSING

1.

King's Crossing
May, 2015

The edge of town was gone, replaced with a thick murky fog, a fog that pushed back. Walking, driving, running into the fog all brought about the same result. After a few feet, something in the mist gently but firmly pressed you out of the fog and back into the town.

Once the residents of King's Crossing realized they were cut off from the outside world, word spread quickly. People knocked on doors making sure their neighbors and friends knew.

Frank heard about it shortly after he and his friends left the shed.

They'd stayed in the shed nearly an hour, talking and wondering about the implications of what had happened with Rayd. Zed had regained a bit of his old swagger, and he let them know he'd be moving on. He had other towns to go to, to use in his fight against his enemies. Frank had grown angry, asking about Zed's promises, about his vows to save

Jake and Logan and Heather. Zed had essentially said, "Tough luck," and walked out.

Frank had followed, fuming. He was still stomping toward Zed when a man ran up to both of them.

"Have you heard?" he asked.

"Heard what?" Frank replied.

The man explained. And Frank felt terror creep into his heart. *My God*, he thought. *Not again.*

It was a different kind of apocalypse than the one he'd experienced in Rook Mountain. Without the presence of the Unfeathered, the town wasn't in any immediate physical danger. They were just cut off. People were scared, of course. But they were also polite and helpful for the most part. Many in town had already seen plenty of strangeness, Frank reminded himself.

They also had the story of Rook Mountain to console them. Like the rest of the world, many in King's Crossing had closely followed the news coverage of what had happened in Frank's hometown. So they at least knew of the concept of a town cut off from the rest of the world. Some of them, Frank suspected, harbored dreams of being famous when this was all over. He was willing to bet that more than a few of them practiced what they'd say on *20/20*.

The Mississippi still moved, flowing out of and into the fog. But any boat that tried to sail it ended up stranded in the river, pushed forward by the current and backward by the fog. It was a source of frustration in the town. They took most things in stride, but the idea that the water could escape town and they couldn't made them insane. There were a million theories on how to leave, and nine-hundred-thousand of them involved some variation on using the river to escape.

Thankfully, the power, like the water, still flowed into town.

Most of the town's electricity came from a power station in Alma, an hour up the river. The question of why electricity could travel between Alma and King's Crossing but the people of King's Crossing couldn't was a popular subject of speculation at the suddenly crowded watering holes downtown.

Still, there were certain realities to face. In some ways, this was *worse* than Rook Mountain. Here they couldn't venture out to the surrounding towns for food and supplies. All they had was all they had. Thankfully, the fog didn't exactly follow the town line. The edge of the fog was jagged, and it left them with six farms, one of which raised cattle. At least dairy wouldn't be a problem.

Communications technology, including cellphone and Internet, didn't work anymore. It was as if someone was purposefully trying to cut them off from the outside world

"If it's any consolation, we've got enough cheeseheads to last us the next seventy years," Sophie said while they were inventorying the shops in town, poking a finger at one of the yellow cheese-shaped hats.

She was teamed with Joe at the moment. Joe rolled his eyes. "Don't remind me. NFL season starts in three months. If this thing isn't solved by then, we're going to have lots of angry Packer fans."

"Like you?"

"Hell, no. I'm a Bears fan."

Zed, for his part, was sullen. He retreated into his home and didn't show his face for the first three days. It was Frank who finally went to ask for his help.

Zed reacted to the town's offer with incredulity. "I don't understand. You *want* me to help run the town?"

Frank frowned. "Don't get any ideas. We're not drawing up

171

Regulations here. But you are the only one with real logistical experience with something like this. Would you be willing to help out? Not lead, mind you, but help?"

Zed hesitated. "I'll help. But just as a man. I don't have any special powers that would come in handy here. Even my compass is basically worthless. It points to things, but nothing beyond the edge of the fog." He looked Frank in the eye. "We haven't been taken out of time. We've been taken out of place. It's like we're out of phase with the rest of the world. And I don't know what to do about it."

Frank paused for a moment. "What if you had the book? What if we find it? Could you use that to get us out of here?"

Zed thought a moment before answering. "Maybe."

So, Zed agreed to help out with logistics.

Mason took a job on a farm. Sophie helped Joe at the library. And Frank worked with the group in charge of resource distribution. It was boring and tedious for all of them, but they were able to eek out an existence.

Six months in, Frank gave Zed the book.

2.

Somewhere in Montana
2016

Alice swung the ax, bringing it down on the log with all the might her ten-year-old body could muster. The wood split with a satisfying crack. She set the pieces in the wheel barrow and grabbed another log, feeling the pleasant ache in her back and shoulders as she did so.

Once, she'd used her sword to split wood. She'd found if she pressed the broken mountain symbol as she swung it, not only did it cut clean through the wood, but all the other wood waiting in the pile was split by her single swing as well. Wilm hadn't been happy. She wanted Alice to learn the value of hard work, not the benefit of using Tools for shortcuts. Alice had a hard time understanding that. Wasn't that the whole point? For her to learn to use the Tools? So she could help them find the towns or whatever?

She'd been here over a year. Wilm had made Alice use the scissors to cut them out of the Away and back into time. At first, Alice had been worried about what Wilm would do when they arrived. After all, she had promised Rayd she'd seek vengeance. But instead, she'd just brought Alice to this remote cabin outside town.

Wilm had disappeared for a few hours that first night—to free her fellow Exiles from the Away as Alice later learned— but after that things had quickly settled into a mundane routine. Alice's education had begun.

After ten minutes of chopping, Alice threw the last of the split logs and her ax into the wheel barrow, and took a long, slow breath of the pine-scented mountain air. Maybe Wilm did have a point about this hard work thing after all. She grabbed the wheel barrow handles and guided it back toward the house.

It had been a strange year. And not an easy one. She'd spent the first few weeks in nearly constant tears. She'd wanted to go home. It had taken her quite some time to accept that there was no such thing as home left to go to. Wilm had shown her on map after map that King's Crossing, Wisconsin, no longer existed. Indeed, it never had. There was no record of it. But seeing a blank space on a map wasn't enough, so Wilm took her to Wisconsin, showed her the empty fields and woods where the town should have been.

Finally, she'd accepted it. She was an orphan. There was no going home. This was her home now, and she'd might as well make the best of it.

The even more difficult thing to accept was that she was the one who'd caused this. She'd held the scissors in her hand and clipped her hometown out of existence. She'd destroyed thousands of lives.

It was almost too big to think about. Every time she did, she felt like she was losing control of herself, of her mind. Wilm told her to put it out of her mind. That if she didn't think about it, the hurt would go away. And most of the time, it worked. It still made her a little sick to her stomach every time she saw those scissors, though.

The wheel barrow hit a root and bounced wildly, causing Alice to loose control. It toppled over on its side and the split wood tumbled to the ground.

Alice bit the inside of her cheek and slowly counted to ten before doing anything. In the old days, she would have Pulled Back, caused the whole thing not to happen, and gone around the root. The urge to do that was still strong. But Wilm wouldn't like it. Pulling Back was only allowed in very specific circumstances, and fixing a minor accident like this wasn't one of them. Wilm was like Rayd; she knew when Alice Pulled Back, so there was no use trying to sneak one past her. Unauthorized use of her power would result in loosing privileges, added chores, and maybe being grounded to her room.

After the wood was once again in the wheel barrow, Alice carefully guided it to the house. She neatly stacked it on top of the wood pile, then put the wheel barrow and the ax away in the shed. A fine sheen of sweat covered her skin by the time she was done. She wanted nothing more than to drink a glass of Wilm's lemonade and relax. Maybe she'd let Alice spend the afternoon reading. The house had a small library, and Alice had read most of the books already. There was no TV and no Internet up here, so she had limited entertainment choices. Still, there were a few old Agatha Christie novels she hadn't read. She liked mysteries, trying to figure out how it was all going to end.

She walked inside and paused as she heard a familiar cackling laugh. A slight chill went through her. San was here.

Normally, it was just Wilm and Alice in the cabin. Things weren't perfect, but they were comfortable. They made a strange little surrogate family. But sometimes the others spent time here. Vee was okay—if a little creepy, even after she'd gotten used to the fact that he had no arms. He just ignored her most of the time, unless Wilm made him interact with her. San was different. She was tall and beautiful and she definitely didn't ignore Alice. It wasn't that she was mean, exactly—Wilm wouldn't have put up with that—it was just that she clearly thought she was better than Alice. She talked down to her in such a condescending way. And it wasn't the usual adult-to-kid condescending. It was something else. She clearly looked down on all of humanity, and Alice was just the representation of what she disliked about life on planet Earth.

Alice carefully eased the door shut behind her. Maybe she could sneak up to her room and do some reading while Wilm and San were talking.

"Alice, is that you?"

No such luck. Wilm had the ears of a much younger woman.

"Yes," Alice answered reluctantly.

"Come in here. We need to talk to you."

Alice stifled a grumble and shuffled into the living room. Wilm and San sat side-by-side on the couch, conspiratorial smiles on their faces.

"Have a seat," Wilm said.

Alice did so. She waited silently. It was better to speak only when asked a question, especially when San was here.

"San and I have been talking," Wilm said. "And we've come to a decision. We think you're ready to perform your first job for us."

Alice felt her pulse quicken. "Really?"

Wilm nodded. "Nothing major. It's just delivering a message to someone in Cleveland. But it is an important message. Think you can handle it?"

Alice had been waiting for this, for a real opportunity to prove herself to Wilm. "Yes. I know I can."

Wilm smiled. "Good. Then let's talk about your cover story."

3.

King's Crossing
2017

Sophie pushed the cart to her least favorite section and began shelving the books. The travel section. Sometimes it felt like she spent half her life there.

The King's Crossing library usage had exploded since what the locals called 'Isolation Day'. With no TV or Internet, entertainment options were more limited. It seemed the majority of King's Crossing had finally discovered their love of the written word. By far the most popular books were those in the travel book section. The good old 910s in the Dewey Decimal System.

They were in their third calendar year of the isolation now, and people were becoming more and more nostalgic for the places they could no longer visit. Not just the exotic places, either. Sure, the books on the Bahamas and Fiji were popular, but other surprise hits included places that had once been much closer but now were just as far out of reach: Chicago, St. Louis, Minneapolis/St. Paul. There was a book on the Mall of America whose cover they'd had to repair three times due to overuse.

Come to think of it, the entire travel section could use a good rebinding.

She silently shelved the last book on the cart, a guide book about visiting San Francisco on $50 a day—Sophie was actually curious how the author pulled that off—and she glanced at her watch. Good. It was time.

She stowed the cart and headed upstairs. She smiled to herself, remembering how she'd been so hesitant the first time she'd gone up these stairs, like she was breaking a rule or something. Now she climbed them ten times a day, easy.

She made her way through the hallway and to the glass doors. She glanced at the sign—*The Rough-Shod Readers, All Welcome, This week's book: Assassin's Apprentice by Robin Hobb*. They mostly posted the book as a joke now. It was no longer a secret that they weren't actually a book club. Once, this meeting had been used to speculate on Zed and his followers' strange activities in the town. Now it was where some of the most crucial decisions about the town's future were made.

She slipped in quietly, all too aware she was the last to arrive. She took her usual seat at the foot of the table.

Joe gave her a pointed look. "Now that we're all here, perhaps we can get started?"

Once, she would have had a snarky remark to shoot right back at him. Over the past couple of years, she'd mellowed a bit. She even kind of looked forward to these meetings. Of course, that may have had something to do with Frank.

177

He gave her a wink across the table, and she smirked back at him.

They didn't see each other as much as they used to. Though they lived in the same apartment complex, their work hours didn't always coincide. And even when they did... Frank spent a lot of time with Matt and Mason. Sophie had her small group of friends from the library. They went out on weekends and had a surprisingly good time. Turned out it was true what they said about librarians. They were all wild at heart.

Sophie also spent a fair amount of time hanging out with Helen. But Matt and Helen were going through a bit of a rough patch, so she rarely ran into Frank at the Campbell's.

Part of the problem was Frank's guilt. She knew he felt responsible for everything that had happened. He felt it was his fault they were trapped in this town. He felt it was his fault Alice was gone. Sometimes, she wanted to shake him and tell him to stop taking responsibility for everything, that people had their own free will and made their own choices. The world didn't spin on the whims of Frank Hinkle.

She did miss him though. And she was pretty sure he missed her. Though his guilt and his pride would never allow him to say so.

Joe led the meeting, as always. He didn't technically hold any political position, but he'd always run the Rough-Shod Readers, so when it morphed into this strange shadow town council, he somehow fell into a leadership role.

The meeting went much like it always did. Very little changed when you were cutoff from the rest of the world. Harlan gave his crop report. Frank gave the state of the town supplies. Ellen talked about the state of commerce—after much debate the town had decided to keep the standard US dollar as their currency. Brandon gave an update on the victory garden program that grew food in people's yards and public parks.

Then there was the final report. The evacuation report.

"Nothing new from me." Zed looked sullen as he spoke, his eyes distant. He too had changed over the past three years. He'd gone inward as if unable to contend with the fact that he'd been beaten. He had done a few things here and there to help out the community. But that spark that had once made him such a powerful and terrifying presence had all but burnt out. He had the book, but he couldn't figure out how to make it do anything. He said he couldn't read it. Not even a little.

Sophie saw the disgust on Frank's face. She knew he didn't like seeing his old enemy giving up like this.

The meeting came to a close and the Rough-Shod Readers began to file out of the room. She grabbed Frank's arm as he filed past.

"Hey, hold up."

He stopped and looked at her, but his eyes were distant. "How you been?"

She shrugged. "Books, you know?"

He looked at her like he did *not*, in fact, know.

"You seen Mason lately? How's he doing?"

Frank shrugged. "Yeah, he's doing well."

He was only half listening. It made Sophie angry. He liked her. She knew he did. But he was too preoccupied with his perceived responsibilities to do anything about it.

She didn't know what she was going to say until she opened her mouth and the words came out. "You want to go to dinner tonight?"

That caught his attention. "Tonight? Oh, yeah, sure. That should work."

There was an awkward pause. She was tired of awkward pauses. "Just to be clear, so there's no misunderstanding, I'm asking you on a date."

His eyes grew wide. "A date-date?"

She groaned. "Yes. An actual, adult date. Like where two people hang out together in order to gauge their compatibility and their mutual interest in pursuing a relationship. You up for that?"

He smiled, suddenly back in the moment, and he looked at her as if he really saw her. "Yes. I'm very much up for that."

4.

King's Crossing
2018

Sophie laughed hysterically when Frank came down the stairs in his ill fitting brown shirt. He took the criticism well enough. He let her have her laugh, then showed her the dress she was meant to wear. That took the smile off her face quickly enough.

They were going to the opening night of a local production of *The Music Man*. Hell, why call it a local production? Why not a world premiere? As far as Frank knew, *The Music Man* had never been performed in this strange new reality. Local productions had become quite the rage in King's Crossing, and Frank and Sophie had been lucky enough to score some tickets. The only catch was the Rough-Shod Readers had decided it would be a nice gesture if they were to wear some clothes by one of the less experienced tailors in town.

Clothes had been in short supply for years now, but with a combination of the stock at the various stores, three truly talented seamstresses, and Frank's careful resource management, they'd been able to keep the town dressed. Time was pushing the limits on that now. Demands greatly outweighed supply. They'd had an apprenticeship program in place for a while now, but even that wasn't keeping up. So Frank and Sophie were nominated to demonstrate the trend of wearing clothes that were less traditionally...good.

"At least it'll be dark in the theater," Sophie said.

Frank smiled and gave her a kiss. "You look pretty good to me."

"Shut up," she said and returned his kiss.

The Hollywood, a hundred-year-old theater in downtown King's Crossing, seated six-hundred. Most of the attendees showed up on foot or bicycle, cars having gone the way of gasoline a few years ago. In fact, the problem of what to do with old cars was a big one. No one wanted the old-fashioned, heavy, useless things in their garage, but there wasn't much else to do with them. Someone had offered up a field to park them in, but the Rough-Shod Readers had shot down that idea. They needed to preserve all the farmland they could. The food supply was holding steady so far, but the population was growing. It turned out making babies was an even more popular form of entertainment than the library and local theater.

Sophie and Frank walked the half mile to the theater hand-in-hand. They didn't say much—that was often the way with them. But they were content to be with each other. Everything else aside, this had probably been the happiest year of Frank's life. He'd had a huge crush on Sophie for years, but he hadn't imagined she felt the same way. Why would a smart, pretty young woman like her be interested in a man with gray in his hair and a face scarred by the Ones Who Sing? But, for reasons he didn't understand, she was. He was so glad she'd asked him out.

The production of *The Music Man* was top notch (all things considered) until the third act, when Willis stumbled out onto the stage.

"Get off!" he yelled, wildly swinging a bottle of moonshine until the actors cleared the stage. The man playing Henry Hill tried to stand his ground for a moment, but Willis knocked him over with a bottle to the head and then kicked him square in the ass, sending him stumbling off the front of the stage and into the arms of the people in the first row.

Frank, Sophie, and six others were halfway to the stage when Willis pulled a revolver out of his belt and waved it at them, causing them to back off quickly.

"Everybody have a seat!" he shouted. His voice carried well throughout the theater. Frank remembered Willis had been in last summer's production of King Lear. When he had silence, he looked out over the crowd and shook his head. "You're a bunch of sheep. A bunch of damn sheep without a shepherd."

He walked to the front of the stage and shielded his eyes with his hand, looking out into the crowd. "We had a shepherd once. Where is he?" He looked left and right. "Where's Zed?"

"I highly doubt Zed's one for musical theater," Sophie muttered to Frank.

Frank agreed, but to his surprise, a man in the back stood up and walked toward the stage.

"I'm here," Zed said. His voice carried even better than Willis', as well as it had in downtown Rook Mountain the day he'd sent Frank Away.

"Get up here," Willis said.

Zed complied. He crossed his hands in front of him and

stood calmly next to Willis.

Willis pulled up his sleeve and thrust it in front of Zed's face. "What's this say?"

"Five," Zed replied.

"That's right! Five! I went back in time five times! I relived years of my life again and again. And do you know why?" He didn't wait for a reply. "Because I trusted you! Because you said you'd save us. But you haven't saved us, have you?"

He raised his revolver and held it to Zed's head with a quivering hand. "You failed us all!"

He pulled the trigger, and Zed collapsed.

The crowd gasped.

Willis looked out at them, as if just remembering they were there. He let out a harsh giggle. "There is no escape. No matter what they tell you, there is no escape." Then he put the gun to his own head and pulled the trigger.

The gunshot was still echoing through the theater when Zed sat up. He struggled his way to his feet. Blood ran down his face, but his head appeared to be intact.

He spoke in a calm, quiet voice that somehow carried through the theater. "We will not give up. We will never give up. We'll find a way to escape." He stared into the stage lights for a long moment before continuing. "And then we will take our revenge."

Frank felt Sophie's shaking hand slip into his.

5.
Boulder Creek, Colorado
2019

Alice was thirteen years old, damn it, and she could do a simple mission without a babysitter. Granted, this was a tad more vital than some of the ones she'd been on in the past, but still. She hadn't liked the way Vee had whined about it. The way he'd tried to insist he should come along. He was jealous of the way Wilm was starting to rely on Alice now, that's all it was. Alice was still a kid—his words. But this *kid* had been the one to find Gavin Point, Pennsylvania, right? The source of the power they'd feasted on last year? The reason they were strong enough to do what they were doing now. So, yeah, maybe it was time to stop looking at her like such a little kid. She wore a bra and had her period and everything, which was more than she could say for him.

That was how she'd laid out her case to Wilm. A little emotional and overly dramatic? Of course. But Wilm, Alice had learned, responded to shows of force. To strong powerful arguments and emotions. She wanted people who would scrape and claw their way to what they wanted over people who could make a calm, solid request.

So here she was, sans Vee. She didn't feel gloaty about it. She felt vindicated that her reading of Wilm and what she would respond to was accurate, but not gloaty. It was all an act. She would prefer to do the job alone. She liked her alone time. But she didn't feel strongly about it. Actually, she didn't feel that strongly about much of anything these days. Sometimes she felt like the better part of her emotions had been cut out by the scissors when she'd cut King's Crossing out of the map. As the scrap of the paper drifted to the ground, so had her humanity. It wasn't that she didn't have emotions, it was more like she experienced them at a distance, as if through a fog.

Boulder Creek, Colorado was a small town in the southern part of the state. Little grew here. Five minutes off the train and Alice already felt dusty. It was certainly beautiful, the way the mountains jutted up in angry, rugged crags. No place she'd ever been so perfectly captured the way she felt. Barren. Jagged. Withered.

She made her way through the streets, using her phone to guide her. She wasn't in a hurry. She was about to make a man's greatest ambition come true. Might as well savor it.

Her lack of hustle had at least a little to do with the object in the long duffle bag she carried over her shoulder. She had her sword, yes, but she also had something else. And having two of the Tools at once? Man, that was some kind of rush.

She reluctantly found the man's house, a beat up old bungalow, and rang the doorbell. The guy was renting the place, she knew that much. No employee of Wilm's organization was allowed to own a home. But it looked like he was pretty embedded. Alice wondered how he'd react to his new, more mobile lifestyle.

It wasn't for everyone. Alice wasn't sure it was for her, but what was she going to do about it? It wasn't like she could quit and go home.

After the third time she rang the doorbell, Alice got a sinking feeling. This guy Clyde had received a note she was coming. No way he'd go out and risk missing her.

Of course, there was always the possibility he'd gone AWOL.

She reached into her duffle bag and pulled out the sword. Many times she regretted having requested this particular Tool. She could have named anything. But she'd picked an unwieldy weapon that forced her to carry a giant duffle bag and made it so she couldn't walk through metal detectors. It came in handy now, though, as she used the handle to smash through a window. She wiped at the sill with a spare sweater from her bag to clear off the loose glass.

As soon as her head was through the window, she knew

Clyde hadn't gone AWOL. Well, technically he had. But permanently. His remains were propped up in an easy chair in the corner of the living room. God, what a smell. Alice didn't know how he'd died, but it'd happened a while ago.

Great. Wilm was going to flip out.

Alice pulled out her cellphone and was about to tap it to initiate the call when she saw something on the coffee table that made her pause.

A United States atlas.

For a moment, she forgot about the dead body and Wilm and the Tool she was supposed to be delivering.

She generally avoided maps. She usually just told her phone where to go, and it took her there. Paper maps had made her queasy.

Still, she flipped the atlas open and began turning pages. She didn't stop until she reached the *W*'s. Wisconsin. The green spot on the map where she spent her first nine years.

The sword in her hand began to buzz in that peculiar way it did when it wanted to be used.

She gently pressed the broken mountain symbol on the sword and felt it click. Slowly, she pushed the point of the sword through the spot in the map where King's Crossing should have been.

She gasped as white light poured through the hole.

She stared at the light for a long time. Then she tried to poke her finger through, but it wouldn't go. Then Alice had a great and terrible idea.

If one of the Tools had cut King's Crossing off the map, would that same Tool still be able to reach it?

She began constructing a story in her head. Maybe Clyde had been alive and well when she got here. Maybe she'd delivered the Tool and the message to him just as instructed.

How often did Wilm and the others check in with their employees? Monthly? If that? How long before they discovered Clyde was dead? And even when they did, would they suspect she hadn't delivered the Tool?

It was a risk. A big risk. But over the last four years Alice had learned *life* was a big risk, one that very rarely paid off.

She took the other Tool, the one meant for Clyde, out of her bag. The scissors with the tiny broken mountain symbol on the handle. She pushed the scissors into the hole in the map.

They fell through with an audible *pop* and the white light went out.

All that was left was a jagged hole in the page.

Alice left, taking the atlas with her. That night, she burned it in her hotel bathtub.

6.

King's Crossing
2020

Matt Campbell had decided to kill himself months ago. The only thing he couldn't settle on was the method.

It had been five years since Alice disappeared. Since everything went to hell. His daughter would be fourteen now, if indeed she was still alive. Frank had told him the story a dozen times, but Matt still had a hard time believing it. Frank and the others had a choice: save Alice or save the world. They'd chosen the second option. And Matt and everyone in town had paid the price.

He wasn't angry at Frank. He never had been, really. He was angry at God, at the world, at the physics that drove the universe and led all of existence to the moment when he would lose his only daughter to an unknowable group of monsters.

It had been hard in the days and weeks after Alice disappeared. So hard. To everyone other than Matt and Helen, those hadn't been the days after Alice's disappearance; they'd been the days after Isolation Day. Everyone had lost people on the outside. People weren't sympathetic in the way they would normally be to someone who'd lost a child. Because she was still on the outside, right? Still alive?

Matt didn't know. That's what he tried to tell everyone. That's what no one seemed to understand. They didn't know what was on the outside. For all they knew, the rest of the world was gone and their little town was the only thing left in the universe.

Helen and Matt had tried to hold it together for four years after Isolation Day. No, not Isolation Day. Screw Isolation Day. To Matt, it would always be Alice Day.

They'd tried, they really had, but it had been too difficult. They were constantly seeing reminders of Alice everywhere they looked, especially in each other. So they stopped talking, stopped having sex, stopped spending time together. It didn't even surprise Matt when Helen told him there was someone else, that she was leaving him. A huge part of him was angry, of course. A smaller, more reasonable part was actually happy for her. Good for Helen. At least someone would make it out of this.

Still, it stung when he saw her in town. So he stopped going out.

Frank still came over fairly often. They had a weekly card game scheduled with a few other guys, but it was cancelled more often than not. Matt felt a little guilty about leaving Frank behind when he killed himself, but, really, the man had Sophie. He was losing a friend, yeah, but it wasn't like he was losing a kid.

Matt had finally decided on how to do it a week ago, and today was the day. He had a little gas stowed away in the garage, and he'd kept the engine maintained. He was fairly certain the truck would start. Yeah, it was going to be overly dramatic and loud, but who cared? If he was going out, he was going to do it big.

He duct taped large rocks to his arms and legs and got in the trunk. The engine roared to life on the first try. He drove through town, windows down, letting the wind hit him in the face, and for a moment he was happy. People looked at him as he drove. They hadn't seen a running vehicle in years. There were a lot of mouths hanging open as he passed through town.

He drove to Volunteer Park and stopped the car at the end of the parking lot right by the small dock where they'd loaded passengers onto the river boats back before Alice Day. He took one last look around his town and said one final prayer. Then he stomped on the gas, crashed through the dock, and splashed down into the Mississippi River.

He'd picked the spot because of its depth. The truck hit the water with an impact that momentarily dazed Matt. He watched with detached interest as the truck sank and water poured in through the open windows.

Damn, he should have closed the windows. Having them open like that gave a man thoughts of maybe living through this.

He fought off his survival instinct and took a last breath.

As the car sank, he saw something strange floating in the water. Something that shouldn't have floated. Scissors. He squinted and saw something on the side of them. A broken mountain. It looked almost like the symbol on Zed's compass. And the symbol on the book.

This, Matt realized, was important. It might be something worth living for. He reached out and grabbed the scissors. Then he looked down and noticed with horror the rocks taped to his arms and legs. It would be almost impossible to swim to the surface.

Thankfully, he didn't have to. Three people in the park had dove in after the truck.

It was a near thing, but they pulled him and the scissors to the surface before it was too late.

7.

King's Crossing
2021

On a December evening in the seventh year of isolation, the unofficial, unelected leaders of King's Crossing, the Rough-Shod Readers, met at the library to listen to Zed talk about the scissors.

"I believe there is a very good chance they can get us out of here," Zed said.

This declaration was met with excited babbling around the room. Matt Campbell, the man who'd found the scissors, albeit during a suicide attempt, received a few pats on the back.

Upon being saved from drowning, Matt had brought the scissors with the broken mountain symbol to the Rough-Shod Readers who had agreed, even Frank, to hand them over to Zed to study. As upsetting as it was to present Zed with one of this new Tools, it only made sense. He was the person with the most experience using one of them.

As soon as he'd received the scissors, a change had come over Zed. After six years of quiet sulking, he had finally snapped out of it. The swagger returned to his step, as did his cheshire cat-like smile.

Zed continued. "Since Isolation Day, my compass has pointed to one spot anytime I ask it to locate anything outside this town. I believe it's where the…let's call it a barrier between us and the rest of the world is at its weakest. Using the scissors, there's a chance we can cut through."

They'd all heard about Zed's tests. He'd tried cutting in various places, and the scissors managed to open strange holes in reality. The only problem was that it was impossible to tell where those holes went. All that came through were beams of white light. Zed had tried sending objects through the hole, but that didn't accomplish much of anything. The objects fell through, the white light disappeared, and that was that. There was no telling where the things ended up. According to Zed, those holes could lead to anywhere in time or space. Or even outside of time and space.

"How do we know if you're right?" Sophie asked.

Zed smiled at her. "I guess we try it and see."

"Try it how?" Joe asked. "Send something else through?"

"I was thinking of sending *someone*," Zed said.

A silence fell over the room.

"And there's no way to tell?" Ellen Kramer asked. "We just send someone through and hope they make it to the other side?"

Zed spread his hands, as if to show he had nothing up his sleeves, then nodded. "Any volunteers?"

After a moment, a half dozen shaky hands were raised, Sophie and Frank's among them.

"Don't be stupid," a voice said from the back of the room. "I'm pretty sure this is my job."

Mason didn't usually join the Rough-Shod Readers

meetings. He didn't have an official position in the group. Frank invited him to dinner once a week or so, but other than that he kept to himself. He seemed to like farming. It was a job he could do mostly in isolation. Even when he wasn't working, he tended to stay in his cabin in the woods near the farm. That made sense to Frank. The woods was where Mason had spent most of his life, after all. It wasn't surprising that he felt most comfortable there.

"Is this why you asked Mason to join?" Frank asked Zed.

Zed nodded slowly. "If he's willing."

"Why him?" Sophie asked.

It was Mason who answered. "I'm unattached. The town needs all of you. You have people who love you." Frank started to speak, but Mason held up a hand to silence him. "I know, I know, I do, too. But it's different. If I don't make it, the town will be okay. No one's waiting up at night for me, if you know what I mean."

"I'd like to throw my hat into the ring," a voice from the other side of the table said. It was Matt. "The only person I love is on the other side. I want to find her. And, just like Mason, I don't have anybody here who'd be devastated if I didn't make it back."

"There's also the matter of what needs to be done on the other side once you reach it," Zed said. "After all, what's the use of sending someone through if they can't make it back."

"And you think I can make it back?" Mason asked.

"Perhaps," Zed said. "Or you can at least find help. What I propose..." He trailed off and took a deep breath. "What I propose is sending the compass through with you. You can use it to find help."

Frank was stunned. Zed willing to give up a Tool? He must be very desperate indeed.

Mason nodded. "I've got a fair amount of experience using the compass."

"My thoughts exactly," Zed said.

"And who's he supposed to find on the other side?" Frank asked.

"I believe that just as a Tool is the only way out, another Tool may be the only way for someone to help put things right with this town. And I think there may just be a Tool that can do it. A Tool that has been known to destroy things created with the same power that trapped us here." He looked pointedly at Frank. "We send Mason to the person who has the knife."

"Christine," Frank muttered.

"Exactly," Zed said. "Dr. Osmond has proven herself quite capable. Between her and Mason, we just might have a chance." He looked down at the scissors for a long moment before continuing. "There's something else we need to discuss. Whether we should do this at all."

His statement was met with a confused silence.

"If Mason is successful in getting Dr. Osmond's help," Zed continued, "and if she is able to free us, our escape could lead to something worse. It won't be long after we're free that the Exiles will come to claim King's Crossing."

The Exiles. Zed hadn't so much as mentioned them since Isolation Day. Anytime anyone else brought them up, he grew sullen and refused to speak about it.

Matt stood up. "Wait a minute. I thought they were locked outside of time. That's the whole reason you couldn't save Alice, right? So they would be trapped?"

"Apparently, I was mistaken," Zed said. "I believe our current situation proves they've escaped."

Frank and Sophie locked eyes. They'd suspected as much,

but they hadn't had the heart to tell Matt his daughter had been sacrificed for nothing.

"I think it's time you tell us what you know about the Exiles," Frank said. "We have to understand what we're facing."

Zed nodded slowly. "Understand that most of what I know comes from things I've managed to piece together. Bits of conversation I overheard. It's far from complete."

"Disclaimer received," Sophie said. "Start talking."

He set the scissors on the table and folded his hands. He looked suddenly pale, like speaking about such things frightened him. Then he started talking.

"They are from…somewhere else. Another…I don't know, dimension. Somewhere outside of time, at least as we know it. In many ways, they are superior to us. They can't be hurt by anything I've ever discovered. They can do things that defy the laws of physics."

"Sounds like someone else I know," Frank said.

Zed nodded. "You're not wrong. I got my powers from them. But that's another story for another time." He turned and looked out the large window for a moment before continuing. "Despite all their superiority, every human has one thing they do not: potential. Time gives us the ability to change. The ability to grow. For creatures without time, this is an alluring concept. If they want to change the way things are, they need that power."

Frank had questions already, but he didn't want to interrupt again. Zed hadn't spoken about this before, and Frank wasn't about to get him off track now. Sophie had once told him his best trait was knowing when to shut up, and he agreed with her assessment.

Zed continued. "Long ago, one of their kind came to our

universe and hid…let's call them batteries. Items that would collect the power, the potential, from humanity. The idea was that when the batteries were full, their kind would come and collect the batteries."

"The batteries are the books," Mason said.

Frank looked at him, surprised.

Zed smiled. "Very good. They hid them in places of great potential and waited. The trouble started when they collected the first book. See, their society had been peaceful. One of the benefits of the lack of time was a lack of war. But when they harvested the first book and suddenly had the potential for change, everything became different. There was a schism in their society. A war. The leaders of the losing side were exiled. They used their remaining power to come here. Their plan was to harvest all the books on Earth and use that power to return home and overthrow the ones who'd exiled them. It wasn't until they arrived here they realized the books were hidden and they had no way to find them."

Zed picked up the scissors and turned them in his hand as he spoke. "They did have one thing though: the Tools. The Tools are a unique creation. They contain a bit of the Exiles' power tuned to specific purposes. But the Exiles can't use the Tools themselves. Only humans can. It takes our potential, you see, to make them work. It's what I've always loved most about the Tools. They're the best of both our species. Their power and our potential combining to do great things.

"So, they had to recruit humans to use these Tools to help them find the books."

"And let me guess," Frank said. "You were one of those humans."

Zed nodded. "I didn't realize what I was doing. Not at first. But eventually I willingly led them to the books. They gained a lot of power and destroyed whole towns because of me. Eventually we…had a falling out."

"Care to elaborate?" Sophie asked.

Zed looked at her sharply. "No. Suffice it to say, I vowed to stop them. I wouldn't let them have the power. That's why I took towns outside time. So they couldn't access them. They are trapped within time, you see. Eventually, if the books aren't harvested when they are full, the power begins to spill out and strange things start to happen. The trees in Sanctuary, for instance. And if you wait long enough, the power decays and fades away."

Frank thought about that for a moment. "So the tree growing in Volunteer Park. Does that mean the book here is full?"

Zed nodded grimly. "They've never harvested a book as full as this one. It's a happy accident I discovered this town before they did. Because if they harvest this town's book, I believe they will have the power to go home."

"Isn't that a good thing?" It was Joe who asked the question. "Wouldn't that mean they'd leave us alone?"

Zed looked down. "When they harvest the book, King's Crossing will cease to exist. As will all the people in it." He let that hang in the air for a moment before continuing. "But that's not the worst of it. When they leave this world, they'll rip a hole in time. A hole that can't be repaired. Then the Ones Who Sing will come through and devour all life on Earth."

A heavy silence fell over the room.

Finally, Zed said, "If we do nothing, they will eventually find other towns and harvest enough power. The result will be the same. But…I believe King's Crossing would survive. It would be a last bastion of humanity. An ark. If we return, we potentially speed up their success and we put the town in danger. But we will also have the chance to fight them. We have some Tools. And I have a plan."

"Okay," Frank said. "Then we do what we've always done in this group. We put it to a vote."

So, later that day, the Rough-Shod Readers gathered in a field outside town to see Mason off on his journey. They'd given him some supplies and enough money to cover him for at least a month of travel.

"There's really no telling where I'll end up," Mason said. "I might go through and just fall into eternity."

"You are truly going into the unknown," Zed said.

"Like an astronaut," Frank said.

"What's an astronaut?" Mason said.

Sophie leaned over and whispered in Frank's ear, "Are we sure he's the guy we want to be sending?"

Frank gave her a squeeze. "I'm sure."

Zed handed Mason the compass, and joy washed over Mason's face. He finally had his Tool back.

"I believe in you, Mason," Zed said.

"It's about damn time," Mason said.

Frank pulled Mason in for a hug, then handed him a letter. "Maybe it'll help smooth the way with Christine. She's not exactly the trusting sort."

Finally, Sophie hugged Mason. "Stay safe, big guy."

Mason smiled. "Whatever happens, I want you to know you were a really good babysitter."

Sophie laughed. "Shut up. I was the worst."

A few moments later, Zed cut into the ground with the scissors at spot the compass indicated, and white light poured out.

Mason took a deep breath and jumped into the hole.

THE BOY WHO FOUND THE WATCH (PART SIX)

East Graver, Texas
1970

They stood in an empty field outside town. It was evening, and a blue dimness was falling over the land. They could see the lights of town beginning to blink on as the sunlight faded away.

"It's too soon," Vee grumbled. He didn't look at Zed as he spoke. He rarely looked at Zed. It was as if he felt Zed was too low to acknowledge.

The five of them stood shoulder to shoulder, facing the town. Wilm, Vee, Rayd, San, and Zed.

Zed shuffled his feet nervously. Never once, in his nearly twenty-two years in their service, had he seen more than two of them in the same place. They'd come today because Zed called. Because he said this place was ready. And because, in all the years he'd been scouting for them, this was the first time he'd put out the call.

"You're right, Vee," Wilm said. "It's ripening. But it's not there yet."

"Damn waste of time, if you ask me," Rayd said, his face

scrunched up in disgust.

Wilm paused for a long moment before replying. Her eyes were fixed on the town. "No…not a waste of time. Not at all." She turned to Zed. "Would you be so kind as to use the watch, please?"

Now it was Zed's turn to pause. They'd never before asked that of him. He nodded and reached into his pocket. He always felt nervous having the watch in plain sight around them, like they might suddenly decide he was unworthy and take it away. He had no doubt they could take it if they wanted to do so, but he would fight them. Oh, how he would fight.

He pressed the broken clock symbol and time stopped. He expanded the circle to include the four beings with him in the bubble that allowed time to pass while the rest of the world around them stopped. Once it had been difficult for him to control the bubble, to expand it beyond himself, but now he did it with merely a thought. He could make the bubble bigger if he needed to. Much bigger.

Rayd watched him warily as he so effortlessly wielded the power of the watch. They couldn't use the watch themselves. He knew that now. That's why they needed him.

Wilm didn't look at Zed. Her eyes were on the sky. After a moment, she smiled. "There," she said, pointing up.

Zed squinted upward and after a moment, he saw what she was indicating. Way up in the sky were three tiny streaks of white. And they were moving. Zed felt a moment of panic. He mentally checked the bubble he'd made. Had he accidentally expanded it so high? No, it ended just above Vee's head. Vee was the tallest of them by a good three inches. But if time was stopped, how were those white streaks moving?

Vee grunted, and Zed looked over to see the big man looking into the sky, shaking his head. "Three of them. And a thousand feet up. Damn waste of our—"

Wilm shushed him. "Listen."

Zed did listen. And after a long moment he thought he heard something. The creatures high above were making a sound. It was almost musical.

There was something terrible about that sound. Something unnatural.

When Zed could barely stand it any longer, he said, "What are they?"

Wilm clucked her tongue. "Nasty creatures, unworthy of a name. They live outside time."

"I've never seen them before. And I've spent plenty of time outside time." He didn't want to admit how long.

San answered, her electric glare turning on him. "That's because you weren't in the right place. They're attracted to the power that gets built up in these special towns. As the place ripens, more of them gather. The more of the creatures, the more ready it is."

"And there's only three of them," Rayd said, picking up the thread. "So, as you might be able to guess, this place isn't ready."

"Only three, yes," Wilm said, the excitement coming through in her voice, "but they are here. How long since we've seen any of them?"

It was Zed's job to hunt down these places. They told him the watch would let him know when they were ready. So he'd called them here. Even though he knew this town wasn't yet ripe. He'd done it because there were things he had to know, and they'd long ago stopped giving him answers.

He drew in a deep breath before speaking. He was afraid to

ask, afraid how they might react, afraid they might even take away his watch—or at least try—but this was the whole reason he'd brought them here. "What if it were ripe?"

Wilm looked at him sharply. "What do you mean?"

"What if it was ready? You said yourself you haven't found one that was ready in a long time. What would my reward be?"

Vee turned and growled at him. "Reward? You have the watch. What more do you want?"

Zed forced himself to shrug, as if he didn't care about the watch. "Yes, I already have that. I'm asking for...an incentive."

Wilm licked her lips. "Zed, if you find us what we're looking for, we'll give you gifts beyond your dreams."

Zed swallowed hard. "Care to be more specific?"

Wilm smiled. "You are feisty today, aren't you? Alright. We'll stop you from aging. Make you unkillable. Allow you to transport yourself anywhere you wish to go in an instant. Give you the power to see into the minds of men. Is that specific enough?"

Zed couldn't help but hide the disappointment on his face.

Wilm's lip curled in a humorless smile. "You want more. Name it."

He knew what he wanted. The pocket watch was just a tiny piece of the power each and every one of them wielded. It was a part of them, not something external that could be lost or stolen. "I want to be one of you."

It was silent for a moment, then San let out a piercing laugh. "Is he serious?"

Zed felt his face grow hot. "You said you need my help. This is my price."

Rayd mumbled, "What a waste of time."

Wilm smiled indulgently, as if speaking to a slow child. "Zed. What you're asking is not only impossible, it's unfathomable. Like a flea wishing to be a man. The fire of distant stars flows in our veins. That is not something which can be gifted. We offer you the ability to live longer than any man has before, as well as other things. You could be rich. Famous. Whatever you want. Let that be enough."

Zed's heart went cold. They'd laughed at him. They hadn't even considered his fondest wish for a moment. But he nodded anyway. "Fine. I agree to your terms. Are you ready for your town?"

San's laugh reached an even higher pitch. "He think's it's that easy!"

While her laugh still hung in the air, Zed pulled back the bubble freezing the four of them.

He looked at them for a long while, making sure one of them wouldn't break through and come after him, the way Rayd had on Wilm's porch so long ago. But he'd gotten better since then. So much better.

Hesitantly, he expanded the bubble, allowing them back into it. San was still laughing.

He breathed a sigh of relief. They hadn't noticed. Though there was something in Rayd's eye. He was looking at Zed strangely, like he knew something was off. But it didn't matter. Zed was committed to what he intended to do.

He concentrated hard and shifted the bubble, pulling it away from the four and expanding it, making it larger than he ever had before. He put the bubble around the entire town.

When the bubble was in place, Zed relaxed. All there was to do now was wait.

So he waited. He waited in the town, among the people. He kept to himself mostly, but he interacted a bit more as the years went by and the town grew accustomed to their strange new circumstances. They eventually grew comfortable spreading out and going into the frozen world for supplies. To Zed's surprise, many in town liked and respected him, as he suggested possible solutions to various problems. It gave him a little thrill to have people turn to him in times of trouble. He'd never experienced anything quite like it.

Slowly, more and more of the strange, featherless bird creatures gathered in the skies above the town. And eventually, they started attacking. This concerned Zed, because it was something he hadn't planned for, and he thought he had planned for everything. He eventually discovered he could protect himself from the creatures by creating a second bubble, a bubble that surrounded only him and moved himself ever-so-slightly deeper into time. It wasn't far enough that it impaired his interactions with the townspeople, but it was enough to confuse the time-sensitive creatures. But there was a problem. Holding one bubble was easy for him now, but holding two bubbles took concentration. Eventually, he figured out a mental trick. He took the second bubble and mentally put it in a box and sealed it shut. The box was in his mind, but he represented it with a real wooden box that he carried with him. This mental trick made things much easier. In fact, he figured he probably could have expanded his protective bubble much further if he'd been so inclined, maybe even large enough to cover the entire town. But he didn't see the use in that. These people were doomed anyway.

So he waited years, watching the number of streaks in the sky grow and watching his fellow townspeople be slowly picked off one by one as the creatures descended each night.

Finally, when the sky was thick with the things, when there

were only a handful of people left alive in the town, he decided it was enough. He walked to the edge of town where the four Exiles remained frozen and expanded the bubble to include them.

San was still laughing, but her laughter stopped abruptly. It was evening now.

"Impossible," Wilm muttered. "You stopped time without us knowing?"

"Wilm," Vee said sharply. His eyes were on the sky. "Look."

Wilm turned her head upward and her eyes widened as she looked at the hundreds of white streaks above.

"I think it's fair to say the town is ripe now," Zed said.

"How long?" Wilm asked, a tiny quiver in her voice. "How long was time paused?"

"Five years, near as I can reckon it," Zed said. He dissipated the bubble, bringing them all back into time.

"Wilm," Rayd said. His voice was thick with emotion. "Who cares how long it's been? Can't you feel it? The town is ripe. Bring Joseph."

Wilm nodded and closed her eyes for a moment. Then another man was standing next to them. Zed was startled not only by the sudden appearance but also by the man's identity. It was the man who'd driven Zed from Santa Cruz to Wilm's cabin in the mountains that day so long ago.

The man was even more startled. He stumbled around in confusion for a moment before his eyes settled on Wilm and he realized what had happened.

Wilm looked at him, urgency in her eyes. "Joseph, listen carefully. This town is ripe. We need you to locate the book immediately, please."

He nodded vacantly. Zed felt a touch sorry for him, not

having a moment to wrap his head around what was happening to him. But just a touch.

Joseph pulled something out of his pocket and Zed nearly gasped. It was a compass. But on the back of it was the broken clock symbol. There were other Tools. Zed suddenly felt dizzy. There was a familiar buzz in the air, the same as when he used the pocket watch, but stronger. Because the two of them were in close proximity, he realized.

Joseph glanced at the compass. "It's this way."

The six of them made a strange procession through town. Joseph led them through the streets like a twisted version of the Pied Piper. He stopped in front of a small house and pointed at a cellar door. "It's down there."

Vee grabbed the door and ripped it off its hinges. He tossed it aside, and nodded for Joseph to continue.

Joseph led them into the cellar. He took a cardboard box off a shelf and pulled out an oversized, leather-bound book. It showed a symbol of a broken key on the cover.

Rayd reached for the book, but Wilm grabbed his wrist.

"No, not here," she said. "We've waited so long. Let's do this under the moon."

Rayd nodded reluctantly, and the group moved back into the street, Joseph carrying the book.

They stopped in the middle of the street. Joseph set the book down on the blacktop and stepped slowly away.

Wilm smiled. "Okay. Now."

The four of them reached down and each put a hand on the book.

And the world warped and twisted around them. Zed felt sicker than he'd ever felt before. It was as if a hole was being cut in reality and something terrible was sticking its head through. That something terrible, Zed realized, was the true nature of his four employers.

It was over in a moment. The book was gone. The street was gone. The town was gone. Zed, Joseph, and the four stood in an empty field.

The skin of the four beings before him glowed a golden orange. All four of them had their eyes closed and even Vee had a smile on his face.

"Where did the town go?" Zed asked.

Wilm looked up at him. She was moving slowly, as if in a drugged-out haze. "It's gone. It never was. We've consumed it, past, present, and future."

This was a terrible thing, Zed knew. But he couldn't help feeling a bit satisfied. He'd done it, and he knew what he had to do next. He took a deep breath and spoke. "You're happy? This is what you wanted?"

"Oh, yes," Wilm said in a lazy voice.

"Good," Zed said. "Then I'd like my reward."

CHAPTER SEVEN: REUNION

1.

Rural Western Wisconsin
January, 2022

They stood in a patch of woods about three miles from the Mississippi. The area was strangely undeveloped. No major highways passed through here. Even the smaller roads were scarce. There were no farms. It was almost as if people were consciously—or perhaps unconsciously—avoiding this area.

Christine looked around with a critical eye. "This is it? This is where the town's supposed to be?"

"It's where the town is," Mason said. "We just can't see it. Or it's on another plane of existence or something. But it's here. Trust me. I was in it less than two weeks ago."

Christine put her hands on her hips and grunted noncommittally.

Will winked at her like he always did when he was trying to reassure her.

It had been a long, strange trip. For all of them. Just three days ago, Christine had been happily plying her trade of podiatry in a private practice, enjoying living with her husband, and anticipating the visits with her son Trevor when he travelled home from college.

Then *he'd* shown up. Mason.

What was he to her, anyway? Step son? No, that wasn't right. He wasn't anything. He was just the son of her ex-husband. If she even believed his crazy story. Which, God help her, she had to admit she did.

Mason had told them about Sanctuary, about how Jake had used a book with strange powers to create a safe place for people, a place from which they could never return. Christine had felt a stab of jealousy when he'd told them about Logan, his mother. But she couldn't stay angry long. It seemed as though she and Jake had both accepted the reality that he would probably never return, and they'd both moved on.

Then came the hardest part. Mason told about the strange creatures in the forest and the people who'd attacked Sanctuary. He'd told of Zed's final battle with a creature named Vee. He'd told of Jake's death.

Mason had also explained everything that had happened since. Escaping Sanctuary with Frank and a woman named Sophie, going to King's Crossing, and being separated from the Earth itself. He'd told of the years they'd spent cut off from the outside world.

Christine listened to all that, but her ability to feel and react appropriately had somehow shut off when she'd heard the details of Jake's death. She'd long suspected it, but the confirmation hit her hard. She felt numb.

Will was great, as he always was in a crisis. He supported her. He held her. This man who'd killed for her and her son, who'd never questioned her love even as she hoped night after night for the return of her first husband. Deep down, Christine wondered if maybe Will had been the tiniest bit relieved to learn of Jake's death. But no. She wouldn't think that of him.

But she couldn't wallow. Frank was alive. That was cause enough for rejoicing. He and thousands of other people needed help. And Christine would help them if she could. There was something else in that town. Zed. She'd feared his return for so long. Now she almost anticipated what it would be like facing him again. It made her wonder if a dark part of her didn't so much fear Zed as miss the fight against him.

Will turned to Mason. He looked at him strangely. Will was always a little slower to react to the weird than Christine. She knew when he looked at Mason he saw a distorted, elderly version of his stepson. It was disconcerting to Christine, too, but Will was having a more difficult time processing it.

"So what do we do?" Will asked.

Mason smiled sheepishly. "Frank said you'd know. He said, if anyone can figure it out, it's Will."

Will thought about that for a moment, then nodded. "You mind?" he asked Christine.

She paused. She knew she had to do it, but she felt strangely possessive about the knife. That was silly, she knew. He'd give it back in a second. He always did.

She passed it to him, handle first.

He took it and an easy smile grew on his face. "Yeah, it likes this place. It's singing to me something fierce."

"You know what to do?" Christine asked.

Will nodded, a wide grin on his face now. He marched to a spot twenty feet away. "Here," he said. He held out the knife to Christine. "You want to do the honors?"

He knew her too well. She snatched the knife out of his hand. "What do I do?"

"This is like a—I don't know—a tether point. You just need to cut it. Push the broken clock symbol and swing the knife like you're cutting a line."

She pressed the button and felt the familiar click. "Okay. Let's do this." She swung the knife in front of her and was surprised when it stopped against something hard, sending a jolt up her arm. "There's something here."

Will nodded. "The knife can feel it, even though we can't."

She swung it again. And again. And again. On the fourth try, there was an audible *snap*.

And suddenly, they were standing on a paved road.

2.

King's Crossing

Another Christmas had just passed and that always made people grumpy. Frank understood. It seemed the only function of holidays now was to remind people of the things they'd lost. Family. Friends. And—less important but still annoying—candy! It wasn't uncommon to run across a group talking in reverent tones and using words like *Hershey's* and *Ben and Jerry's* and *Reese's Peanut Butter Cups*.

Frank felt the loss of those things. But maybe not as acutely as the others. He'd spent seven years in prison, followed by who-knew-how-long in the Away eating only the flesh of the Unfeathered, before this current isolation. He was used to coping, and at times coping with far less.

He arranged the few remaining boxes in the storeroom for the thousandth time, verifying everything was in its place. Of course it was. There was so little left here he probably would have noticed at a glance if anything was missing. They still had a nice supply of canned beets. So there was that.

Still, he came here every day. His empire had shrunk substantially over the last seven years, but he felt possessive of it.

A frantic pounding on the door roused him from his thoughts.

Odd. No one knocked on this door. Not ever. That was part of what he liked about coming here. When he was here, he was forgotten.

He marched to the door, and pulled it open. Garrett, one of the police officers in town, was standing there. Frank's first thought was that something must be wrong. Maybe someone was hurt. Had Matt tried to kill himself again, maybe succeeded this time? Then he noticed the look on Garrett's face. The police officer wore a wide smile, and his eyes were bright and happy.

"Frank," he said, and Frank could have sworn there were tears in the man's eyes. "It's happened. It's finally happened. We're back." His message delivered, Garrett ran into the unusually crowded street, letting out a whoop as he went.

Garrett hadn't said what had happened. He hadn't needed too. Frank understood.

Mason had succeeded.

Frank stumbled down the concrete steps of the old warehouse and into the street, ignoring the bite of the cold January air through his tee shirt. Patty Gossel was the first person he saw. He grabbed her by the shoulders.

"Are they sure?" he asked. "The mist's gone?"

She nodded furiously. "It's gone. Jim Franklin walked a mile past where it used to be, and nothing stopped him. There's some gas at the police station. Word is they're filling up one of the old cruisers to venture out farther."

He pulled her in for a hug, which she returned with just as much enthusiasm. Frank wasn't sure he'd ever exchanged a word with her before, but that hardly mattered now.

The streets were filling as the news spread. It was strange

to Frank. After seven years of being trapped in town, the first thing they did on their release was push closer together to celebrate. Maybe it made a certain type of sense. They'd been through something together, something no outsider would ever understand. And they needed that one last time to be together in a way they never would again.

Frank followed the flow of the crowd moving toward downtown, toward Volunteer Park, toward the Mississippi. He felt an arm slip around him and turned to see Sophie. He pulled her close in a tight hug.

"Can you believe it?" Frank asked. "The old bastard did it!"

"Probably my babysitting influence," Sophie replied, a wide smile on her face.

They had just reached Volunteer Park when a cheer went up in the crowd. The people parted to let the new arrival through.

"You did it, Mason!" someone called.

"Tell us what happened!" someone else yelled.

But Mason didn't reply. He just kept walking forward, acknowledging them with a nod and a sheepish smile. Frank felt his heart swell as he saw his two old friends behind Mason.

Will had a bit of gray in his hair now, and it seemed to Frank he'd put on fifteen or twenty pounds. Christine had gone the other direction, becoming thinner, perhaps a little too thin. Despite the lines on their faces, they still had that old spark in their eyes.

He ran forward, pushing past the other onlookers, and embraced them.

They held their group hug for a long time, none of them saying anything.

Finally, Frank pulled away and looked at Christine. "You

heard about Jake?"

She nodded, tears filling her eyes.

"I'm sorry," he said. "I tried to save him."

"I know," Christine said.

Frank felt someone nudge his shoulder. He turned and put his arm around the woman behind him. "Sophie, this is Christine and Will Osmond." He grinned at his two friends. "And this is Sophie Hinkle. My wife."

Christine's jaw dropped. "No way. Frank Hinkle got married?"

Mason rubbed his chin. "Yeah, sorry about that. He made me promise not to tell."

Frank said, "No way I was going to miss seeing that look on your face."

Handshakes and introductions followed. There were plenty of other people who wanted to meet Christine and Will, and plenty who wanted to shake the hand of Mason Hinkle, hero of King's Crossing.

Frank didn't know how long they'd been standing around basking in the presence of their fellow townspeople. It might have been five minutes, it might have been an hour. All he knew was he didn't want it to end. Not yet.

So, of course, it did.

A voice boomed through the crowd. "My people."

They all turned toward the voice. Zed was standing in a pavilion, using it as a make-shift stage. He was holding the book with the broken man symbol.

"Your lives are in danger," Zed said. "The decisions we make in the next few minutes will determine whether we live or we die."

Christine said, "I really hate that guy."

* * *

3.

"This *should* be a time for celebration," Zed said. "I would like nothing more than for us all to revel in each other's company. We've waited so long for this moment. And we should be allowed to enjoy it. We're free. However, our freedom could also be our downfall."

Sophie squinted up at Zed. The sun was behind him, shining in such a way that he almost seemed to glow. She wondered for a moment if he'd planned it that way. Who was she kidding? Of course he had.

His voice filled the park, as if amplified. Sophie remembered Frank's stories about how Zed used to control the crowds in Rook Mountain.

She turned and saw Frank was looking at her.

"You've never seen him like this," he said.

Sophie turned back toward Zed. They'd spent so much time with him over the past seven years. He'd sat in the Rough-Shod Readers meetings with them. Sophie and Frank had often speculated about whether he'd somehow changed.

Seeing him standing up there, she had a sinking feeling in her stomach and she knew he hadn't. Seven years? That was nothing to Zed. The man claimed to have waited nearly a thousand while Sugar Plains, Illinois slowly decayed into Sanctuary. He hadn't changed at all. The true Zed, this Zed, had merely been hibernating, waiting for his moment to come alive.

Maybe that wasn't such a bad thing, though. Maybe they needed the real Zed right now.

"For seven years we've been hidden away," Zed continued. "Yes, we've been locked away from the rest of the world. My good friend Frank Hinkle used to be a lock builder, and he once told me the name of the type of lock that can only be opened from either side with a key. A deadlock, wasn't that what it was called, Frank? This town was locked away from the rest of the world as if with a deadlock. It trapped us, yes, but it also kept things out. The things that were chasing me. The things I warned some of you about so long ago."

Sophie's eyes scanned the crowd. They were eating it up. Every eye but hers seemed to be fixed on Zed. She saw her boss at the library, Joe, his jaw set with determination. She saw Matt Campbell, his eyes wide.

"Make no mistake, they are coming for us, and the world will pay the price." He leaned forward and spread out his hands to them, showing his vulnerability. "I have one question for you, my townspeople, who have stood so strong through everything that's happened. Will you stand with me one more time? Will you help me save the world? Will you fight?"

He stopped, letting the silence hang in the air. The atmosphere was electric with tension.

To Sophie's surprise, it was Mason who stepped forward.

"No," he said. His voice sounded weak compared with Zed's, but it carried through the crowd like a shockwave. The man who had just saved them was now standing up to Zed.

Zed's smile wavered. "You don't think it's important to save the world?"

Mason licked his lips. "I think it's important to keep your promises. And you made us a promise. Before the final fight, you promised to bring my parents here. And Sophie's sister."

Sophie's heart nearly stopped. That had been so long ago. So much had happened. She hadn't dared hope.

Mason waved toward the book in Zed's left hand. "Come on, don't tell me you haven't figured out how to use that thing over the past seven years."

Zed slowly nodded. "I have learned. I may be able to do what you ask."

"Not what I ask. What you promised."

Zed nodded curtly. "Yes, yes. Mason, Frank, Sophie, come with me."

They followed him to the shed. Christine and Will came with them, even though they hadn't been asked. That seemed fair. It was Christine's husband—or ex-husband, Sophie was never clear on that—who might be back from the dead in a few moments after all.

Sophie had a hard time concentrating while she walked. Thoughts were slippery. One image filled her mind. Heather. Not the picture they'd shown on the news after she'd been killed. Heather as a girl, her hair flying in the wind like it had when they'd dared each other to lean off their parents' balcony and yell *sanctuary*. Could Zed actually do it? Could Sophie be moments away from seeing her sister again?

And if so, what would her sister be like? If Zed pulled her here from just before the murder, she'd be a confused sixteen-year-old who'd suddenly jumped nearly twenty years into the future.

But that didn't matter. She'd be alive.

Zed led them into the shed, and Sophie saw the small twisted tree was still there, same as it had been on the day they'd pulled Rayd through. It didn't seem to have grown at all since then.

Zed pulled the door shut and looked around the room at each of them. "If I do this, I have to know you're with me. You have to join in this fight. No matter what comes of it."

He looked at Sophie for confirmation, and she nodded. God help her, she nodded. She didn't hesitate, not for a moment. Anything to have Heather back.

Mason agreed just as quickly.

When Zed turned to Frank, there was a pause.

"You can do this?" Frank asked.

"Yes," Zed said. "I believe I can. Over the years, the book slowly started to reveal itself to me. I can't use it as well as I used the one in Sanctuary, of course. But I had a thousand years to study that one." He flipped open the book. "We'll start with Jake."

Zed took a deep breath and moved his finger in a complicated shape across the page.

A hot white light suddenly burst out of the tree and an opening nearly the size of the tree trunk appeared.

"My God," Will said. "He's actually doing it."

Zed shot him a look. "Please be quiet. This is rather precise work."

Will mumbled an apology.

They all stared at the tree. The hole suddenly seemed larger than the tree itself somehow. A dark shape blocked the light coming out of the tree.

Sophie glanced at Zed. His finger seemed to be moving at impossible angles on the page.

A man fell through the hole in the tree and hit the floor with a thud.

"Jake!" Frank cried out.

And there he was. The man Sophie had seen die in the woods. Jake.

Jake lifted his head and looked around the room, confused. "What's happening? Frank?"

Sophie had a sudden sinking feeling in her stomach. There was blood running from his ear onto the floor.

Christine gasped.

Sophie had seen him like this before. "When?" she said,

217

staring up at Zed. "When did you pull him from? Where was he just before you brought him here?"

Zed sighed. "It was complicated. I had to get him at a very specific moment."

"What are you talking about?" Christine asked.

"We needed to cause as little disruption as possible to the chain of events. After all, Jake died after turning Vee into a tree. We couldn't pull him through after he was dead, of course. But we couldn't bring him over too much before it, either. We couldn't have Vee not be transformed, after all. That would mess up all sorts of things."

"Wait a minute," Frank said. "Are you saying he's dying? You brought him over as he was dying?"

"Frank," Jake said weakly. "I was just talking to you. Through the tree."

Frank grabbed Zed by the collar and slammed him against the wall. "What the hell have you done?"

Zed smiled. "Please be careful. There is a time-and-space-spanning portal hanging open right next to us."

"This is not what I asked for!" Frank spat the words in his face.

"Come on," Zed said. "I gave you what you wanted. He's alive. There's always a chance he'll stay that way. We do have a doctor in the room, after all."

Christine was already on her knees next to Jake, cradling his head in her hands.

Jake looked up at Christine, his eyes wide. "Christine... what are you doing here? Am I home?"

"Yes," she said. "You're home. I've missed you so much."

He nodded weakly. "Is Trevor—" Before he could finish the question, a coughing fit took him. He spasmed and coughed wildly, spraying Christine with a mist of blood.

Christine spun her head around toward Frank and Zed. "What happened to him? What's doing this?"

It was Sophie who answered. "I was there. I saw it. He was using a book, the Sanctuary book. And he, I don't know, he used it too hard or something. It was like something broke inside of him."

"Wonderful," Christine said. "Thanks for the super helpful diagnosis."

Sophie resisted the urge to snap back at her. That wouldn't help.

Frank slammed Zed against the wall again. "Do something! Fix this!"

Zed sighed. "I can't."

"Then bring him through sooner. Before he's hurt."

"What's done is done. Besides, even if there was a way, I wouldn't do it. I do that, and maybe Vee kills us all before we even get to this point in time. I won't risk it."

"Kills us all?" Frank asked. "I thought you couldn't be killed."

"Oh, it's difficult," Zed said, "but I can be."

"Good to know," Christine muttered from the floor. She reminded Sophie of Logan. Jake certainly seemed to have a type.

"Look," Zed said, "I've given you a little more time with him. That's all I can do without putting the entire world at risk. Fix him if you can. If you can't, enjoy the last few moments before he passes on."

Frank grabbed the book off the floor and shoved it into Zed's hands. "There's got to be something in there to fix it."

"Afraid not," Zed said.

Frank pulled Zed toward the tree. "Then I'm pushing you through. Good luck with whatever the hell's on the other

219

side."

Zed sighed. "That's quite enough." He backhanded Frank, sending him reeling across the room.

Frank hit the wall and crumpled to the ground.

Sophie ran to him.

Frank looked up at her, his eyes wide, blood from a split lip running down his chin. "I'm okay."

Zed took a step toward him. "You and that temper. And you don't even have the evil little coin to blame it on this time."

Jake started coughing again. Will held his head while Christine ran her hands along him, inspecting him for any sign of injury.

All eyes were on Jake now, but something out of the corner of her eye made Sophie turn. The door to the shed was opening.

"Um, guys," Sophie said.

"Thought I'd find you here." The voice was female. A tall, blonde teenage girl stepped through the door. She was holding a thin sword with an air of familiarity that said she knew how to use it.

"I don't know what you did to get King's Crossing back here," the young woman said, "but they are *not* happy. And they're coming."

4.

Alice looked around the room, squinting, trying to place everyone.

"Alice," the man in the corner said. "Alice Campbell."

She turned toward him. Something about the way he held himself was familiar. She'd only met him once before, and then only briefly, but she knew him. Her lip curled up in a half smile. "You were in our house the morning I was taken."

The man nodded. "My name's Frank."

Another man stepped forward, his gaze fixed on the sword in her hands. "What is that?"

Alice had never met this man, but she knew him from Wilm's description. She spun the sword around in her hand and held it so he could see the broken mountain symbol. "Come on, Zed. You of all people should recognize a Tool."

He squinted at her. "You work for them?"

"I do. Well, I did. I guess I just unofficially resigned when I came here to warn you."

Up until about two hours ago, she'd been enjoying a day off, which as usual involved hanging out in a small town waiting for her next assignment. In this case, it had been Rupert Falls, Idaho. The town was a dud. One of the lower level scouts had suspected it of being a place of power, of having a book.

This particular scout was a fifty-three-year-old with white hair down to his shoulders. He passed the message through the official channels, but Alice watched him through the whole process. He'd never seen her, of course, and had no idea who the random teenage girl was at the coffee shop. Or the movie theater. Or the church. She'd kept a low profile and he hadn't looked at her twice any of those times. No doubt he had no idea he was passing the message to someone nearly forty years his junior. But that was part of the reason she was so effective. Nobody ever suspected who she really was.

She'd investigated the situation and followed the checklist. Strange but scientifically explainable land form or weather pattern? A history of showing up in folklore and historical documents more than should be expected for a town of its size? An unusually small percentage of residents move out of town? A large number of residents who do leave town end up in powerful positions?

Rupert Falls was borderline on three of the four, so she understood why the guy had reported it. It made sense on an intellectual level. But this town didn't have the right feel. She didn't know how to explain it. She could just *feel* when it was right.

So, she'd gotten some time off while she waited for her next assignment. She hoped the down time would last a while. If not, she could always Pull Back a few times so she could relive the days of relaxation all over again before going back to work. She'd gotten pretty good at Pulling Back. When she was a little kid, she'd tugged on the rope in her mind. Now she just sort of eased it back, leaned against it until time rolled back to where she wanted it to be. It still burned in her mind a little when she did it, but she didn't mind the pain. It had gotten so she kind of liked it. She could do it without the bosses having a clue. They thought they still had her locked down on that front, and she played it up like she never used it without their permission, even asking, begging for permission sometimes, and pouting when she didn't get it. But it was almost a reflex now. She didn't even have to picture the rope most of the time. She just mentally leaned back.

Then, on the second day of her time off, all hell had broken loose. One minute she'd been in the theater watching some dumb superhero movie about a guy with a green ring fighting a guy with a yellow ring, and the next she was in Wilm's cabin, a furious Wilm staring down at her.

"Somehow they got out," Wilm said without preamble.

Alice had no idea what Wilm was talking about and said as much.

"Your people," Wilm said, the disgust clear on her face.

"King's Crossing."

Holy hell, Alice thought. They'd done it. It had to be the Tool she sent through. It had to be.

There was a crash and the stomping of feet that could only mean Vee was entering the house. After all these years, all the time she'd spent out there on her own, all the creeps she'd faced down and scrapes she'd gotten in, and even with her magic sword, she had to admit: Vee still scared the hell out of her.

He came through the door, his armless torso almost too large to squeeze through the standard size frame.

"When are we leaving?" he asked.

"As soon as San gets here," Wilm said. "Shouldn't be long."

"Good," Vee said. "I'm going to tear Zed's head off."

Alice resisted the urge to ask how Vee intended to rip anyone's head off without any hands.

A moment later, the statuesque, raven-haired San stepped into the room, as quiet as Vee was loud.

"We ready to go?" she asked.

Wilm nodded. "Let's begin."

Alice knew Wilm was about to teleport them. She had to act. She took a deep breath and Pulled Back to one day before. It was a slightly risky move, but it couldn't be helped. She needed to get to King's Crossing. And if they lost track of her, they couldn't teleport her to Wilm's cabin. At least she thought they couldn't.

She drove all day, through the night, and into the next day, making it to King's Crossing in a cool nineteen hours. Plenty of time.

Then she waited for the town to reappear, and, when it did, she headed for the shed. She knew it would have to be the shed. That's where the tree was, and the tree might be the people of King's Crossing's only advantage. And the book. If they had figured out how to use it. Now she was in the shed, facing these people, some of whom she used to know and some she'd never met. If this crew was King's Crossing's best shot, Alice didn't like their chances.

Zed smiled at her. "I used to have your job, you know. I knew a lot of others who did, too. It never ends well."

"It wasn't my choice," Alice said. "They drafted me."

Mason took a step forward. "We tried to save you. We really did."

Jake moaned.

Alice turned and looked at him. "What's the matter with him?"

"He's dying," Zed said. "He used a book, one of their books. In the end, it used him up."

Before she could answer, there was a cracking sound like thunder.

Alice gripped her sword. "Okay, Zed, I hope you have a plan. Because they're here."

THE MAN WITH THE WATCH (PART ONE)

Rook Mountain
1983

Zed met with his fellow Toolsmen and Toolswomen in a small diner on the outskirts of town. They sat around a long table. Zed had slipped the owner one thousand dollars to close the restaurant and leave them alone. He sat at the head of the table, partly because he'd called the meeting and partly because he had achieved things the others hadn't. He was one of them, but he was also the best of them. The first among equals, some might say.

He'd done what the others had failed to do. He'd brought their masters a ripe and ready town—not once, but four times now— and he'd been rewarded accordingly. As far as he knew, the rest of them around the table were normal humans. Which meant they were killable. But they also had Tools, most of which Zed had never seen with his own two eyes. It would be stupid to attempt to kill them outright.

It hadn't been easy to bring the group together. Their masters were careful to keep them isolated. But over the past decade, Zed had slowly wormed his way into the network of communication, asking a question here and another there.

Each carefully crafted to be innocent on their own but add up to something more. The beautiful thing about the network of informants, the vast majority of whom didn't carry a Tool, was that they each had so little information about each other that they couldn't gossip about the inquisitive bald man who showed up a bit more frequently than he should.

The others around the table looked nervous. They'd come because he'd called. They didn't know each other, but they all knew him. Knew of him, anyway. What he'd done.

Cindy, a woman with black hair piled on her head in an unfashionable beehive, was the first to speak after they were seated. "You gonna tell us what's going on?"

Zed smiled. He'd been doing that more and more lately. He'd found that he'd mellowed with age—he was technically nearly one hundred now after spending so long outside of time— and he found things humorous that he would have once found annoying. Besides, he'd learned the disarming power of a well-placed smile. And now, with all of them gathered in one place, he was feeling a little giddy. It was making his head swim.

"Before we get down to business, let's take a moment to enjoy this," he said. He closed his eyes, feeling the electric energy in the air. The feeling of power. All the Tools in one place.

When he opened his eyes, they were all staring at him blankly. They couldn't feel it, he realized. His heart sank a bit. He'd thought these people were like him, and maybe they were, a little. But if they couldn't feel it in the air, the immense power, then they weren't tuned into the Tools.

He sighed and decided he might as well begin. "Thank you for coming to hear my proposal. I'd like to start by laying our cards out on the table." With that he took out his pocket watch and set it on the formica in front of him.

A few of them gasped. Most had never seen another Tool before. They might not even be aware others existed.

Slowly, they all followed suit. Henry, the bearded man at the foot of the table was the first. He set his knife on the table. A handheld mirror soon joined it. And a key. Then a lighter. Then Joseph laid down his compass. Then Rachel set down her hammer.

All the Tools were on the table but one, the only one that had been in plain sight since the start.

Zed looked at Donald, a man with stark-white hair. He clutched a cane with the broken clock symbol in his hand.

"You all may not know this, but Donald has a special roll in our organization. He's what you might call...quality assurance."

"What do you mean?" Joseph asked. The man looked at Zed with a bit of awe. Maybe it had something to do with the fact that Joseph kept aging, and Zed didn't. Zed considered the man an idiot. His compass was as critical to helping their masters as Zed's watch. He should have demanded a bigger reward, like Zed had.

"That cane of his can sense other Tools. So Donald's job is to track us. To watch us. To make sure we do as we're told."

Donald grimaced but he didn't deny it. He took a look around and saw hard looks coming at him from all directions. He reluctantly set his cane on the table.

Zed graciously nodded his thanks. He turned to the others and said, "I've been thinking a lot recently about our role. And I was curious if some of you might be as tired as I am of being sent out to pick ripe towns like migrant workers pick oranges."

It was so quiet Zed could hear the slight wheeze in

Donald's breathing.

When no one spoke, Zed continued. "There is quite a lot of power in these towns. Perhaps we shouldn't be so eager to hand them over to our masters. People who don't trust us enough to give us the barest of information."

Henry shook his head slowly. "You're crazy. You want to go up against the Exiles, but you're afraid to do it alone, is that it?"

Zed's smile widened. "Yes. It is. They would crush me like a bug."

Cindy tilted her pale face at him. "So you want us to die with you?"

"Not exactly. I know I can't beat them alone, but I believe the Tools are more than the sum of their parts. If we all worked together, we would have a chance." He checked their blank faces before continuing. "There's something else. The power our bosses are trying to collect seems to be learning to protect itself from the Tools. Isn't that right, Joseph?"

Joseph paused for a moment, then nodded. "The first town you brought me to, East Gravers, Texas, the compass led us right to the book. But the last couple...it hasn't been so easy. We searched for days. We had to be very close to the book before it even registered on the compass."

Donald scowled at Zed. "What's that have to do with any of this?"

Zed was honestly disappointed the others couldn't see what he could see. "It means we're nearing the end of our usefulness. The bosses only keep us around to use the Tools. If the Tools aren't going to help them reach their goals, they don't need us. It's only starting with the compass, but I'm thinking long term here. Let's take the power while we can."

"I can't believe you brought us here for this!" Joseph said.

If Joseph wasn't on board, this was not going well.

Zed held up his hand. "Please. Hear me out. I'm not advocating killing them. Merely…negotiating a profit sharing arrangement." He turned to Joseph. "You can't tell me it feels good to know they could take that compass away at any time. We need to have a little power of our own."

"Says the man who can read minds and can't be killed." It was Rachel. She was the youngest of them. She'd only had that hammer of hers for five years.

"That's borrowed power, too," Zed said. "Don't think they can't take it away. But there is one kind of power we do have." He tapped the pocket watch. "Knowledge. We each know how to use one of these Tools. They've kept us away from each other so we don't share, but I suggest we talk about our Tools. We know what the compass does for them, but what about the other Tools? If we have all the information in one place, I'll bet we can find a way to use it against them."

No one said anything. They were all looking at him in disbelief.

"I'll start," he continued. "This pocket watch can stop time. Even better, it can create pockets where time moves in different ways and rates. It's how I've been able to get the towns ready. I take them out of time and let them ripen. Ten or twenty years go by in an instant." He looked around at them. "Who's next?"

After a long silence, Henry picked up his knife. "This is my knife, and I'm thinking about jamming it into your heart."

Zed considered saying that wouldn't do much of anything, but thought better of it. "Come on, Henry. Information is power."

Henry twirled the knife lazily in his hand. "Here's what

bothers me, Zed. You had to know all of us wouldn't go along with this. I doubt you believed any of us would. You also knew you'd be a dead man if word of this got back to the bosses. So why ask us in the first place?"

Zed waited, feeling the eyes of the others upon him. He'd half-hoped it would go the other way, but he'd known it wouldn't. That was okay. Because this was his moment. This was when he stopped being the boy who found the watch and started being the man who owned it.

When the silence was so heavy in the air Zed knew one of them was sure to break it, he spoke. "Henry, you misunderstand the situation. I'm not asking. I'm telling. Consider the possibility I'm offering or face the reality of being my enemy."

"Your enemy?" Cindy was half standing now.

Henry picked up his knife off the table and twirled it in his hands. "I owe the Exiles everything. We all do. They gave us our lives. Made us what we are. And now I'm going to take the Tool they gave me and see if you really are unkillable."

Zed leaned back in his chair and reached casually for the pocket watch. "That's the difference between me and the rest of you. They gave you your Tools. I took mine. Now I'll take yours."

He hit the button on the pocket watch.

Fifty years passed in an instant.

When he returned to time—many years later for Zed, but only a moment later in reality—he was alone. He sat for a long while, just looking at their empty seats, his anger simmering. The last fifty years hadn't gone the way he'd planned. Not at all. Fifty years locked out of time and what did he have to show for it?

Worse, his work wasn't done. The harder phase was next.

And then, with no warning, the harder phase was sitting right in front of him, in the seat Henry had occupied only moments ago. He hadn't seen her appear. It was as if she'd been here all along. The look on her face was more troubled than angry.

"Hello, Wilm," he said. "You made it here fast."

She shrugged. "Please. You think the others didn't tell us about your little meeting? I decided to let it play out to see what you were up to, but I never expected..." Her voice trailed off for a moment. "I came when I felt you use the watch. Vee, San, and Rayd will have felt it, too. They'll be here soon, I expect, and they won't be as eager for discussion as I am. Vee in particular would love the opportunity to hurt you. So let's see if we can get this sorted out." She leaned forward and folded her hands on the table. "What did you do with them?"

Zed realized he was clutching the watch very tightly indeed. "I took them out of time. They lived out the rest of their lives and died, some by natural causes, some not so much."

Wilm's face was even, but Zed saw a fury behind her eyes. "Not the people. There are plenty of people. What did you do with the Tools?"

Zed frowned. "They hid them. Turns out they were very good at hiding. I expect they used that compass to find places where I'd never look. I searched for them for years, but..." It hurt admitting his failure to Wilm. "Anyway, they are dead and the Tools are lost. They're in Rook Mountain somewhere, I'd imagine. Which makes it all the more frustrating that I can't find them."

Wilm's already ghostly face turned a shade paler. "You realize that's a problem? We sense the Tools when they're used. But if they're dead, they won't be using them."

"That *is* a problem, then."

Wilm sighed. "Do you have a solution in mind? Offer it up. Otherwise, hand over the watch before the others get here. They might decide to let you live."

Zed said nothing.

"Those powers of yours, your long life, it can all be taken away."

Zed grinned at her. "That's why I'm doing this. I seem to remember you laying hands on me to grant me these powers. I'm betting you have to do the same to take them away."

"That's a big bet. When the others arrive—"

"They're not coming," Zed said. "Or rather, they are coming, but it's not going to help you any."

Wilm squinted at him. "What have you done?"

"I've taken us outside of time. Very far outside of time, in fact. I call it the Away."

She shook her head slowly, and Zed thought maybe he saw the tiniest flicker of fear in her eyes. "That's not possible. I'd have been able to feel it if you used the watch."

"Yeah, I've been working on that. Seems I've found a way around it."

She looked around suspiciously.

"Oh, you knew there were layers within time, didn't you?" Zed asked, unable to keep the sarcasm out of his voice. "Well, there are, and we're in a deep one. I wanted to make sure we had time to talk."

"Fine," Wilm said. Her eyes were hard little things now. For a moment, Zed thought she might let the illusion of her humanity fall away and show him what she really was. But she maintained her composure. "Let's talk. Do you want to start with how the hell you think you're going to get out of this alive?"

"Sounds like a wonderful place to start. After this conversation, I'll disappear and you'll never see me again."

"You make it sound easy."

"Not easy, but doable." He held up the pocket watch.

"You plan to hide from us outside time? Spend your life in a frozen world?"

"Not exactly. See, I got to thinking about those towns of yours. And the way you talk about the power within them ripening. And I started wondering what would happen if that power wasn't harvested. What if it was left alone? Would it eventually turn rotten? Unusable?"

Wilm said, "That's just an analogy." But Zed could see in her eyes it wasn't.

"You've told me you need that power. So what will happen to you if it's all used up? How many towns are there? Not more than a few dozen, I'll bet. Whatever you did to me is permanent. I don't need that energy to survive. But you do. You need it to stay alive here on Earth. So I'm thinking I'll just wait you out."

She shook her head sadly. "It won't work. For a single town's power to go rotten could take a thousand years."

Zed shrugged. "I've got a thousand years."

"And a rotting town will not be a pleasant place."

"I'm a man of simple needs."

"Sounds like you've got it all figured out. Why tell me?"

Zed stood up. He wanted to be standing over her. "Because, when you're weak and dying, I want you to know who it was that beat you."

She opened her mouth to speak, but then stopped. She cocked her head, as if listening.

There was something. Zed heard it too. It was like a distant chorus of voices singing.

"*Zed.*"

Wilm's lips curled into a smile.

"*Zed.*"

The door to the diner eased open, and a swirling black shadow slipped inside. It circled the room.

"*Zed. We know of you. You step in and out of the river of time, but we smell its stink upon you.*"

Zed's eyes tried to follow the swirling mass spinning around the room, but it made him dizzy.

"You've made a mistake," Wilm said. "Just because you can drive a car doesn't mean you know how the engine works. And time is a pretty damn big car. It just so happens I know my way around it very well." She reached out her hand and brushed it against the passing black cloud. The creature or creatures let out a sound like a purr. "The Ones Who Sing were among the first we encountered when we came here. We have a certain understanding."

"*Zed,*" the creatures sang, "*you do not belong here.*"

Zed took a hesitant step backwards.

"*You do not belong in the river, either. Not anymore.*"

The cloud was closing in on him now, he could feel it.

"*You do not belong anywhere.*"

He'd wanted to stay longer, to rub it all in Wilm's face a bit more. But these creatures. The Ones Who Sing.

"*You are a vile thing, a creature no longer human.*"

The cloud contracted and wrapped itself around his arms. It flowed over him like a thousand razors. He let out a scream as they slid over his skin. If he survived this, he would heal. That was his gift. But, damn, did it hurt now.

Enough messing around. Time to go. He pressed the broken clock symbol on the pocket watch. And nothing happened.

His eyes grew wide with horror.

"Oh, yes, these creatures have a bit of power over time themselves," Wilm said. "If they don't let you go, you're not going anywhere."

The creatures flowed over his chest and back. His clothes had been cut away and he felt his skin falling away in ribbons.

"Sometimes," Wilm said. "It's a bad thing not to be able to die."

He couldn't move. They were gripping his arms, legs, and neck, holding tight even as they rolled over him with their razor bodies.

Wilm took a step toward him. "I may get tired of watching this in a few days. Then I'll think of something else to do with you. Unless you'd rather I took away your powers and let you die now?"

Zed grunted in frustration, and it came out as a scream. His face was the only part of him not covered in the black mass.

"Oh that's right," Wilm said. "You love your power. You'd do anything to keep it."

Zed reached out with his mind. The usual electric-sweet buzz of the pocket watch was muted. But it was there, he realized. It was there. If only he could reach it.

"See, what you don't understand is that the best you can ever hope to be against me and mine is a mild annoyance," Wilm said. "And I don't say that as an insult. It's more than anyone else has ever done. You've hidden the Tools, and that's something."

She leaned close as she spoke. "But we will find them. And that pocket watch of yours will go to some other pathetic little boy. Hopefully one that minds."

Zed felt it, the power of the pocket watch. He felt a tiny

thread of it wiggling out from the black cloud of singing creatures. He grabbed onto it with his mind and pulled as hard as he could.

And then the Ones Who Sing were gone. It was just Wilm and Zed standing in the diner, one of them with a smirk on her face and the other naked and barely looking human through the ribbons of ruined skin and streams of running blood.

Zed felt the room spinning and knew he was about to lose consciousness. Before he did, he squeezed the pocket watch, pressed the symbol on it, and took himself out of time. He didn't go as deep as he had been—no, he hoped to never go that deep again. He just went down one level. Far enough that Wilm would be frozen in the present.

His last thought was that he'd won. It hadn't been how he'd envisioned it, not at all, but, at least for the moment, he'd won.

He collapsed to the floor in a thick pool of his own blood and passed out.

CHAPTER EIGHT: THE QUARRY

1.

Alice gripped her sword. "Okay, Zed, I hope you have a plan. Because they're here."

The muscles in Zed's jaw stood out as he gritted his teeth.

"I do have a plan. But it's going to take a few minutes. Can you hold them off for a bit?"

Alice blinked hard. "You want me to fight them?"

"That wouldn't be my approach, but you do have a big sword. Just distract them. Keep them busy."

Frank said, "I'll go with her."

"No," Zed said. "I need you here. You're part of my plan."

Mason said, "She's not going alone."

Zed nodded curtly. "Fine. You go, Mason. The rest of you stay."

Alice glanced at Mason. She remembered the old man looking up and seeing her in her hiding place at the top of the stairs. No other adult had ever noticed her up there.

"I don't suppose you're armed?" she asked.

Mason shook his head.

"You really brave or really stupid?"

He held up a compass. "This is a Tool. It'll point to

anything you ask it to. I just asked it to show me a safe place, and the needle didn't move. So I'm thinking out there is just as good as in here."

They left the shed and joined the crowd gathered in Volunteer Park.

The first thing Alice noticed was the stillness. Groups of people this large were always in motion. Like a body of water, they swayed and swelled. But this group was perfectly still. Their eyes were on the sky. Alice followed their gaze.

Wilm, Vee, and San floated thirty feet off the ground. Wilm had her hands stretched out like a benevolent god. San had hers crossed over her chest. The hulking, armless, Vee floated to the left of the other two.

Never had the three of them appeared less human. The way they held themselves, the way they almost glowed, was a glimpse past their human disguises and into what they really were. It made Alice sick to her stomach. She'd been working with them for so long now, she often thought of them as people. But they weren't. They were deadly parasites here to feed off the Earth until there was nothing left of it.

"People of King's Crossing," Wilm said in a booming voice. "We have come seeking a book. It has a symbol on the cover. An object with a crack through it. Give us the book, and we will leave."

"Seems unlikely," Mason muttered.

Vee leaned over and whispered something in Wilm's ear. She nodded, and he smiled.

Suddenly he shot through the sky like a bolt.

Vee slammed through the roof of the shed like it was made of paper. The crowd listened in silence as the sound of shouts and screams came from the shed.

"No," Alice whispered.

A moment later Vee emerged, floating through the hole he'd blasted in the roof. His face and torso were covered in blood. The book with the broken man symbol floated next to him.

"It's done," he said.

"No," Alice whispered again. It couldn't go down like that. She wouldn't allow it.

She Pulled Back.

"Give us the book, and we'll leave," Wilm said.

Alice took a step forward. If she distracted them, maybe Vee wouldn't notice the shed.

"Hey boss!" Alice yelled at the sky. "I've always wondered what my sword could do against one of you. Want to find out?"

Wilm looked over at her. Fire burned in her eyes, but her voice was calm. "Ah. We were looking for you. I'm afraid we're going to have to let you go. Vee?"

Vee rocketed through the air toward her. He snarled the word, "Traitor!" as he flew.

Alice gripped her sword. She had no idea if it could hurt Vee, but she really wanted to find out. Only downside was, if the sword didn't work, she was dead.

She heard a voice through the crowd, a voice she hadn't heard it ten years. Her father. "Alice!"

She couldn't risk it. What good would she do if she died two seconds into the fight? Besides, she suddenly wanted to live through this, if she could. For her parents.

She Pulled Back.

"Give us the book, and we'll leave," Wilm said.

Okay, clearly a direct challenge wasn't going to work. She briefly considered Pulling Back a bit further, back to when they'd been standing in the shed. That way she could wait with the sword raised, let Vee impale himself when he came crashing through the roof. But, no, that wouldn't work either. Even if she succeeded in killing Vee, there were two others to deal with.

She had to make them believe she was still working with them. She had to trick them.

Easier said than done when your bosses were mind readers.

Still, hadn't she done it before? Hadn't she Pulled Back hundreds of times without their knowledge? The trick, she knew, was to not out-and-out lie to them. They could tell when she was lying, and then they'd go digging around in her head. She couldn't give them a reason to do that.

If she could tell the truth, but spin it so it sounded like what she wanted them to hear, if there was no *actual* lie, they might not be tipped off and they'd have no reason to read her mind. It took them time and effort, and at the moment they had neither.

She had to make them think she was still working for them.

"Hey boss!" Alice yelled at the sky.

Wilm looked over at her, the fire burning in her eyes just like last time. "Ah. We were looking for you."

"Yeah, I know," she said. "Sorry about that. I Pulled Back and came here on my own."

Wilm squinted at her. "I didn't feel that."

No lies, Alice reminded herself. "Yeah, I can do that now. I've been doing it for a while." She paused only for a breath, not wanting to let Wilm respond. "Listen, this whole thing didn't go so well the first time around, so I needed to come back for a redo." Not technically a lie.

"Is that so?" Wilm asked.

"Yeah," Alice said. "And I have good news. I know where the book is." Not a lie, but, crap, now what? If she gave them a false location, they'd know she was lying.

This wasn't going to work, either. She tried to Pull Back, and realized she couldn't.

San smiled. "Let's just see how this plays out, okay?"

2.

Frank knelt on the floor next to Jake and put a hand on his forehead.

My God, Frank thought. *Zed actually did it.*

Jake weakly opened his eyes.

Something was keeping Jake alive, Frank realized. Jake had been dead the moment Frank stepped through the tree in Sanctuary. Now Jake had been laying here almost five minutes. He wasn't exactly looking his best, but he wasn't dead, either.

"Frank, are you with me?" Zed asked. "We need to pull this together very quickly. Those things out there, my former bosses, they're not slow at killing."

Frank nodded, then paused. "Wait. You said you'd bring back Sophie's sister and Mason's mom first."

Zed looked a little annoyed. "Let me explain the situation. We are moments away from dying. Us and everyone we've ever cared about. So, no, I don't have time to bring your friends back from the dead." He paused and his voice grew a bit softer. "I will later, if we live though this, but not now."

Frank looked at Sophie. There were tears standing in her eyes. She wanted her sister back just as badly as Frank had wanted Jake. It didn't seem fair that he should get his wish and she shouldn't get hers. On the other hand, what would it matter if they were all dead in five minutes?

Sophie nodded, showing him it was okay through a forced smile. Frank appreciated the effort.

"Okay," Frank said to Zed. "You said you have a plan."

"I do," Zed said. "It's you."

"Wait. What?" Frank felt his heart begin to beat faster. "No, no, no. You've always got a plan. If you don't have anything better than waiting for me to come up with something, we're all toast."

Zed stared into Frank's eyes, and Frank felt the crawling sensation of something squirming over his brain.

Frank tore his eyes away from Zed's. "Don't do that."

Zed smiled sadly. "There's something in there. Something big. I see it every time I look into your mind. Ever since that time I knocked on the door of your cabin in Rook Mountain. There's something hidden away. And I don't think even you know what it is. But I have a theory."

Frank shook his head violently. "You're wrong. There's nothing hidden in my head." He wasn't sure why, but the very suggestion made him unreasonably angry.

Zed took a step forward. "Remember the deadlock. The lock that can only be opened with a key. Most minds are more like deadbolts. We control the bolt ourselves. But I think your mind, parts of it anyway, are a deadlock. Not even you can get into it."

"No. You're talking crazy."

"I've been searching for the key for a long time now," Zed continued. "I was hoping I could find it and take whatever power's lurking up there. But I give. We're out of time. I don't have the key." He looked around the room. "But maybe someone here does."

They all looked at Zed, their eyes wide.

"We have your brother," Zed said. "Your wife. Your former sister-in-law and her husband, the people who helped you take me down in Rook Mountain. If anyone knows what's inside your head, it's one of them. But," he turned to Jake, "I'm guessing it's him. Because he has it too. Not nearly as badly as you do. But there's a block in his mind I can't quite see around."

Jake stared up at Zed, a combination of fear and anger in his eyes.

"So tell us, Jake. What is it Frank doesn't know?"

Jake's forehead felt hot and dry under Frank's hand. He looked up at Frank. His voice was weak when he spoke. "I was just talking to you. Through the tree." Jake chuckled. "Who was that girl with the sword?"

"Long story." Frank nodded toward Zed. "Tell this idiot. Tell him there's not something locked in my mind."

Jake smiled. "There's nothing I like more than telling Zed he's wrong. But…" He trailed off, looking at the ceiling. "I don't know, man. When I was talking to you a few minutes ago, I mentioned the quarry. You acted like you had no idea what I was talking about."

Frank felt like the room was spinning. Something was tickling the back of his mind. He'd felt it before, the first time Jake had mentioned the quarry and again when Zed claimed Frank had burned the Rook Mountain book. It didn't feel nice. It made him nauseous, actually. He wanted to push it away.

He suddenly knew Zed was right. There was something in there. Something he didn't want to face. "I don't…" Frank said. "I don't know what the quarry is."

Jake reached up with a weak hand and touched his brother's arm. "Yes, you do. We used to go there every day after school."

Frank felt a stabbing pain behind his eyes. "I don't. I can't."

He felt Sophie's arm slip around his shoulders.

"Yes you can, Frank," Zed said. "And I think I've given you a way in. I brought Jake here. Which means that he was gone when you walked through that tree. But also that he wasn't."

Frank groaned.

"Picture it, Frank. Remember."

Frank did. He remembered stepping through that tree and seeing Sophie for the first time. His dead brother was at his feet. He also remembered stepping through the tree and Sophie telling him Jake had vanished a moment before Frank had stepped through.

"Now," Zed said. "There are two sets of memories. See if you can peek between them. Look into the secret part of your mind."

Frank didn't want to. It hurt to think about it. But he had to. He knew he had to.

He forced his way into the gap, and a flood of memories hit him.

3.

Rook Mountain
1996

They left school and headed toward the quarry. Frank wanted to swing by the house and get a Mountain Dew and maybe a granola bar or something, but Jake wouldn't hear of it. If they went home, Sean Lee would likely spot them. And if that happened he'd either try to talk them into playing a game of pick-up basketball or want to follow them wherever they were going. Playing basketball with Sean wasn't much fun due to his aversion to playing defense—No D Lee they called him—and he certainly couldn't follow them where they were going.

The quarry was Jake and Frank's secret.

They rode up Baron Mills Road, nine-year-old Frank pedaling as hard as he could trying to keep up with his eleven-year-old brother. Jake didn't wait around, and Frank didn't blame him. They were both excited to get there.

They turned onto a tiny trail. It was so small you might not have noticed it if you were walking past, and you definitely wouldn't notice it if you were driving. It was a sickly, winding dirt thing. Leaves and branches smacked against Frank's bare arms as he went down the trail. It didn't hurt, exactly. He wasn't going fast enough for it to really make a difference. In fact, it made things even more exciting. He felt like Indiana Jones, blazing his way toward the idol, dodging traps and pitfalls every step of the way. Sometimes he even muttered to himself, "This belongs in a museum." Never when Jake was too close, though.

By the time Frank reached the small clearing where the trail veered off to the right, Jake was sitting on the ground, arms crossed over his legs, bike on the ground next to him as if he'd been waiting for hours. Only the small beads of sweat on his forehead and his heavy breathing betrayed the fact that he'd put any effort into getting here so quickly. Frank had recently gone through a growth spurt that had cut the height difference between he and his brother to an inch or so. Now Jake was having to push himself to make it seem like he was still so physically superior.

It made Frank feel a little good, catching up to Jake. He knew it wouldn't last. Jake would hit his next growth spurt and shoot ahead of him again. But it made Frank feel slightly sad, too. His big brother wouldn't always be bigger. At some point, Jake would stop having growth spurts and Frank would catch up with him.

But that was a long way off. For today, they had the quarry.

Frank hopped off his bike before it stopped rolling and let it fall to the grass. Jake jumped to his feet. It was a race to the quarry. Both boys held nothing back. Frank had a slight head start, but even though his legs were almost as long as Jake's now, they weren't nearly as strong. Jake jetted past him and squirmed his way through the entrance to the quarry.

Frank sighed. Always second place.

They'd discovered the quarry two months ago while playing in the woods. No, Jake didn't like to   call it *playing* anymore. He was too old for playing. Exploring, then. Or hiking. Whatever you wanted to call it, they'd been riding down Baron Mills Road on their bikes when Frank had wiped out while trying to do a wheelie. The downside was he'd scraped up his right knee and elbow pretty good. The upside was they'd discovered the trail.

They'd followed the trail, ignoring the blood running down Frank's arm and leg. It had seemed so strange. How many times had they been down that road? They were less than a mile from their house, and there was a trail they didn't know about? It seemed impossible. Worse, it seemed wrong; it was an affront to their dominion over their neighborhood kingdom. That rebellious trail had come into their land and set up shop without even a courtesy hello to the land's rulers.

Once they'd gotten over the initial shock and indignation, they'd been quite happy about the trail. After all, if they hadn't known about it, it was a safe bet that none of the other kids in the neighborhood did, either. The trail was theirs. The Hinkle boys. And woe to the kid who tried to encroach on their precious territory.

It wasn't until their third day exploring the trail that they'd found the hole in the hillside, and it wasn't until the fifth trip that they worked up the courage to climb into the hole.

It was a cave. Not a huge cave, not the Batcave or anything, but a big enough cave that you could stand up and move around in there. The ground was rocky, and it sloped away from the entrance in a way that made Jake think of the piles of rocks at Fred's workplace at the beginning of the Flintstones. So they'd dubbed the cave *the quarry*. Neither of them knew exactly what the word really meant, but it had a nice ring to it. And giving the cave its own name made it feel even more special.

They began visiting the cave, exploring there on a regular basis. It was a kid's dream. A cave of their own. They came home, night after night, the cave's red mud covering their clothes. Their mom wasn't exactly the hands-on type, so as long as they started their own laundry, she didn't much care.

And, beyond all reason, they actually managed to keep the place secret.

Somehow, it wasn't until their fourth time going inside the cave that they found the shelf. It was built into a wall, tucked back in a corner. To call it a shelf was a bit grand. It was actually just a level surface dug out of the mud, creating a little space. And on the shelf, there was a book and a knife.

Frank was immediately drawn to the knife. It was sharp as all hell as he quickly and painfully learned, and it looked like it would slide between a pirate's ribs without too much trouble. Best of all, there was a strange symbol on the knife's handle. A clock with a crack running down the middle.

Frank liked to pretend it was some ancient Cherokee weapon, never mind the clearly modern clock carved into it. Maybe it was left by a dying Cherokee chief as he held off his enemies while the children of the tribe huddled in the cave behind him. Or maybe it belonged to a Cherokee princess who'd used it to cut her own throat after her father had forced her to marry someone she didn't love.

Mostly, Frank just used it to whittle sticks into slightly sharper sticks.

But Jake, he only had eyes for the book.

The book was at least three inches thick and bound with a rich red leather that almost perfectly matched the color of the mud in the quarry. It too had a symbol: a river with a crack running through it. A broken river. That didn't even make sense to Frank, but Jake seemed to like it.

The fact that both the knife and the book carried similar symbols and they were found together made it hard to deny they were somehow related. That complicated Frank's Cherokee fantasy, but whatever. Maybe the book had belonged to the chief's dorky brother.

The curious thing about the book was that the pages were blank.

But that didn't stop Jake. He looked at those pages under the pale beam of his flashlight like they had naked women on them or something. Jake was like that with books. Frank only read when forced by threat of failing school, but Jake read for fun. Jake loved stories. Frank made his own.

Staring at blank pages, that was just weird.

But whatever. Frank played with his knife and Jake looked at his blank book, all by the light of a couple flashlights. He'd thought that sitting around a damp and—to be honest—kind of smelly cave would have gotten old fast. But it didn't. Something about the place was exciting. They were drawn there. Frank couldn't stop thinking about it when they weren't there, and he knew it was the same for Jake. So they'd started going every day.

Then things had started to get weird. Not with Frank; he

was still just sharpening sticks business as usual. With Jake. He swore some of the pages had words on them.

Frank checked. They most definitely did not.

But Jake wouldn't be talked out of it. He started talking about how the words were there, Frank just couldn't see them. They hadn't revealed themselves to Frank.

It got so Frank stopped looking forward to going down to the cave. Not so much that he *stopped* going, but enough that his feelings about the place were mixed at best. Despite his concern for his brother, he found he couldn't stay away. That knife was just too cool.

Frank stood by the entrance to the quarry. He saw a dim light inside and knew Jake would have already moved to his usual place in the corner and would have the book in his hand. Weird.

Frank squeezed through the entrance and took the knife off the shelf. He sat down, pulled a stick out of his backpack —he carried them with him everywhere now—and started whittling. He didn't ever do anything with the sharp sticks except throw them into his backpack. If vampires ever attacked Rook Mountain, he would totally be ready.

Frank whittled and let his mind wander.

That was one of his favorite things about working with the knife. Normally he had a hard time relaxing. It felt like his mind was always going a million miles per hour, thoughts, worries, feelings, rushing through his head. But when he held the knife, it felt so easy to just let all that drift away.

He didn't know how long had passed before a strange groaning sound woke him from his wanderings.

It was Jake.

Jake was staring straight ahead, unblinking. Frank's first thought was, *Is that how I look when I'm spacing out?* His second was, *Something's not right.*

The strained groan came from Jake's throat again. It was a deep, gurgling sound. A sound that shouldn't come from an eleven-year-old boy. His finger was moving across the page of the open book in a strange, methodical fashion.

He groaned again. It sounded like he was in pain. Then Frank noticed vines growing up from the ground, slowly crawling up Jake's leg.

Frank watched in silent terror as a vine curled itself around Jake's leg. Jake groaned again, and Frank realized it was squeezing.

"Jake," Frank said. He meant to whisper, but his voice sounded loud in the silence of the cave.

Jake didn't move. His eyes stared straight ahead and his finger kept moving across the page.

"Jake!" Frank said, louder this time so it echoed off the walls.

Still nothing. The vine was crawling upward, and it didn't seem to be moving so slowly now. It was almost at Jake's knee.

How was that possible? A killer vine growing in a cave? It had to be caused by that damn book.

Frank shook Jake. Nothing. He tried to pry the book away from Jake. Even though Jake was only holding on with his left hand, his grip was like iron.

Frank blinked back tears of panic and desperation. "I don't know what to do."

Except, suddenly, he did.

He scooped up the knife and gripped it tight. His brother was going to be *pissed*, but he didn't see what other choice he had.

He brought the knife down, stabbing the book.

Then he began to scream.

It felt like being electrocuted. Or rather, what he imagined being electrocuted felt like. Something was flowing out of the book, through the knife, and into him. It hurt—bad—but there was something else there, too. He felt strong. Under the pain there was power coursing through him.

Jake blinked and looked up, staring at Frank with wide eyes. He looked as helpless as Frank had felt a few moments ago.

The book in Jake's hands burst into flames. Frank had his hands inches away from the book, but he felt no heat. Jake didn't seem to be feeling the fire either, even though he was holding the book on his lap.

After a moment, all that was left of the book was a pile of ashes.

Frank staggered back, dropping the knife, and gasped. The pain was gone now. All that was left was the power. But that power…

Frank took a breath, and it seemed like he could feel each and every molecule of air. Not only feel them. He thought, if he'd wanted to, he could rearrange them. He heard a voice— *What's happening to him*—and realized he was hearing Jake's thoughts.

He reached for the knife, and before he could get to it, it came to him.

It was too much. Too much power. He could hear things. Earthworms digging. Birds adjusting their balance on the branches outside. The electricity buzzing through the power lines by the road.

He couldn't handle it. His mind felt like it was on fire. It was all too much.

He felt the pain of a rat as it lay dying from a wound a muskrat had given it the day before. He tasted the cigarette smoke being exhaled by a man in a cabin half a mile away.

And above all, he felt something else. A power even greater than his own. No, four powers. He could see the things they'd done. My God, they'd devoured stars.

And if they noticed him...he knew they would consume him. And how could they not notice him? His power was singing at the top of its lungs. It couldn't happen. It had to stop.

He needed to quiet the power. But even then, it wouldn't be enough. What if they heard his thoughts? He had to hide it. So he did. He used the power to hide itself. He built a brick wall in the back of his mind in a place no one, not even he, could see.

They left the quarry, leaving the knife and the pile of ashes inside. When they were outside, Frank noticed a tiny bit of power still floating around. The wall in his mind was still solidifying. He used the power to build a similar wall in Jake's mind. Jake couldn't remember either, not if they were going to be safe.

As he was still building the wall in Jake's mind, Frank began to forget. What was he doing? What were they doing there?

They wordlessly got on their bikes. By the time they'd arrived home, Frank had forgotten the quarry had ever existed.

4.

King's Crossing, Wisconsin
January, 2022

Frank snapped his head up. It had all come back to him in a moment. How had he forgotten? All that time they'd spent there. What did it mean?

He looked down at Jake. "I remember," Frank said. "I

remember the quarry."

Jake nodded. Was it Frank's imagination, or did Jake look a bit stronger than he had a moment ago?

"Good," Jake said. "It's strange when I think about it. I know we used to go there. I can remember us riding our bikes there day after day, and I remember going in the cave. But I don't remember anything that happened inside the cave. It's like there's a cloud over it or something."

Frank smiled weakly. "Yeah, sorry, buddy. I think I was the one who put that cloud in your head. Only I didn't finish. That's why you remember part of it."

"We went back, you know." Jake looked at Christine. "You remember? Where we found the knife?"

Christine nodded and smiled. "You wouldn't go in there. I thought that was pretty weak, making your wife go in the dark cave because you were too scared."

"Yeah. I didn't know why I did that. It was like I couldn't make myself go in."

"But the message you gave to Sally Badwater," Frank said. "Why'd you tell me to meet you at the quarry?"

Jake looked off into the distance. "I don't know. I was confused, going through the mirror. You've felt it. You know. It's disorienting. I wanted to give Will the message about Sean. But also..." He looked into Frank's eyes now and put his hand on his brother's shoulder. "I remember being safe in the quarry. I remember you saving me. Not the details, but the feeling. The feeling that you would do anything to help me. And I needed to feel that again."

And suddenly, Frank knew what he needed to do.

The books absorbed the potential of humanity, and Jake was hurt because he'd overused the book. Could it be the book had absorbed too much of him?

But Frank had absorbed an entire book. The potential of an entire town.

And Jake had regained a bit of his strength when Frank had touched him, both when he'd first come through the tree and again when Frank touched his forehead a few moments ago.

If Frank could somehow share the energy with Jake...if he could give back what the book had taken...

Frank concentrated on the hand resting on Jake's forehead. He focused on letting the energy flow out of him and into his brother.

Jake's eyes suddenly shot open and he gasped.

Frank pulled his hand away and Jake visibly relaxed.

"Holy hell, Frank," Jake said. "Whatever you just did...I think you fixed me. That was some strong stuff."

Frank grinned, love for his brother suddenly washing over him. "I think I almost gave you an overdose." Frank's eyes were filled will tears. His brother was back. For real this time.

Zed crouched down next to them. He was smiling wide now. "I knew it. The book here in King's Crossing hid itself away from the compass. The only other thing I've seen do that is your locks. That was my first clue. I tested the theory by trying to open a portal here in the shed to bring Rayd through. That worked, even without the book. Because you were here. The same power that's in the books is in you." He put a hand on Frank's shoulder. "What did you see? What did you remember?"

Frank hesitated. He'd come to trust Zed over the last seven years more than he'd ever thought possible. He'd given Zed the book willingly. He'd trusted him with his life today.

But it was still Zed. Frank wasn't ready to share everything with the man who'd sent him Away. Who'd tried to kill him and everyone he cared about. Who'd tried to steal Rook Mountain from time itself.

"It was like you said," Frank replied. "I remember burning the book in Rook Mountain."

At that moment, the door flew off the shed, as if ripped free by a tornado. This was all the more confusing when Frank saw the man standing in the doorway had no arms. Vee.

Vee glared at them and growled, "Zed."

He stepped inside, followed quickly by a woman with blonde hair and a tall, muscular woman with black hair.

And behind them was Alice. The girl stumbled into the shed. "Sorry," she said, tears in her eyes. "They read my mind. Then I couldn't Pull Back. They locked me down."

Frank had no idea what she was talking about, but that hardly seemed like the worst of his problems at the moment.

The blonde woman smiled when she saw the book in Zed's hand. "Ah," she said. "You've found the book for us."

5.

Sophie stood statue still.

Sophie didn't consider herself someone who scared easily, but Vee frightened the hell out of her. She'd seen Jake turn him into a tree, and he'd still managed to kill Jake. Well, not kill him, she supposed. He was alive now. This whole time travel thing still confused her.

The blonde woman stepped forward. She carried herself with such authority that Sophie realized she had to be Vee's boss.

"Zed, it's time," she said. "You've been on the run a good long while. You put up a respectable fight. And taking out Rayd…well, I didn't think you had it in you."

Zed's smile widened. "Wilm, you don't know the half of it."

Wilm returned his smile, and Sophie had the strange idea that maybe this woman had taught Zed how to smile through the pain. "What I don't understand is why? You let Sugar Plains rot and lived in the decaying town for a thousand years just so we wouldn't get the power. Why? What did it get you?"

Zed took a step forward and looked her in the eye. "Because fuck you. That's why."

She shook her head sadly. "We gave you life. Endless life."

"No," Zed said. "That's not true, is it? You gave me life that would last as long as this Earth. And this Earth isn't lasting much longer."

Wilm shrugged. "What did you want from us?"

"I wanted to be one of you. You could have made me like you, taken me with you when you leave. Instead you made into some sort of Renfield to your Dracula. Doing your bidding and waiting to be cast aside."

The woman with black hair stepped forward. "You're lucky you got that much. If I had my way—"

Wilm held up her hand. "Let's not be dramatic. Give me the book, Zed."

Zed snaked out his tongue and licked his lips. "Listen, this book…" He held it up. "This book contains more power than you've ever consumed at once. Enough to get you off this world and back to your homes. If give it to you, you'll go and leave this world to the Ones Who Sing."

Wilm shrugged. "If that's so, it's so. This world has taken two of our own. The first was my husband. We made Tools out of him when he died. His people were a whimsical sort; they chose the clock as their seal in a land without time. And now Rayd is gone too. This world takes too much and gives too little. Its people squirm under our thumb, never satisfied. Always wanting more. You are the perfect example. You could have served us far longer than you did. You could have used your powers to seek pleasure, but instead you only used it to try for more power."

"Our people call that ambition," Zed said.

"Our people call it stupid," the black-haired woman said.

"These people you've surrounded yourself with," Wilm said. "Did it feel good to lead them? These meaningless toads? As if anyone other than you and Alice are even worth so much as a glance. And I'm beginning to have my doubts about you."

Sophie tightened her grip on her husband's arm. Worthless. That's how these aliens or demons or whatever they were saw the rest of them in this shed. As worthless.

And suddenly Sophie realized that might not be a bad thing. They didn't know about Will and Christine, how they'd spent years hiding the Tools in Rook Mountain before finally facing off with Zed on the roof of city hall. They didn't know about Sophie and the great and powerful evil that Zed claimed lived inside her. And they didn't know about Frank. About his fight against the Unfeathered. Or his fight in the Away and the against Ones Who Sing. Frank had survived them all.

Christine, Will, Frank, and her all together? Plus Zed and the weird teenager with a sword? That seemed like a pretty formidable force against even these creatures.

Wilm stepped toward Zed. She reached out a hand and placed it gently on his arm.

"Did you feel it?" she asked in a voice that sounded almost kind. "Did you feel it flowing out of you? Everything we gave you? All the power? You're a normal man now. You'll age. You can be hurt or killed."

Zed's lip quivered as he glared at her, but his voice was steady. "What do I care about aging if the world is going to be gone by the end of the day?"

Wilm shrugged. "Just thought you'd want to know."

Vee rolled his head in a circle and his neck cracked sharply. "Can I rip off his arms now?"

"What's the point?" Wilm asked. "He fought us, and he made a good effort of it. But he's powerless now. Might as well let him watch the end. He's got nothing left."

"You're wrong," Zed said. "I've got something you've never seen before. I've got Frank Hinkle." With that, he dropped the book into Frank's hands. Both Frank and the book disappeared.

"Frank," Zed said. "Run. Run and never come back."

THE MAN WITH THE WATCH (PART TWO)

1.

Sugar Plains, Illinois
Sometime after 1985

Zed walked the deserted streets of the place that had once been Sugar Plains, Illinois. It was strange, the way it was happening. He'd expected decay over time. He'd expected things to fall apart once no one was around to fix them, or even to care if they were broken. But he hadn't expected this. The signs of civilization, of the town ever having been there, were simply fading away. The street under his feet was dirt now. Not long ago it had been blacktop. One morning, the blacktop had simply been gone. It had startled Zed a bit, but probably not as much as it should have.

He'd spent years outside of time before, decades in each of the four towns he'd ripened for his former masters. But this was longer. Near as he could tell, he'd been in Sugar Plains for three-hundred-twenty years. Yet still the white bird creatures gathered outside town each night, more of them every year. If they were his canary in the cage when it came to gaging the ripeness of the town, it was far too healthy for his liking.

Still, he believed in the soundness of his plan. The energy would eventually spoil. Or dissipate. Or something. It would become unusable to his former masters. He would wait for however long it took. And then he'd move on to the next town. And he'd repeat the process until there was nothing left for them to draw from. Then he'd watch them slowly lose power and die.

That thought alone gave him strength to get through the long, lonely days.

The last of the people of Sugar Plains had died two years ago. It was a young girl. She'd been sick for a long time. Zed might have been able to save her if he'd put enough thought and research into the matter, but it hadn't seemed important then. Now, he was surprised to discover he missed the people. Not individually. One-on-one, people were annoying, like a bit of food stuck between his teeth. But over the last three centuries, he'd come to find he enjoyed people en masse. And he had a skill for speaking to them, for persuading them to his way of thinking. Communities of people, especially gathered together in a crowd, had an energy that was not unlike that of the pocket watch.

When he was being honest with himself, he had to admit it wasn't the people he missed at all. It was their admiration.

He brushed his hand along the trunk of a tall twisted tree as he passed it. The things had been springing up all over town for the past couple hundred years. He wondered how huge they would get before it was all done here. He understood that the trees were the natural expression of the overripe energy within the town. Something had to be done with that energy if powerful beings from God-knows-where weren't going to show up to devour it. And so the trees grew.

The book with the broken world on it had taught him that.

It had taught him so much more, too. Sometimes he wished there was someone else here to talk to about it. Preferably a large group.

He had set out this morning from his mansion on the edge of town—the mansion his people had built for him hundreds of years ago—with no clear destination in mind. But somehow he found himself where he always did on his daily walks. Downtown. It was vain perhaps, but he liked to take his lunch while looking at the statue they'd built of him.

He stood for a long moment, staring at the statue, before coming to the same conclusion he always did: it was a fair representation. The statue might not look exactly like Zed in the strictest sense. It was an idealized version of him. In the statue, he looked in the way his people saw him. And, even though his people were gone, this memory was a nice reminder of the feeling they'd given him.

"'Look upon my works, ye Mighty, and despair.'"

Zed started at the sound. It was so strange, so unexpected, that he had absolutely no idea how to respond. It had been years since he'd heard another voice.

The sound had come from behind him, so he slowly turned around.

Vee was even taller than Zed remembered, and his beard was even thicker. Zed was usually the tallest person in the room, back when there had been people and rooms, but Vee towered over him.

"This is what it's come to?" Vee asked. "You lording over a kingdom of rats? Making them build statues in your honor?"

Zed opened his mouth, trying to remember how to speak.

"It's pathetic," Vee continued. "You're king of a dead town."

"'Better to reign in hell than to serve in heaven,'" Zed said finally. He figured one classical reference deserved another. His own voice sounded strange in his ears. Oddly formal and distant.

Vee grunted. He brushed past Zed and walked to the statue. For a moment, Zed was sure the big man was going to attack the statue, maybe punch it or pull it down. Zed had no doubt Vee could do it. The man was built like a tree trunk.

"It's not a bad likeness," Vee said. He turned to Zed and looked him up and down. "You're in a spot of trouble, and I'm trying to figure out how to deal with you. Wilm would say to bring you home. She'd argue this display of initiative proved you were worth reforming. Rayd would demand satisfaction. He'd consider it an affront to his honor. San would probably just rip your face off."

"And you?" Zed asked in his strange, weak voice.

Vee shrugged. "I've always seen eye-to-eye with San in most respects. I'm not above being persuaded though."

"How'd you get here?" Zed asked, partly because he wanted to steer the conversation in another direction and partly because he was genuinely curious.

"You're not the only one who can manipulate time a bit. I noticed the stutter when you stopped time. I kept myself in that moment until I could muscle my way through."

Damn. Zed thought he'd corrected that problem. If things had worked correctly, Vee and the others shouldn't have been able to even tell he was gone. He had been so sure he was safe here.

His heart was racing. He eased his hand into the satchel hanging from his shoulder.

"Weren't expecting that, were you?" Vee didn't smile, but the way the skin wrinkled around his eyes gave Zed the vague impression that he was pleased. "After I tore myself free, it was simply a matter of following the bird creatures. They're drawn here. Though you've hidden the town from them, they still feel the pull of it now and again." He ran his hand over the calf of the statue of Zed. "And here I am."

Zed asked, "What about the others? Will they find their way here?"

"Perhaps. But I wouldn't count on it. You bound us up tight."

"And you always were the strong one."

Vee was staring up at the sun now. "Even though time is stopped, the sun keeps moving. Days and nights move here. But outside the town, it's always dusk. I crossed half the country with the setting sun in my eyes."

Zed held up the pocket watch. "I'm very good with this thing."

Vee chewed on that for a moment, as if trying to work it out. "What's it going to be, then? You want to take us back to the others? Start time again and let Wilm try to protect you? Or should I handle this here?"

Zed licked his lips. "I'd like to propose a third option."

Vee said nothing, but he was listening, which was a good sign. Zed was beginning to get the feeling the bearded man was more impressed with Zed than he let on. Impressed, and perhaps intrigued.

"I take it you can feel that?" Zed asked, indicating the air around them. There was no need to clarify what he was referring to. Zed could feel it whenever he touched the pocket watch. The energy in the air. It had been a long while since he'd used his powers of persuasion. It was comforting to see how fast they came back.

Vee nodded stoically.

Zed took that as another good sign and continued. "The

others towns we took weren't this ripe. Not by half. The energy here crackles." He paused for a moment, looking off into space as if he could see the power hanging in the air. "You gave me a choice, so now I'll give you one. We can go back to the others. I won't resist. Or, if you prefer it, you could keep all this energy for yourself."

Vee's eyes betrayed nothing. The man was stone. "We don't have the compass. Finding the book would be…difficult."

Zed released his million-watt smile, the one he reserved for his moments of greatest need. "That won't be a problem." He pulled the book with the broken world symbol out of his satchel.

Vee drew in a sharp breath. It was quiet, but Zed heard it. And when he did, Zed knew he had won.

"You found it," Vee said. It may have been Zed's imagination, but Vee's voice sounded a hair weaker than normal. "Without the compass. That must have been some search."

Zed shrugged. "I had three hundred years and a town of adoring people to help me. You'd be surprised what can be accomplished. It was hidden under a pew at the Lutheran church. A janitor found it. I rewarded him with three wives and the ability to read minds. I can share my powers now. Did you know that?"

Vee's eyes were on the book, a look of hunger on his face.

Zed casually flipped the book open. It sprang to just the page he'd needed. Of course, it had. God, he loved this book.

"This book is the embodiment of the power of this town," Zed said. "It's a thing of wonder. And it could be yours."

Vee seemed to come out of his daze. The big man took a step forward.

Zed ran his finger over the page, tracing the illustration

drawn there. "But it never will be."

Vee tried to take another step but was jerked backwards. It looked as if something was holding on to his foot. He looked down and his eyes widened. His foot was changing, burying itself in the ground. "What are you doing?" he groaned.

"I'm using the book," Zed said. "All these years, all this power, and all you idiots thought to do was consume it? You didn't stop for a moment to consider that it might be more useful in its current state than as fuel?"

Vee's body was lengthening now. It was truly something to behold. The book had said what would happen, but Zed hadn't fully believed it would work. Seeing it with his own eyes was something different.

Vee groaned as he transformed.

"Tell me," Zed said, "does it hurt?"

But he'd waited too long to ask. Vee's mouth was gone. A few moments later, there was a tree standing there. It looked no different from the dozen others throughout the town. Zed noticed with slight dismay that the statue had been knocked over during Vee's transformation. It lay on the ground in a dozen pieces.

But it didn't matter. This tree was the tribute to Zed's power now. He'd done the unthinkable. He'd beaten one of his former masters.

He hoped the rest of the Exiles *would* show up here so he could do the same to them. But they didn't. So he waited almost a thousand years, until the trees were thick and every trace of the town that had been was gone. His clothes fell apart and he forgot to replace them with new ones. He sometimes forgot his own name. But the book always reminded him.

Over time, the book faded. It still worked, but it had lost

the crackle of power it had once had. Even the words on the page seemed to fade in and out.

When the white bird creatures stopped coming and the Larvae began to appear, Zed knew this place was done. His former masters wouldn't be able to syphon any energy from it. The town had stopped producing the power, and the power had devoured it. The place no longer existed, at least not in the world it once had.

He used the book one last time to open a portal in a tree, and he travelled through time and space to the next town on his list.

He stepped out, naked and barely remembering how to speak, and looked at his new home. Rook Mountain, Tennessee.

2.

Rook Mountain
Sometime after March 27, 2014

Frank moved the knife toward Zed. "What happens if I open it?"

Zed looked at the box, the one with the lock on it. The Cassandra lock. But he wasn't paying attention to that. He was barely paying attention to conversation. He was attempting, not for the first time, to look inside Frank's mind. It was a maze in there. No, that wasn't quite right; it was a lock. A lock without a key.

They were in Rook Mountain City Hall. Frank had come here in the night seeking the box that now sat in front of him. The box that Zed used to store the bubble that kept the Unfeathered away. It was a mental trick and nothing more, a bit like a more extreme version of the memory palace technique orators had been using for centuries to remember seemingly impossible amounts of information. The box was Zed's mental trick, but opening the box would destroy the bubble nonetheless.

Zed tried to worm his way into the cracks in Frank's mind, but it wasn't working.

"What?" Christine asked. "Frank, don't open it. We don't know what will happen." The good Doctor Osmond had burst into the room a few moments before. Zed had barely noticed.

Something about Frank's mind, the lock without a key, sparked an idea in Zed. A lock with out a key. A box that had a bubble.

"Yeah," Frank said. "That's why I'm asking. So how about it, Zed? What happens if I open it?"

With that, it came to Zed. What if the box couldn't be opened? Not by anyone at all? "If you open that box, I leave. You are on your own. I'll leave this town to the Unfeathered."

"That's all I get?" Frank asked.

"That's all you get."

"How about if I start cutting you?"

Zed shrugged. "I might say a few more things, but would you believe them? You already know the important stuff. That box keeps the Unfeathered away. What else do you need to know?"

Zed waited, knowing what would happen, knowing Frank would open the box. He'd created the Cassandra lock after he'd seen it at the top of Frank's mind that day so long ago when they'd first met. Zed had put it on the box as a precaution because it would be so difficult to open. But it *could* be opened. What if there was a lock that couldn't be opened at all? Imagine what he could do with such a thing.

"Frank, no," Christine said.

Frank reached for the lock and twisted it, squeezing in exactly the right place and pulling at just the right angle. The lock snapped open. He lifted the box's wooden lid.

The four sides of the box collapsed outward onto the desk. The box was empty.

"That will be very difficult to replace," Zed said. It wouldn't. But he wanted to see how Frank would react if he put the potential death of the town on his head.

The room was silent for a long moment.

Christine put a hand to her mouth. "Oh, Frank. What have you done?"

"He's killed you all," Zed said.

Frank turned to Christine.

"No, it's okay," Frank said. "There was nothing in the box. That couldn't be what was keeping the Unfeathered away."

Zed twisted his face into a grimace. "It wasn't what was in the box. It was the box itself." This was true, after a fashion. It was the box that allowed Zed to hold two bubbles in his mind at once.

Christine looked at Zed. The gun hung from her hand. "You can fix it, right? You can fix the box?"

Zed picked up one of the pieces of wood and turned it over in his hand. "No," he said. "I can't. Whatever power it had is gone."

Frank looked at Christine. "Listen, it's all going to be okay."

"No, you listen," Christine said.

The sound came again. The sound of singing.

"The Birdies," Zed said. "Isn't that what you call them, doctor?"

Christine didn't answer.

"First they'll come in the night for people who happen to be outside," Zed said. "But then they will grow bolder. It won't be long before your homes aren't enough to protect you. Then they'll start attacking in the daytime." He turned the piece of wood in his hand over and over.

Zed set the piece of wood on the desk. "I'm leaving." He held out his hand to Frank. "Give me the knife. I need it where I am going."

Frank hesitated, then said, "No way."

Zed stood up. "That's what I figured. I suggest you two stay here for the night. It's going to be ugly out there."

He took one last look into Frank's mind. And there, right at the edge of things, he saw something that truly disturbed him. It was a still image and nothing more.

A book. The Rook Mountain book. And it was burning.

The image made no sense. Zed felt the power still building in this town. It had to be gathering somewhere. Had this man actually destroyed the book? Seemed impossible, but…

He marched across the room, giving Frank and Christine a final frown as he slipped through the open door. There was a flash of blue light as he shut the door behind him and transported himself across town.

Zed appeared a moment later in the basement workshop of his large home. He worked for a few hours, ignoring both the song of the Unfeathered and the screams of the Rook Mountaineers they were devouring. He crafted three small square boxes, an inch wide and tall, by soldering together scraps of metal. They didn't have to be strong. They just had to be without an opening. That done, he drilled tiny holes in them and ran a string through each, making them into necklaces.

He let the necklaces dangle from his fingers and surveyed his work. It was a rush job, that much was clear from looking at it, but it would do. He wasn't out to win any awards for craftsmanship. What he needed was functionality.

Zed drew a deep breath. He wasn't looking forward to transporting himself so far, but it had to be done. And then he could finally be at peace, for the first time in over a thousand years.

He materialized moments later outside a cabin deep in the Rocky Mountains. He kept his eyes shut for a few long moments, taking slow breaths and steadying his stomach. Traveling so far made him a bit ill.

Zed opened his eyes and was momentarily surprised to find it was dark. He'd forgotten it had been night when he'd taken Rook Mountain out of time. For the rest of the world, it still was nighttime.

His stomach flipped and flopped, twisting and cramping painfully, but is was nothing he couldn't manage. Back when he thought about such things, he'd wondered what traveling such long distances actually did to a person. His selectmen could travel, sure, but only across town. And even that had the strange result of melting and reconstructing their bodies. To travel as far as Zed just had…he wondered if the stomach pains he was experiencing were a sign of something much worse happening inside of him. He wondered if maybe his invulnerability was the only thing that kept him alive through the process.

He walked toward the cabin, enjoying the cool air on his face. If he hadn't known time was stopped, he could have thought this was just another night at Wilm's cabin. He'd spent many such nights like this back when he'd been in her good graces. He'd spent hours just sitting on the porch, the pocket watch in his hand—just being. Unlike those nights, it was silent now. The Unfeathered were far from this place. He was likely the only animated being in a thousand miles in any direction.

He pulled open the screen door and walked inside.

Sure enough, there she was, sitting in her favorite chair, an open book in her lap. Something non-fiction, undoubtably. She worked so hard to understand this world, both her source of power and her adopted home. She learned about the science and the history. But never the people. She never made an effort to understand what really made them tick. They were beneath her notice unless she needed something from them. Then she would bribe or coerce them as needed.

That was what made Zed better than her. He might not love the people—even the ones who loved him—but he did understand them. And that made all the difference.

Still, this woman had made him what he was. Without her, best-case scenario, he would now be a very old man, looking back on a futile life and trying to find the meaning in it. He owed her something for that, didn't he?

He put a hand on the woman's rock-hard shoulder, and he was reminded of the statue that used to stand in the center of Sugar Plains before Vee knocked it down while changing into a tree. That statue and this woman were both equally as useful. Items that served only to remind him of past glories.

Nostalgia was all well and good, but Wilm's time had passed. She'd lived a long life. How long exactly Zed didn't know, but surely as long as anyone could expect. She'd spent it consuming power. It was Zed's time now. And he didn't intend to just consume power. He intended to cherish the power. Wield it. Put it to good use.

He put one of the necklaces around her neck. The tiny metal box thudded against her frozen chest.

He admired it there for a moment, admired the idea of it.

The question of how to deal with his remaining three

ormer masters had long weighed on him. He could send them deep in time, as he had with his fellow Toolsmen and Toolswomen, but he would have to remain with them. And unlike his fellow Tool bearers, his former masters would certainly find and kill him.

But if he created a bubble of time and put it in a box, a box that could not be opened, a lock without a key, if you will, he could allow the box to function independently. He could stay here while sending them there. He could even create another bubble to make the box slightly out of sync with their timeline so they couldn't destroy it. It was genius.

Even after a thousand years, Zed still managed to impress himself now and again.

He looked at Wilm one last time. He considered bringing her to life for a moment so they could talk. So she'd know who'd done this to her. But that was madness. Vanity. She might crush him in the few moments he spent talking to her. Anyway, she'd know who had done this to her. She'd know.

He reached out and tapped the box, mentally activating the bubbles inside, and she disappeared.

She'd live out the rest of her existence in a deep hole in time, the type of place where the Ones Who Sing lived. They might not kill her, but she wouldn't be able to escape, either. At long last, he was safe from Wilm.

Now all that remained was to find San and Rayd. He had some ideas where they might be. They too were creatures of habit. But finding them could potentially take a while. He decided he'd better get started.

As it turned out, finding and disposing of San and Rayd only took seven days. They were both in their favorite haunts, St. Louis, and Seattle, respectively. He sent both of them to the Away without so much as a word to them, same as he had

272

with Wilm.

Then he returned to Rook Mountain. He had an idea for another way the boxes could be used. He could use them to punish people. Enough of brandings and maimings, from now on whenever anyone broke Zed's rules he would send them to the Away to serve out their sentence. It would be a new rule. He'd call it Regulation 19.

CHAPTER NINE: THE LOCK WITHOUT A KEY

1.

"Frank," Zed said. "Run. Run and never come back."

Frank stood perfectly still. He carefully controlled his breathing even though any sound he made was hidden by the lock. He clutched the book in his hand. Zed clearly expected him to do something. Did he really want Frank to run?

Wilm looked around the room, her eyes wide. "How? What did you do?"

Zed chuckled. "Frank's been a thorn in my side for a long time now. I thought it was time you felt the pain."

Wilm looked at San. "Can you push through?"

San hesitated. "No. Whatever power he's using, it isn't ours."

"Smells familiar, though," Vee said. "There's a stink to it."

"Yes," Wilm said.

Frank's mind was still reeling from the memory of the quarry. Was that why he had the power to make the locks? Because of whatever it was he'd absorbed from the book? And was it that same power that had locked the memories away, even from himself?

And what exactly was he supposed to do with this book?

He could destroy it like he had the Rook Mountain book. He had the knife, after all. But what would that do to him? The Rook Mountain book had clearly messed with his head. Would his mind be able to hold another huge helping of that power?

Or maybe he wasn't supposed to destroy it. It was, after all, their only weapon against Wilm and the others. Not that he knew how to use it.

He needed to understand more about the book.

Wilm and the others were still distracted, trying to figure out what had happened to him. He reached out and touched Alice on the arm.

She let out a yelp of surprise as he suddenly became visible to her.

"It's okay," he said. "I've locked you away with me. They can't hear or see you."

"How are you doing this?" She spoke in a whisper. Frank understood. It was difficult to wrap your mind around the fact that you could speak openly in front of someone without them hearing you.

"I make these locks." He didn't have time to explain. "Look, you spent the last seven years with them, right? I need to understand more about the books. Zed said they're like batteries. What's this power they're trying to collect?"

She looked at Wilm for a long moment before answering. "Can we go outside?"

Frank suddenly realized the girl was terrified of Wilm. And who could blame her? She'd been kidnapped by the woman, after all. Frank nodded, and they slipped out the door.

The people of King's Crossing were chattering, confused.

Alice glanced up at the faces around them. "They can't see or hear us, either?"

Frank shook his head. "So you know about the books?"

Alice nodded weakly. "I know what I saw. And what they told me. They talked a lot about Zed and what he was trying to do. The way I understand it, the books are absorbing some kind of potential energy from the town. Or the people. And when the Exiles harvest the energy, it destroys the town. And if they don't harvest it, it slowly begins to decay, eventually destroying the town anyway, like what happened back in Sugar Plains, Illinois. That's what Zed was trying to do. Take the towns out of time so the batteries would eventually decay."

"And that's what he was trying to do with Rook Mountain," Frank said. Zed must not have known Frank had already absorbed the power from the book.

A thought occurred to him: the town hadn't been destroyed when he stabbed the book.

"Listen," Frank said, taking Alice by the shoulders. "I think I know a way to make it so they can't get their hands on the book. They'll never be able to get their hands on it."

"What are you gonna do?" she asked.

"I'm gonna destroy the book." He held up a hand before she could object. "I can do it without hurting the town. But is there anything we can do with the book? Any way we could use it to our advantage?"

She shook her head. "Not that I know of. Do your thing. Now."

He took a deep breath. "Hey, there's a chance this might not…I might not make it through this. I don't have time to say goodbye to Sophie."

Alice nodded quickly. "Yeah, I'll tell her you said all kinds of mushy stuff. Get on with it."

Frank gripped the knife and raised it over the book.

Before he could bring down the knife, a sudden shooting pain in his head sent him reeling.

A booming voice filled the air.

"That smell. I recognize that smell." It was San, the statuesque woman with black hair. She was floating over the crowd, searching it with her eyes. The people of King's Crossing stared up at her, frozen with fear and awe.

Another shockwave hit Frank's brain and he doubled over and let the book slip from his fingers. It felt like a wrecking ball hitting his skull from the inside. He realized he was lying on his back on the ground now, though he hadn't felt himself fall.

"It's a book," San said. "You're using the power from a book. But how?"

The pounding came again, now from another direction. Frank squinted up into the sky and saw Vee floating to his left. "We will break down the walls. You are like a child. You might be holding power, but you have no idea how to use it."

Frank wanted to say that the use of power assaulting him wasn't exactly subtle either, but he didn't think he currently had the power of speech. Another impact slammed into his head and drove him to his knees.

"You're somehow using the power to mask yourself from us," San said. "If I didn't recognize the taste of that power, I wouldn't have been able to find you at all. Despite what my brother Vee says, it's actually very nicely done."

Frank felt a cool hand on his shoulder. He turned his head, nausea rolling through him as he moved, and looked up, expecting to see Alice. Instead, he saw Wilm looking down at him.

"I'm very curious where you got that power," Wilm said.

A wave of pain rocked Frank, putting everything he'd felt

before it to shame. He lost the ability to even open his eyes. It felt like his mind was a gaping hole. He could barely hold a thought.

"Ah," Wilm said. "That's better. We can see you now."

"My guess is he was doing it instinctively," San said. "Probably didn't even realize how he was doing it. More the power protecting itself than him using it."

"And you, my dear Alice," Wilm said. "After everything we've done for you? I must say, I'm rather disappointed."

Frank still couldn't open his eyes. The world was dark, but he heard a squeal of pain or maybe terror that could only be Alice.

"Shall I burn out her mind?" That was Vee speaking, his distinctive low rumbling voice banging around in Frank's head like a gong.

"I hardly see the point," Wilm said. "She'll be dead in a few moments. They'll all be dead."

Frank let out a tiny moan. He managed to roll onto his side. A major accomplishment, as far as he was concerned. Maybe he should celebrate by resting for a moment or two.

"Ah," Wilm said. "The broken man."

She must be holding the book now, Frank realized. Soon this would all be over. The thought terrified him, but there was something sweet about it, too. An end to the pain. Not just his, but everyone's.

Wilm continued. "Did you know, Alice, that the symbols on these books represent the great families of our home? The icon of a lone man was the symbol of a proud family of warlords. I was briefly engaged to their second eldest son. They're long dead, of course. That's what the crack means. The family is no more. Jorrick, our old friend who built the books, did it as a way to honor the old families."

Alice yelped again. Frank wished he knew what they were doing to her. Or maybe he didn't.

"My husband's family symbol was the clock. They were a quirky bunch. Rayd's symbol was the mountain. So many families. So much history. All lost forever." She sighed.

"I can't wait to see what your symbol is," Alice said in a strained voice. "I'm gonna use your bones to make a plunger. I'll think of you every time I use it."

Wilm made a tsking noise. "Shall we?"

Frank forced his eyes open.

Wilm held the book. Her hand rested on the cover. San was reaching toward it. A silver, shimmering construct of an arm suddenly appeared on Vee's right side, and the hand reached toward the book.

Frank wanted nothing more than to close his eyes and wait for the end. He didn't know if it would be painful, but he was pretty sure it would be fast. And that was all he wanted. For it to be over fast.

He'd been through so much. So much pain. So much loneliness. And now it would be over.

Then he felt the heavy, cold weight of the knife in his hand. He remembered Christine and Will and Trevor risking everything to try to save him the day he was sent Away. He remembered Jake fighting to the death to turn Vee into a tree back in Sanctuary. He remembered Alice battling her way back here to warn them about Wilm. He remembered Sophie standing up to Taylor, the man who'd killed her sister.

He couldn't let this happen. Not while there was even the sliver of a chance left. His friends trusted him. Against all odds, even Zed trusted him.

And trust was a must, yes. But even more important was what you did with the trust people gave you. It was a gift.

That's what Zed never understood. He asked for the people's trust in Rook Mountain, and when they gave it to him, he betrayed it. He took that most precious of gifts and he sold it to buy another chance at the power he so coveted.

Frank wouldn't do that. He wouldn't be like Zed. He would give their trust the respect and the honor it deserved.

He'd do this one thing, and then he'd finally be able to rest.

Frank struggled to his feet, the world spinning around him. Wilm and the others didn't notice. Their eyes were locked on the book, on the power they were about to drink. Frank gritted his teeth and raised the knife.

Vee's hand touched down on the cover of the book, the final one of the three, and they all opened their eyes wide, looks of ecstasy on their faces.

The color seemed to drain out of the world. Sounds grew faint. The town was fading.

Frank buried the knife deep into the book and fire poured into his mind.

It was worse than it had been with the Rook Mountain book, so much worse. If the Rook Mountain book had been like drinking from a fountain, then this was drinking from a fire hose. He didn't know if the screaming he heard was coming from him, Wilm, Vee, San, or all four of them.

Through the haze of pain he saw the three Exiles, their looks of ecstasy now replaced with expressions of terror.

Frank realized he wasn't just sucking the power out of the book. He was sucking the power out of *them*. Somehow, he was draining their power.

The three godlike beings in front of him seemed to be *diminishing*. They looked gaunt, like they'd gone weeks without eating. A moment later, they were inhumanly thin, skeletons with paper-like skin.

And then, they were gone. All that remained were three shimmering pools of metallic liquid on the ground at his feet.

The book burst into flame, but just like with the Rook Mountain book, he didn't feel it. Or maybe he did feel it and he just couldn't distinguish it from the agonizing fire burning inside him.

He looked down and, to his surprise, he saw the people of King's Crossing looking up at him. He was thirty feet in the air.

There was Matt, Alice's dad, his eyes wide. Frank realized he could hear the man's thoughts. *Please let my daughter be okay. If Frank has to die to make that happen—*

Frank stopped listening. Maybe he didn't want to hear it.

There was Joe, fearless leader of the Rough-Shod Readers. His thoughts were full of quotes from Milton's *Paradise Lost*.

And there was old enemy stepping out of the shed. Zed's thoughts…they were different than everyone else's. He wasn't thinking in words at all. As he stared up at Frank, Zed's thoughts were only of a terrible hunger. Zed bent down and picked up something off the ground, but Frank didn't notice what it was. Because his friends and family were coming out of the shed now, and Frank was overwhelmed with love for them.

He looked down at his hands and saw they were glowing. No, not just his hands. All of him. The fire, Frank thought. It was seeping out through his skin.

Frank took one last look down at the people of King's Crossing. The people who'd taken him in over the past seven years and given him a home. The people he'd saved. The people who'd saved him.

And he smiled.

The world went dark, and Frank tumbled out of the sky.

* * *

2.

Sophie stumbled out of the shed and saw Frank floating in the sky. His skin was glowing. It was the strangest, most terrifying, most beautiful thing she'd ever seen. God, how she loved him.

Then he fell from the sky and landed with a loud thud.

They'd waited in the shed for a while, Sophie, Zed, Jake, Christine, Will, and Mason. They hadn't believed Wilm and her friends would be able to find Frank. No one could see through Frank's locks, not even the Exiles.

So they'd been shocked when they saw the world beginning to fade. It felt to Sophie like all the air was being sucked out of her lungs. Something pulled at her. It was like an undertow, and she knew that in a few moments she and everything else in this town would be washed away.

Then, suddenly, it had stopped. It was as if the world were even brighter and more alive than it had been before. It was like the wave crashing, pushing her back onto the shore. Then, there was screaming. And a ball of light, like fire, flashed through the air.

They'd followed Zed outside. And she'd seen Frank, shining like a light in the sky.

She ran to where he lay on the pavement. He didn't seem to be injured, not visibly anyway. There was no blood. That didn't mean anything, though. He could have a broken neck, or a broken back, or internal bleeding, or who-the-hell knew what.

His skin still glowed. She reached out and caressed his cheek. It was cold.

He was breathing, but his breaths were shallow with long pauses between them.

She looked up at the others around her. She saw Alice hugging her dad, her golden sword on the ground at her feet. Jake, Christine, and Will all looked down at Frank with troubled stares.

"What's wrong with him?" Sophie asked.

No one answered.

Zed stood apart from the rest of them. "He did it. I don't believe it. He actually did it." He touched Alice's arm. "Tell me exactly what happened."

Sophie saw the sunlight glint off something in Zed's hand. It was the knife. Somehow he'd gotten ahold of Christine's knife.

Alice shook her head. "I don't know. It was all so fast."

"Just tell me what you saw. Anything you can remember."

Her voice quivered as she spoke. "Wilm was holding the book. They all touched it the way they do when they devour a town. Then things went all swirly like usual. Except this time was different. I wasn't just watching. I felt like *I* was being sucked in too."

"That's because you're part of this town," Zed said. "You weren't an outside observer. This is your town. Tell me what happened next."

"Okay. Frank was lying on the ground. Then he got up and stabbed the book with that knife. Then everything changed. I didn't feel like I was being sucked in anymore. Frank started glowing and the rest of them..." She trailed off and waved a hand toward other metallic pools of liquid on the ground. "Then the book caught on fire and Frank floated into the sky. You saw the rest. He fell."

Zed's eyes were lit up. "Of course. The only thing that can draw the power from a book is one of the Exiles. And the Tools are made from their remains. Stabbing the book with the knife drains the power from the book, same as when the Exiles touch it."

It suddenly struck Sophie that they may have just wiped out an entire alien race. But now, with her husband lying half dead on the ground, she found it hard to care about that. They were trying to destroy the Earth, after all.

Zed crouched down next to Frank. "I should have known. Back in Rook Mountain, I knew the power was still there and it was still building. But I couldn't find the book. That's because there was no book. His mind became the trap for the power. All the power of Rook Mountain was hiding inside him all along."

Zed laughed, and Sophie felt a chill run down her spine. She'd heard Zed laugh before, but never like this. Never like he was so close to losing control. "Do you know why Jorrick put the books where he did? Wilm had a theory. She told me once a long time ago. She said Jorrick hid the books centuries ago at the sites that were destined to become the greatest cities in our world. They were supposed to be places of great learning, great innovation. Rook Mountain, Sugar Plains, King's Crossing. All these places should have been centers of earthly culture and the birthplaces of humankind's greatest achievements. But the books gathered the potential of these places and trapped it. All that power in one place attracted strange things like the Unfeathered and the Ones Who Sing. After Wilm and her people consumed the potential from the book, it would be as if the town never existed."

He tapped Frank's forehead. "It seems there's a more perfect storage device." He looked up at the rest of them, his eyes wild with excitement. "Can you imagine it? Inside his head is the potential of two cities, plus the energy Wilm, San, and Vee were carrying. No wonder he's out cold! He has no idea how to use it! How to even deal with it."

Zed was holding the knife so tightly the tendons on his arm were standing out and his knuckles were white.

"He has no idea how to use the power," he said, "but I do. I've tasted it. I practiced using it for a thousand years! Albeit in a smaller dosage." He gently rested the blade of the knife against Frank's forehead. "Imagine what I could do with that power."

Sophie couldn't breathe. Zed had a knife against her husband's head. A man who destroyed countless lives. There was no question in Sophie's mind Zed would kill Frank to get to that power. He'd kill all of them if he had to.

Something welled up inside her. Something she hadn't felt since she'd killed Taylor back in Sanctuary. Before she realized what she was doing, Alice's sword was in Sophie's hand. She pressed it against Zed's neck.

"If you don't set that knife down in the next three seconds," Sophie said, "I will kill you."

Zed hesitated. He spoke slowly when he answered. "Think very carefully before you do anything. Frank is dying. We can't stop that. His mind has not had a thousand years to prepare for this moment. Mine has. Don't let his death be for nothing."

"Put down the knife," she said.

"Sophie," Zed said, "I can do so much good. Humanity is not safe. Consider the Ones Who Sing. You think they'll never break into time? Consider the Harbinger's Song. And the mirror lands."

"I don't know what any of that means," she said.

"Exactly! But I do! I can stop those dangers and a thousand others. I can lead humanity into the next millennium. I can do so much good. Kill me if you must, but know humanity is losing its chance to step into the future safe and free."

The sword quivered in her hand. Maybe humanity did need someone to lead them. But it sure as hell wasn't Zed. "You told me something a long time ago. You told me I'm capable of great evil. And I think you were right."

Sophie slashed the blade across his neck with one quick motion. It sank deep into his flesh and blood poured out around the wound.

She staggered back, shocked at how simple it had been, at how easily the steel had cut his throat and how deep of a gash it had made. She let the sword fall from her hand and it clattered to the ground.

Zed's eyes widened, and he touched his neck. He brought up the hand and squinted at the blood. He looked from Sophie to the blood on his hand as if he was having difficulty connecting her with what was happening to him.

He opened his mouth, but all that came out was a weak gurgling sound. He wouldn't speak, not ever again, and the look of horror in his eyes showed he knew it.

But he never let go of the knife. Not even at the end.

He collapsed onto his side as he passed out. A few bloody moments later, Zed was dead.

Frank quivered on the ground.

Jake stepped forward and held out his hand to Sophie. She took it and he pulled her to her feet. "I don't think Zed was lying. Frank's not looking good. All that power in his head. It's trapped in there."

"It's like a lock without a key," Christine said.

What had Zed called that earlier? A deadlock.

Matt looked up suddenly. "Wait. I think I know something." He took Alice by the shoulders. "Frank said it himself the day we talked up on the bluff. The morning before all this started. He said *you* were the key to all this."

"That was just a figure of speech," Sophie muttered.

But Alice didn't seem to think so. There was a distant look in her eye. "We have to let the power out. It's trapped in there, like you said. If it really is humanity's—I don't know, potential—like Zed said, it needs to be released back into the world, right?" She picked up the sword and a bit of Zed's blood dripped off the blade and onto the ground.

Sophie raised an eyebrow. "If you even *think* about stabbing Frank with that sword of yours—"

Mason put a hand on her shoulder. "I think it's okay. She's the key, remember? Frank's head is like a deadlock. And she's the key."

"That's what my sword does," Alice said. "It releases things. It's what allowed me to get the scissors to King's Crossing."

The girl stood over Frank and set the point of the sword against his forehead. It was so similar to what Zed had done with the knife only a few moments ago that Sophie had to suppress the urge to tackle Alice to the ground.

Alice took a deep breath and paused, her eyes scrunched shut. She pushed the broken mountain symbol and gingerly pressed the sword into Frank's head.

A beam of light poured out around the sword. It shot into the sky, widening as it went.

Alice pulled the sword out of Frank's head with a grunt and stumbled backward. She clutched the sword to her chest.

Sophie tried to follow the light's path into the clouds, but it was too brilliant to look at. She hoped it scattered as it hit the clouds. Whatever the Exiles had taken out of the world was flowing back into it. The potential. That's what they taken.

Human potential. A small part of it, anyway. And now it was escaping back into the world.

A moment later the light was gone. The only evidence it had ever been there was the dazzling pain in Sophie's eyes, like she'd looked directly at the sun. She blinked a few times and that too went away.

But Alice wasn't done. She walked over and—one by one —stabbed the pools of liquid metal. The remains of Wilm and Vee and San. These reacted differently to the sword. Instead of the light, there was only a bit of smoke as the pools dried, crackled, and turned to dust.

Alice spit on the ground and walked back to her father.

Frank sat up and put a shaky hand to his head. The place where Alice had cut him wasn't bleeding. The skin was whole and undamaged. Sophie dropped to the ground next to him.

"You okay?" she asked.

"Yeah," he said. "I think I am." He looked at Zed's body. "Your work?"

She smiled, blinking back the tears. "You know me too well."

It was late afternoon in King's Crossing. Soon there would be questions to be answered. There would be decisions to be made. And someone would have to do something with Zed's body.

But for now Sophie and Frank Hinkle sat on the grass in Volunteer Park next to the Mississippi River, surrounded by their friends. They were alive and unafraid, and they held each other.

THE LAST OF THE HINKLES

1.

Jake opened the door and took a deep breath. This would be the first time he'd driven a car in…how long? It felt like a hundred years. He was a little nervous.

Or maybe the nerves stemmed from the fact that he was alone with his son for the first time since their strange reunion. His sixty-something son.

"You ready to do this?" Mason asked.

Jake considered the question. Ready to drive across the country with his son, a boy he'd treated distantly at best and who'd grown into a man he didn't know at all? "Yeah. I'm ready."

"Just to let you know, I get car sick."

Jake smiled. "You get that from your mother."

Mason's eyes widened. "Really? I didn't know that."

Jake put the car in reverse and eased out of the driveway. "Yep. That's what she told me, anyway. We were never actually in a car together. She said any time she wasn't driving she felt like she was gonna throw up."

"Huh. Maybe you should teach me to drive."

"Well," Jake said, "it is kind of a father-son tradition. Let's take it slow, though."

A weight hung in the air as they drove toward the highway, and Jake knew what it was. The same thing that burned in his gut like a furnace. It was a serious topic to start the drive on, but Jake had to talk about it. He felt like he couldn't go another mile without saying it.

He looked at his son. "Mason. I'm so sorry."

Mason screwed up his face in surprise. "Sorry for what?"

Now it was Jake's turn to be surprised. "For abandoning you. I didn't protect you. I left you alone in Sanctuary with that monster."

Mason looked out the window. "Well, you were dead at the time."

Jake let out an involuntary laugh. "Yeah, as excuses go, I guess that's a good one."

"Best I've heard." Mason turned back to his father, a slight smile on his face. "You know something I learned from Frank? It was right after he'd proposed to Sophie. Everybody knew they should get together. Everybody but them. Then they started dating and it was going well and everybody knew they were made for each other. He finally proposes, and I ask him, 'Frank, why'd you wait so long? We were here for years before you even made a move.' You know what he said?"

Jake shook his head, a sad smile on his face.

"He said, 'I don't know, man. And I don't care.' He said, 'there's no use looking back. You gotta enjoy what you have and not fret over why you didn't have it sooner.'" He rapped on the window with his knuckles. "Did I have a messed up childhood? Yes. But, you know, now I'm taking a cross-country trip with my dad in his prime. How many old timers can say that?"

"Let's not go crazy," Jake said. "You never saw me in my

prime. I was something back then. The Unregulated, they called us. Zed spent years trying to figure us out."

"I heard."

"Oh no, you heard Zed's version. You haven't heard the truth." He reached out and patted his son's knee. "Sophie told me you used the book in Sanctuary. She said you could move the trees with it. That you opened a door to Rook Mountain."

Mason let out a laugh. "Now *that* was something. You should have seen me."

A few quiet miles passed. Mason kept his eyes on the fields rolling past the window and Jake kept his on the yellow line in the center of the road.

"The University of Denver," Jake asked. "Nineteen hours and forty-five minutes, according to my fancy phone app."

Mason grinned. "My brother. I can't wait to see what he's like."

A shadow fell over Jake's face. "Me too. Two sons, and I missed both their childhoods."

"Remember what Frank said. Eyes on the future."

Father and son drove west, crossing the country they'd helped save and enjoying the sights and the sounds of it. They stopped at too many scenic overlooks and ate too many greasy roadside burgers. The conversation grew easier as they went. They found they had similar senses of humor. Jake wondered if that was genetics or if they just shared a certain gallows humor common to men who had lost so much.

Neither of them mentioned that Will and Christine lived out in Colorado, too.

Jake hadn't even said goodbye to Christine. She'd moved on with her life, and he had to let her. After all, he too had moved on back in Sanctuary. Mason was living proof of that. And he could see she was happy. Will was the right person for her. Jake wasn't going to get in the middle of that. He wasn't going to make her choose.

They met up with Trevor at a pizza place near the university. They stayed in town a few days and got caught up a little. But Trevor needed his space and time to understand everything that had happened.

So, Jake and Mason returned to Rook Mountain. It turned out there were two vacant cabins at the old Hinkle Resort. Jake took Will's old cabin, the one where the Unregulated had met so many times.

Trevor came often to visit, and he eventually fell back in love with his childhood home. It wasn't long before he was looking at apartments in town.

Rook Mountain, it seemed, had a way of bringing folks back.

They stayed in Rook Mountain from then on. Jake, Mason, and Trevor. Survivors of Zed. Wielders of books and Tools. Family.

2.

It was two years before Frank started making locks again. For a long while, the idea was too heavy in his mind. It carried too much weight, too much baggage. But every once in a while, usually when he was least expecting it, out for a walk or in the shower, an idea would pop into his head. It was never a full lock, only a concept that could eventually lead to a lock. A feeling almost. Something he couldn't put into words.

But he knew from experience that if he pursued that idea, it could eventually lead to something. That process, creating something new, used to fill him with so much joy.

Still, he never did anything with the ideas. Not for two

years. When he finally sat down to work on one, everything about it felt clumsy. His fingers felt too big and he couldn't quite get them to do what he wanted. The lock didn't come together the way he'd thought it would. When he finally got it working, he realized it was clunky and derivative.

He tossed it out and started over. The next one was a little better. The one after that was better still. And after a couple months he had two new designs he didn't hate.

His locks didn't have any special powers now. Whatever had allowed him to do that had leaked out when Alice stabbed him with the sword. His locks were just locks. But most days that was enough.

He never did get back to the pure joy of creation he'd had when he was younger. He aways held a little back, like he was afraid to get lost in the process. Sometimes he caught glimpses of that old mental state of pure creation, but he never gave over to it. Of all the scars he bore from the things he'd been through since meeting Zed on that day so long ago, that might have been the one that hurt the most.

Sophie had scars too, he knew. Killing Zed had damaged her, but her greatest pain came from the thing she *hadn't* been able to do. Frank had his brother back. Sophie's sister was still dead. What was worse, she might not have to be.

Heather had been killed in 2010. Alice would have been four at the time. If Alice Pulled Back to the morning of the day Heather was killed, she could dial Sophie's parents' phone number. Sophie had thought of a dozen things Alice could say to stop Heather from going out that day. To save her life. She'd shared them all with Frank, usually late at night. They both had trouble sleeping sometimes.

But Sophie knew it wouldn't be worth it. Who knew what other things might change? Maybe the domino effect would make them lose their chance to defeat the Exiles. Maybe millions would die because Sophie missed her sister.

Even if nothing changed, was it fair to ask Alice to relive everything she'd experienced?

Still, sometimes in those late night conversations Sophie admitted she believed she could talk Alice into it if she tried. And that she wondered if maybe things could turn out even better than they had this time around. But those thoughts were always gone by morning.

Frank knew Sophie still believed what Zed had told her. She believed she had the capacity for great evil.

But didn't they all?

Frank trusted Sophie. And the fact that she shared these dark thoughts with him at night proved she trusted him back.

They'd decided to stay in King's Crossing. After spending seven years fighting to hold the town together, it felt like the right place to be. Rook Mountain was the past. King's Crossing was the life they'd built together.

Sophie still worked at the library. She'd gone back to school to get her bachelors and eventually her masters in library sciences. Her dream was to take Joe's job when he retired in a few years. She still attended every meeting of the Rough-Shod Readers, though Frank had dropped out after things had gone back to normal in King's Crossing. They actually discussed books now, and Sophie even convinced them to slip in some sci-fi and fantasy every once in a while.

They visited Tennessee every fall to see Sophie's parents and the southern Hinkle clan: Jake, Mason, and Trevor. Rook Mountain was as beautiful as ever when the leaves were changing. They made it out to see Christine and Will in Colorado every few years too.

But Frank's favorite pastime was sitting on the front porch

with Sophie in the evenings. Sometimes they read books or took turns strumming the guitar. Many nights they just sat in silence, Sophie often sipping a cup of tea, and Frank with the compass in his hands.

He couldn't explain exactly why he'd saved the compass from Christine's knife. The tree in the shed had withered and died. Christine had taken the knife back to Colorado. Mason had keep the scissors. Alice still had her sword. Maybe Frank just wanted a little piece of magic to call his own.

He held the compass on those nights and watched the needle spin as he thought of destinations. He said them aloud, enjoying the way it always made Sophie laugh.

"Denmark," he'd say, and the needle would spin.

"Bill Clinton," he'd say, and the needle would turn again.

"The first girl I ever kissed," he'd say, and the needle would move as Sophie slugged him in the arm.

They ended every night the same way. After Sophie had finished her tea, or they'd closed their books, or they'd put away the guitar, he'd say, "Home."

And the needle would point to Sophie.

Then they'd go inside, lock the door, and keep each other warm.

The end of the Deadlock Trilogy

AUTHOR'S NOTE

We'll leave Frank and Sophie there. I think they've earned a bit of privacy, don't you?

Frank, Sophie, and Mason's journeys are over, but I will likely return to this world in future novels. Other heroes will rise to face some of the threats Zed listed in his final moments. And Alice still has that sword and the ability to Pull Back. I assume she'll put them to good use. Maybe she'll let us tag along sometime.

Thanks for reading this trilogy. I hope it was as much time-hopping, genre-bending, never-back-down-in-the-face-of-evil fun as I intended.

As a way of saying thanks for reading, I've also included some bonus features.

- 'The Broken Clock' music playlist
- And (coming soon) a video Q&A where I answer reader questions about the trilogy

Visit *pthylton.com/broken-clock-bonus-features* to view the bonus features.

If you enjoyed **The Broken Clock**, please consider leaving a review wherever you bought this book. As an indie author, I count on reader reviews to help my books reach a wider audience.

If you just want to say hello, email me at pt@pthylton.com

If you're wondering what to read next, check out my fantasy novella series about the assassin Zane Halloway. The first installment, **Thorns and Tangles**, is absolutely free. Visit pthylton.com/books/thorns-tangles for details

Thanks once again for your support!

ACKNOWLEDGEMENTS

This book would not have been possible without support from the following people:

My wife, who is always supportive and holds me accountable for writing each day.

My daughter, who asked me, "Is that nine-year-old girl in your book based on me?"

My editor, Kirsten D, who played a huge role in shaping this trilogy.

My friend Andy, who is a wonderful daily sounding board for my crazy ideas.

My dad, who gave me my love of story.

My beta readers, who I will not call out by name here. You all rocked it once again.

My fellow indie authors, who supported me and advised me via dozens and dozens of email conversations.

And thanks to you, dear reader, for your continued support.

ABOUT THE AUTHOR

P.T. Hylton is a writer, podcaster, and instructional designer. He lives in beautiful Eastern Tennessee with his wife and daughter. Check out his blog at *pthylton.com*.

Made in the USA
Middletown, DE
22 December 2017